WINTER GRAVES

by Luke Walker

A HellBound Books Publishing LLC Book
Austin TX

A HellBound Books LLC Publication

Copyright © 2021 by HellBound Books Publishing LLC
All Rights Reserved

Cover and art design
By HellBound Books Publishing LLC

No part of this book may be reproduced, stored in a retrieval system, or transmitted by any means, electronic, mechanical, photocopying, recording or otherwise without written permission from the author
This book is a work of fiction. Names, characters, places and incidents are entirely fictitious or are used fictitiously and any resemblance to actual persons, living or dead, events or locales is purely coincidental.

www.hellboundbookspublishing.com

Dedication:

This one is for my friends.

Winter Graves

Acknowledgments:

Once again, thank you to James, Xtina and the Hellbound team for their support and hard work. As always, my thanks and love to friends and family. As with everything I create, this book wouldn't have been written or published without the constant support and encouragement from my wife Rebecca.
Thank you so much..

Other Books by Luke Walker

Die Laughing: 2015.
Hometown: 2016.
Dead Sun: 2018.
Ascent: 2018.
The Unredeemed: 2018.
The Mirror Of The Nameless: 2018.
The Day Of The New Gods: 2019.
The Dead Room: 2019.
Pandemonium: 2020
The Kindred: 2021

WINTER GRAVES

Winter Graves

Chapter One

The ground below Loui Cameron's back, the ice-cold air and the almost complete darkness marching away down the long path beside the river had all been frozen in time by the hammer held over the centre of her face.

Moments before when the jarring pain from her impact on the path had eclipsed her fear, Loui had summoned reserves of control she had no idea she possessed and listened to the gruff voice of her dad telling her to do as he would and take no crap from her attacker.

"You hurt me and my dad will tear your head off. You know who my dad is? Carl Cameron and he'll kill you."

She'd barely heard herself, the croak of her voice like an old lady on forty a day, so there was no way the figure who'd thrown her to the riverside path would catch much of it.

Apparently unperturbed by her threat or the mention of the name, the figure had remained motionless. They were as much a part of the night as the black of their surroundings and the silent river not fifteen feet from her head while Loui blinked away the droplets of sweat dribbling out of her hair, and her thoughts collapsed into snapshots of memory.

A walk home from Becky's after a late one with the boys in the park and some tins; two in the morning come and gone, then three and four and knowing she needed to sneak back into the house before either of her parents or Uncle Steve got up. A walk of half an hour towards the estate and its dark alleys. No fear or trepidation because she knew who she was and her place in the town. People knew her dad. They knew his history and that meant there was nothing to fear late at night. Even the boys she and Becky had been with in Willow Park knew the score and not one tried their luck after she said no.

But all that had proved to be a lie soon after the boy with the smile slightly visible in the shine of the moonlight had come from the other direction, pulling away when he saw her and apologising if he'd made her jump. Said he was surprised to see anyone out here so late. Said he was new to Lawfield and had gone into the town centre to check out the nightlife. Said he was twenty and worked in the Ford dealership out where Albion Way merged with a massive industrial estate.

Asked if he could walk her home and he was cool with her saying no because she didn't know him.

But she'd said yes.

Then their talk and her stolen glances his way to see his nice mouth and his head free from a hat despite the freeze of a winter that had dragged on for months. Hair strong, thick; jawline not buried in layers of fat as seemed to happen with any guy older than about twenty-five but still there in a way that was alien to boys her own age, and his questions about her not too probing or at all aggressive.

Just a nice guy.

But then the world spinning and the air rolling with her as he took her from the ground and threw her to the path.

And now time set on pause because the hammer was right over her face and the word please was coming again to her lips, coming in place of any promises of revenge on him, the guarantee of his own death at the hands of her dad. The sweat still trickling down her forehead, each drop as cold as the inside of the freezer in their kitchen; her armpits soaked, her stomach turned into a fiercely hot tennis ball ready to punch its way out of her body, and the shameful surety she was literally a second from wetting herself. But then all of that fading into silence and stillness while she lay motionless but somehow also moving. Insane or not, she existed in both states at the same time. While she knew she remained on the ground, she rose to meet the tops of the dropping willows trailing their long branches in the riverbank, turning over to see her own body prostrate on the path.

Loui Cameron understood.

She no longer belonged to her flesh and blood. She was less than either; she was reduced to sight and touch and she'd been taken above, drifting gently in the currents. The spread of long grass bordering the path and the rear of the expensive houses on Water View stretched in all directions, and there was the taste of ice a hundred feet up. Lifeless January swam over the fields and roads as she did, floating further out and taking in the open land forming the empty acres to the east of Lawfield, the cycleway that twisted through the green now turned jet-black, and the small woodlands growing closer together as the land neared Oxford. Loui's vision drifted north, passing the curve of roads where the only cars were parked in wide drives or locked behind garage doors. Further out to New Road as it bisected Lawfield's centre, further north and her bird's-eye view of a demolition site: the great mounds of rubble and glass, the three squat buildings close to the fence blocking the site from Mansfield Road; the few remaining buildings with the boarded windows of their lower floors, and the looming bulk of the main hospital still untouched by the machines.

And Loui saw the tiny shape of the man crossing the uneven ground, heading to the gates and she thought:

That's who's going to save me.

Time started again.

The hammer rose sharply, then swung down, and all Loui could do was try to scream even as blood flooded her throat and the hammer crashed down again.

Scream and let her fear turn to rage inside the cannon-fire of agonies because the boy with the soft voice and suggestion of a nice smile was killing her.

Chapter Two

As Andy locked the gates to the site behind me, I did my usual thing of checking both ends of Mansfield Road. Dozens of old houses; hundreds of sealed windows and only a few lights shining behind curtains. Frozen puddles on the pavements and in the gutters, their surfaces polished black. A couple of hours to go before dawn and nothing moved. Even the taxis were gone. For the most part, Lawfield slept.

Behind, Andy's steps faded as he crunched over the stones and frost on his return to the staff cabin. Warm in there. Warmer than anywhere in the exposed outdoors and my walk home with the millions of gleaming stars high overhead and even the bulk of my heavy coat not quite enough to keep out the winter. As always when leaving work, I asked myself why I didn't just drive here. And again as always, I knew it wasn't because the flat was only a twenty-minute walk from my job as overnight security for the building site's grounds. It was because I liked to see Lawfield peaceful, liked it in a way I couldn't articulate to anyone—not that anyone had ever asked. That walk before most people were up and ready for the new day was a chance to be alone and free from the hassles of life, chance to welcome that freedom.

There were no more sounds of Andy; he'd be in the cabin, probably having a shot of Scotch and readying himself for a shift as boring as mine. The dispute with the developers and council had kept the men away, the tools downed and the machines quiet for weeks and that argument showed no signs of a resolution. Good for my temporary job if nothing else.

Gloved hands deep in my pockets and breath rising like smoke, I left Mansfield Road, crossed New Road and started down a cut between the side of a high fence and a wooded area. While it was relatively isolated and almost completely silent, that wasn't why I came to an abrupt stop, my boots snapping the edge of a solid puddle.

Someone was watching me.

I kept still, moving only my eyes and made out nothing beyond a couple of feet in any direction. The fence formed a barrier of long gardens and the wood petered out probably thirty feet in. New Road remained vague beyond the gloom at the opening to the cut and the open patch of grass at the other end might as well as have been the other side of the world.

The feeling of being watched, of eyes considering me in the pre-dawn light, sent chills over my back and the fresh cold had nothing to with the winter. Breathing through my mouth (and fighting the need to suck in deep breaths of the icy air in case I was forced to run), I listened and caught only a distant sound of traffic. It faded into silence in seconds, but the creeping freeze up and down my spine remained with its many fingers. While I had a bit of height, I wasn't built like Andy or the site manager Tom. If anyone was close by and planning on mugging me or simply wanting to start some shit for no reason, I'd have to run.

A tiny gust of wind blew through the low undergrowth before dying. The thought of heading back to New Road and trekking all that way into Lawfield's hub needled at me and I dismissed it. That route home would take twice as long as usual, and I needed sleep. I needed my flat where I could shut the door and, once again, keep the world out.

Figuring it was probably nothing more dangerous than a city fox but still taking my hands from my coat pockets, I got moving again, striding purposefully and entering the almost invisible area beyond the end of the fence while I checked all directions with quick jerks of my head. Icy grass crunched below my boots and the air, already sharp, grew much colder the closer I came to the river.

Back on autopilot, I joined the path that ran alongside the Evenham, using the moon as a guide, listening to the gentle lap of the water on the bank. Dozens of old willows formed a border between the path and the playing fields beyond, and their branches rustled in tiny whispers.

A thud straight ahead made me freeze. Staring that way was no help; the moonlight turned my immediate surroundings white but didn't reach more than another five steps in front.

A second thud, then a third, then a fourth: a flurry of terrible blows and cracking sounds.

I moved forward and even now I wonder what would have happened if I'd run.

The girl crashed right at my feet and her blood splattered my jeans. Blood turned black in the white of the moon. So much black on the shattered hole that had been her nose and mouth.

She reached for me, making a noise I'd never heard before; something choking and wet and dying.

Movement ahead.

He came out of the dark, a young man maybe twenty-one or twenty-two with blood coating his fists and his coat. He pocketed a thin object, something I couldn't quite identify and what I later learned was a hammer.

Without the slightest indication he'd exerted himself, he came for me and I went for him.

Swearing, raging, I punched without aiming and hit his ear. Pulling back, I landed another one near his nose and felt no impact at all. It was like attacking fog. Spitting my fury and horror, I got a weak hold of the collar of his coat, yanked him close and smelled the rich, salty stink of so much blood. Howling, I shoved hard and the kid went down, legs splayed, falling on his hands.

He was still grinning.

Running to the girl, I realised I was shouting at the attacker and had been for the last few seconds.

"Stay there. You hear me? Don't fucking move."

The girl rolled over and looked at me.

Ella was looking at me. My sister. My dead sister.

I think I screamed. It's hard to be sure now. Either way, I went down on my arse and couldn't do a thing as my sister peered from a ruined face coated with black and tried to breathe through a load of broken bones and the kid was no longer on the ground, but was coming straight for me, fist raised a moment before it struck my cheek.

I crashed down, my surroundings spinning and shaking. The river could have been in the sky; the ground was a dancing wave and the stench was a clammy stink all over my tongue.

A hand grasped my hair and yanked me to a sitting position. The fresh pain made me cry out and the world danced.

"Hello, Jimmy."

He said it right in my ear without moving closer. That wasn't the worst part.

He said it in Ella's voice.

I screamed and while he repeated hello, Jimmy, I screamed until I ran out of breath and shadows that had nothing to do with the closing in dawn drowned my vision.

He gripped my throat and twisted me, looming closer at the same time. "I like you, Jimmy. I always have. You're. . ." He seemed to consider while my insides shrieked. "You're interesting." He rose, still gripping my hair. "Don't forget how much I like you."

His hard punch into my eye immediately halved my vision with a detonation of agony. The ground, as crisp as a freezer, welcomed me as I dropped and he strode away. The girl, no longer Ella but instead a small stranger, a child, faced me with blood running from wounds all over her head and face.

She didn't see me, though. The girl was dead.

I fell fully flat and the moon was skimmed with a red growing closer to black.

From somewhere in the thick gloom and frost, a voice called.

"Loui thought you were the one to save her, Jimmy. She really thought that."

Chapter Three

Neither man in the van had spoken in long minutes, the passenger silent through apprehension edging closer to outright fear with each moment. At the same time, the driver's thoughts alternated between what had happened beside the river and the small object in the rear of the van. He cared no more for his companion's dread than he did for the events at the river and what he'd done to Loui Cameron.

Or, for that matter, what he'd done to Meg Freeman.

They took the turning from Church Way into St Michael's Street at exactly a minute past eight. Keeping his speed at a constant fifteen miles per hour, the driver passed half a dozen estate agents, all empty and quiet, and slowed as he drew nearer to the last business on the right. The long wall of windows at the front of The Black Boar ended at a narrow alleyway between the pub and the largest of the estate agents. The van drew level with the Boar's entrances and reversed without hesitation. With a smooth manoeuvre, it backed into the opening of the alley and stopped.

Seconds later, the rear doors swung open and the driver gripped a small bundle wrapped in bin bags. From the front of the van, a voice, high-pitched and already slurring despite the time, called:

"This going to take long?"

The driver, somewhere in his early twenties and dressed in a clean pair of overalls, replied without taking his eyes from the three industrial waste bins wedged against the wall of the pub, specifically the space below the bins.

"Shut up."

In the passenger seat, Bill Lister shut up. While the drink had claimed him long before and the years since had collapsed into an unlit hole, he knew enough to do what the man in the overalls said. He also knew he put himself in danger every time he spent any time with his nameless associate despite their age difference, but Bill was a firm believer in needs must, and right needs most definitely were must. His lips, permanently dry from being rubbed ached for a taste of the drink he'd been promised. His throat felt like a brick wall baking in a nasty summer.

Give it a bit of time, he told himself. There was work to be done today. He'd been told the plan several times; he'd repeated it to himself and to the man in the overalls, and while his mind did not work with any real degree of clarity, he knew what was needed. More importantly, he knew what he'd gain from the day's work.

Fully aware of Bill's thought processes, the man in the overalls held his smile inside, dropped to the dirty puddles and potholes of the alley's floor and inhaled. Damp, cold and secret all around him. But not secret for much longer.

Squatting, he placed the bagged object on the ground and shoved it as hard as possible to the underside of the nearest bin. The plastic bags tore as he pushed, revealing a glimpse of blue for a moment when he turned the bundle over to its side. The upper half of the shape managed to fit below the bin before refusing to budge. Satisfied, the man rose, took another few breaths to taste the little space and returned to the van's interior. Doors slammed at his back, he clambered to the driver's seat and pulled out into the road.

The sun brightened briefly as the clouds parted, momentary rays doing little to warm the men against the ever-present chill. While the driver stared at the road ahead, unblinking eyes drinking in the image of Jimmy collapsing to the pathway, Bill held a hand over his mouth and nose, unconsciously sniffing for the remaining smell of vodka. He watched the driver without turning his head. Work to be done, he'd said; work connected with whatever had been left in the alley all wrapped in bin bags. Bill didn't like to think about what the object might be; he didn't need to think about that when the promise of a drink and plenty of cash was so close. Only another few hours, but Jesus Christ, his throat and tongue itched.

"Soon, Bill," the man in the overalls muttered. He'd left the window open a fraction and the numbing wind slipped fingers into the van. While the sun tried to break through low clouds, there was no more warmth at eight than there'd been two short hours ago beside the river.

The driver's face twisted, caught somewhere between a grin and a sneer as if pained. Forgetting about the river and whoever might be drawing close to the girl's body (a dog walker, perhaps. It was always some old fart walking his dog who found the bodies), the man checked the road behind. A few pedestrians were in sight down near Church Walk, but none paid any attention to the van as he took it to the end of St Michael's Road. Too early for them, the air too sharp, and too much of their own lives in their fresh coffee from the nearby Starbucks or on the screens of their phones. They didn't see. They never did until he was right in front of them.

Both men were silent as the van followed a slope to Carling Way which encircled the bulk of Lawfield's core. Joining the traffic, the driver kept his focus straight ahead and ignored Bill's occasional twitching leg and shifting in his seat as if he needed the toilet. Slowing as a bus ahead pulled into a stop, the driver opened his window further and took a deep breath. So much chill to the day, so much threat of the winter rolling on and on into the months ahead. And who knew? Depending on how things went over the next few days, perhaps it would.

Still in silence, they drove on and took a turn off from Carling Way. Ten minutes after the drop off beside the pub, the driver brought the van to a halt on a bus stop on Oxford Road. He knew the schedule in detail: there wouldn't be another bus passing for five minutes. Cars streamed by. The section of the road they'd parked on formed the beginning of a sloping bridge. Below, the shadowy water of the Evenham flowed, its surface rippling as the wind picked up for a moment. Ahead from where the van was parked and the traffic passed, a turning into a new development of expensive homes was lined with smooth green. And further on, the focus of the man driving the van: the flats of Oxford Place. Ten floors tall, clean and shiny and pleasant and all the mod cons. Exactly the sort of place he knew Jimmy would call home.

"This is it," the driver told Bill who had come close to zoning out while the non-stop stream of traffic passed them. "The top floor. That's where he is right now."

Bill nodded, not having a clue who lived up there and caring even less. Whoever they were, they'd obviously pissed off his strange associate; the plan for later proved that if nothing else. He smelled his fingers again. Vodka, fading and Scotch and gin ahead. Jesus bleeding Christ. A drink. A proper fucking drink and all this weird stuff—whatever it was—would be done.

"The top floor," the driver mused. "That view. All that. . .exposure. Seems strange, doesn't it?"

"Yeah," Bill croaked.

"A man who doesn't like to be around people, who doesn't like company or want anything to do with the world and he's got a view of the town like he's king of it."

The driver laughed and again, the odd mix of pain and humour crossed his face. "What do I know? Maybe he got a deal on the rent. I'll have to ask at some point." He showed his teeth in a wide smile. "Should have mentioned it earlier."

He turned towards Bill who shrank towards the door and window as fear broke through the fog in his head and the need for a drink. Even registering the focus of the driver's eyes didn't help. So what if the man was looking beyond Bill and even beyond Oxford Road to the edges of the river to whatever the hell would be out there at this time of the morning? So what to any of that? Bill knew danger and threat. He was trapped in the van with his life on the line.

"Get out," the driver said and his voice was new. Despite his youth, it had become the flat, lifeless whisper of a man in his nineties. To Bill, it was like hearing the January air come to life and given flesh.

He reached for the handle without looking, caught it and the door swung open. Without raising his voice beyond the noise of the road or the wind, the driver spoke and Bill heard him clearly as he left the vehicle.

"Do your job properly. The pub at one o'clock."

Nodding and grinning, Bill staggered to the high wall overlooking the river and turned back.

The driver was grinning.

But his eyes.

His eyes had turned over fully, turning the orbs into the white of golf balls.

Screeching, Bill jerked away, smacked into the wall and the driver waved, his eyes utterly normal.

The sensation there and gone in a second, Bill thought he heard someone crying out in weak protest. If there had been a sound, he was much too unnerved by what had to be his imagination of his young companion minus his eyes.

Seconds later, the van joined the traffic, headed over the bridge where it turned into Oxford Road, not stopping as it passed the flats where someone Bill did not know lived on the high tenth floor.

Chapter Four

Keeping totally still with my eyes shut didn't do any good. Everything hurt. Even the load of painkillers I'd necked a minute after staggering through my door weren't much help. Worse than the cuts or the memory of the tearing sting in my hair as the man grabbed me or the grenade going off in my head when he decked me in the eye, worse than the pain in my body was the throb of old injuries inside. And I didn't have any pills for those.

"Ella," I whispered, making myself jump, then groan. The name had come without warning. It came to mind often, but almost never further.

Still with my eyes shut, I reached out and found my phone on the arm of the sofa. Hitting three nines would take no effort at all. Even explaining to the police why I'd run wouldn't take much. Whether or not they'd believe me or nick me for deserting a crime scene, I didn't have a clue. In the end, it wasn't going to matter because I couldn't call them. Couldn't say to another person what had happened on that silent path beside the Evenham.

"He killed her." I whispered it to the gloom filling my flat, the light still murky because the curtains at the living room windows were open no more than a crack and the late morning couldn't break in.

"He killed that girl and he kicked the shit out of me while she died right at my feet."

The empty flat didn't have much to say back to me about that.

"And he knew my name. He said it right to my face and the girl changed and—"

I broke off, eyes opening for no reason.

The sight lasted for barely a second—movement against the long curtains on the other side of the room. Something small and thin formed from the shadows pressing on the curtains and making the material ripple, something no larger than a child and the top half twisting, turning towards me.

I closed my eyes again before I saw the face I knew was only in my head, counted to ten and looked back at the now normal curtains.

Standing was an effort, but I managed it. Walking the few steps to the window hurt more than I wanted to admit, and letting in the grey daylight was no small miracle. Whatever I thought I'd seen on the curtains was gone; I put it down to stress, the poor light and the horrible, mad business beside the river.

"He knew my name," I told the room. It was easy to picture myself saying the same to the police and their suspicion that a young man who killed a teenage girl and who knew my name meant I was somehow involved.

Easy to picture that and easy to accept there was no good I could do by telling the police what I'd seen.

So, you ran from a crime scene? So, what? Who wouldn't? It's not like you could have done anything to stop it. It's not like you're guilty of anything or you know who he was. Right?

Curtains open fully, I stood in the window with the massive sheet of sky above and away while ten floors below, Oxford Road made its way for long miles to the north. The Evenham streamed below the bridge, its pitch-black surface dotted with the white of swans and ducks. Cars, vans and a double decker bus followed the section of road directly outside my block of flats, always moving underneath the low clouds and I was rising, rising, rising.

Into the sky.

Like a bird, I moved with the currents, and Lawfield spread out in all directions below. Oxford Road and all around it with its pubs and shops and old narrow streets full of shadows, and the nice streets and avenues on the other side of the centre—none of that interested me. None of that was in my eye as I banked with the currents and came low towards the pavement opposite my block of flats. Skimming the surface, I shot between a few pedestrians, rose again and sped over the high wall that blocked road and pavement from the riverbank.

Dark water below; dark water flowing and me flowing with it. I raced next to the same bridge I'd run over a few hours before, convinced I'd be seen and the blood on my clothing and shoes would mark me as a killer. Beyond the bridge to the other side of the river and then like a bullet nearer the ground, streaming further away, level with the messy tangle of greenery and the massive field on its far side, now level with the first of the old willows and their branches trailing in the river and speeding faster and faster, higher again, blasting from the path with its lines and thin cracks and tiny puddles to the grey ceiling of two hundred feet, three, four, higher and Lawfield, my home, a sheet of greens and browns and thousands of houses and lives sitting underneath.

And then I was a falling stone, heading straight towards the tent erected over the pathway while dozens of police officers in their uniforms and the clean white of their forensic clothing searched the undergrowth for any signs of the monster who'd left the hurt remains of a child for the morning to find.

At the last second, I came back to my flat, back to the exact spot where I'd stood before whatever the hell the mad vision was. No sweating or shaking or nausea. Nothing out of the ordinary unless I counted the bag of bloody clothing in my bathroom.

Holding my chest as if my heart pounded, I spoke to the living room. "What the fuck is happening?"

The answer was a tired whisper from miles below.

Let the world go.

Everything inside shoved that whisper out of reach, refusing to hear it or consider the words. It belonged to the dead past.

Knowing what I would see, I clicked the TV on and switched to a rolling news channel.

The smooth white of the tent was exactly as I'd seen a moment before. Same with the officers standing guard around it and searching the area or on their phones. The whole thing was a mirror image of seconds ago.

I watched for a few minutes; there were few facts to report. A man walking his dog had found a body, believed to be that of a teenage girl, and the police had quickly arrived on scene. The public were being asked to stay away (presumably they were out of shot) and the voice-over described the area as a lonely, bleak part of the town as the camera tracked over the riverbank and the Evenham.

Telling myself that I should have called the police as soon as I'd been able to stand after the attack did no good. I'd run like a scared kid, fleeing from the horror of what I'd seen and the man knowing my name like we were old friends. The police wouldn't want to know about that. They'd care about the first person on the scene leaving a dead child. They'd care about the blood on my clothes and why I'd bagged everything, including my underwear, as soon I'd sneaked into the flat like a burglar.

Pacing around the flat while the news repeated their little information didn't help. The image of three or four officers coming up to the tenth floor in the lift while the one in charge told the others I was a suspect played over and over, and I spent a few minutes staring at the door, waiting for the knock.

It didn't come. Minutes passed and I was still not even close to being in control of a single thing.

Unaware I was going to speak, I said: "I am going out. I'm not hiding here."

Let the world go.

"Shut up," I told the memory.

Ten minutes later, I was out the door despite wanting to close the curtains and keep it all away.

And I couldn't think of anything other than the echoed words still not fading even after seventeen years, their power to wound undiminished.

Chapter Five

Detective Sergeant Michael King kept his hands in his pockets and his back to the river as he gazed across the grass to the man walking his dog. It wasn't the old guy who'd reported the body, struggling to speak through his tears. That gent was giving a statement. Doubtless welcoming the shot of Scotch in his coffee as he went over his dog running to the path and his lumbering chase that ended in realisation, then horror.

"Christ." King muttered it under his breath and wished for a thicker coat. The day was uncomfortable enough without standing next to a freezing river with fuck all to protect him and all the others from a non-stop breeze blowing over the water. Even King's hair, still thick enough at forty-one, was cold.

Could be worse.

Too right. He eyed the tent and the officers standing at its perimeter, their hands folded and their simple presence telling the crowd on the other side of the grass that they were to come no closer. Could be a lot worse. He could be inside the tent where that smell would be growing with each passing minute. Not that it was too bad right now. Death only being a few hours old and the low temperature meant the remains were almost refrigerated. Unless they really were refrigerated soon, the stink would begin to touch everything. Grass, path, trees, air. That reek of a body beginning to fall apart and there wasn't a pissing thing he or anyone else could do to stop it because it was beyond too late for the dead girl.

King saw his own great anger and disgust mirrored on the visible faces as officers spoke to their radios or each other, and even on the little he could make out of his SIO, Detective Superintendent Fulcher, as the older man stood at the tent's edge, talking rapidly into his phone. Fulcher, as big and hard as any lead officer King had seen in countless cliché cop dramas on TV, looked like he might start throwing punches soon. Either that or weep on this little piece of Lawfield where the miles of trees and damp grass and all the cut-throughs up and down overgrown slopes were permanently shadowed filled. Where anyone could be watching and enjoying the sight of the police beginning their investigation.

"Sir?"

King focused on the shape in the white suit at his side. With almost no facial features visible behind the mask and the figure lost in the smooth paper of the clothing, he couldn't take a guess who'd addressed him.

"Bryce, sir."

King nodded. "What you got?"

"Partial shoe print."

The forensics officer led King along the path, both men treading with care, to a section of riverbank where the long grass and shrubs parted in a small curve around muddy earth still damp from the morning's frost. King peered. Bryce was right. The distinct pattern of a shoe lay in the mud, or at least some of the pattern. The upper half by the looks.

"Nice." King wished for another word. Not a thing about this whole ugly business was nice. "With a bit of luck, that will give us something to go on."

Bryce nodded; the paper of his clothing crinkled and rustled. Behind him, other members of the forensics team sifted through tiny sections of the riverbank and around the grass. Two more entered the tent, vanishing into what King knew would be a horrible atmosphere. No bad jokes to try and win one on life's shittiness; no gallows humour here. All the ugly side of people was around King, around everyone, and no amount of jokes or forced piss-taking would do a thing to help.

Life had won. No. Death had won.

Banishing those thoughts, King gestured to a nearby officer and pointed at Fulcher. The officer got the older man's attention with a discreet murmur. Seconds later, the SIO strode from his spot near the tent, still on his phone. He wound up the conversation fast, spotting the look on King's face. Phone clasped in one chunky hand, he eyed the DS and Bryce.

"Anything?" he asked and puffs of fog blew from his mouth.

"Hopefully." King nodded to the ground and Fulcher spotted the print immediately.

"Trainer?" he asked Bryce. The other man nodded.

"Could be something. Could be fuck all and the way things are going, it's fuck all." He took a look to either direction of the path, still wet with puddles and dirty lines of frost. "It's not as isolated as it looks out here. Lost count of the number of people walking their dogs. Not to mention that lot." He was careful to make no gesture to the crowd, growing as the minutes passed. Dozens of bodies filled the grass beyond the cordon. A hundred feet from the tape and officers standing sentry, the public tried for a decent view, some making no attempt to hide their desire to see a body while others held their mobiles aloft, recording the images to upload seconds later. King swallowed his anger. Even after close to twenty years, he couldn't always believe the callous, unthinking nature so often prevalent to groups of people.

It wasn't only that and he had to admit it while Fulcher told Bryce to get all he could from the print and to make sure the photographer currently working in the tent got enough shots. No, not just anger at all or the struggle to keep himself shut off and controlled as always. Crime scene of murder or rape or mugging or a kicking, King knew about control. He knew about looking at the facts and only the facts. No need for an emotional reaction, no use for one. If he was to be any good when it came to nicking the right person, facts were all he needed.

But this one.

This one was not right. Here, in the unending grey light and the lap of the Evenham against the rotting weeds and long strands of the willows sinking into the water, this one was all sorts of shit. All sorts of not right. And it made no difference that there was no sign of sexual assault. The girl's head was still in pieces.

"You okay?" Fulcher asked, voice low as Bryce crouched to the print, the smaller man dismissing his colleagues from his thoughts.

"Sir?" King said.

"You in control, Mike, yeah?" Fulcher's voice remained quiet, soft. For a big man, he knew how to control volume and he knew the power of doing so.

King nodded and blew out a long sigh. "Sorry. Just. . ." He shifted his lips, licked the upper one and took a mental step back. "Just not a fan of this one, sir."

"No. Me, neither." Fulcher placed a gentle hand on King's arm and led him to a patch of the path between two of the skinnier trees. Above the men, narrow branches trembled as a wood pigeon, curious of the gathering of the people, watched them.

"I know this is as shit as it gets." Fulcher kept his rage buried under a sea of outward calm, the sole exterior indication a flush brightening his cheeks. Like King, the scene felt all sorts of wrong to him. He had ten years on King and that meant a decade's more experience of facing stuff he shared only with a select few colleagues; a decade of keeping it away from his family and his home. No way was he bringing the shit to his door. No fucking way and that wasn't about to start now. Even the thought of his wife and two kids being any direct part of this here in the shit and the worse business coming soon made Fulcher want to sink his fingers into the flesh of the man who'd destroyed the child not thirty feet away.

Breathing normally, not sweating and with a steady heartbeat, Fulcher said: "We've got a bad one here, Mike. I know the kid. Her name's Loui. Cameron."

"Oh." King had his own poker face as his SIO did. "Shit."

"Yeah. Shit."

"You telling them direct? Carl and..." The mother's name came to him without much effort as did her face. Hard, all lines and a big pair of staring eyes. As well-known as Carl Cameron was to the force, Erica Cameron was not a woman King wanted anything to do with.

"Erica," King finished.

"Not me. Carl doesn't need to know I'm part of this right now. We'll need a formal from them on the girl, but we know it in any case. Loui." He stared across to the opposite bank, grateful that side was even more overgrown and wild than their immediate surroundings. A small mercy no looky-loos were gawping beyond the water, or worse, snapping shots on their poxy phones.

"I've sent uniform there," Fulcher muttered. "They'll have to get Carl or maybe his brother to do the deed. I—"

Fulcher's phone, still in his hand, rang. He answered it with the same breath in which he'd been speaking to King.

Fulcher's face, relatively unlined for a man of his age, changed in seconds. Fulcher's mouth opened into a black hole. Teeth and gums were gone; the man's tongue became a shrivelled piece of meat, curled and useless on a dry seabed. Cry of disgust a second away, King stepped back. His SIO's features were normal again if he could call the terrible paleness and the lines around the man's lips and eyes—lines that had been much less defined only a short while ago—normal.

You get a grip on this shit. Right now.

King got a grip on this shit. Right now. But he couldn't get a grip on Fulcher turned into an old man, not a big bastard who knew the score when it came to anything.

Fulcher hung up. He met King's eyes and all the control in the world was back in the D/Supt's hands. It had to be if he had any chance of getting through this.

Fulcher said: "There's been two more."

Chapter Six

A few steps from the front doors of the pub, the urge to be back in my flat was as much a need as the need to eat. I stumbled, watched by three guys smoking on the pavement, and pretended I'd hit a loose slab. They studied my battered face with undisguised interest while their fag smoke drifted away.

"You all right, mate?" the oldest one asked. His totally bald head gleamed even with the lack of sun.

I nodded and that was all because words wouldn't come.

You need to do this. You need to be out.

Knowing the interior voice didn't really make sense (it wasn't like I was a suspect; I just had to feel as if I was a normal person and not someone who'd walked straight into a murder scene hours before), I pushed on the doors and entered The Black Boar.

Straight off, it was a bad idea. One o'clock on a Saturday afternoon and the world in the pub for a lunchtime drink and a cheap meal. Again, I needed to be away, to turn the world off. Standing in the entrance and scanning people, I pictured myself in a quieter, backstreet pub with no row of TVs on the wall, no kids, no noise other than a few old farts telling stories. It was no good. Lawfield's pubs catered to the family market. In any case, my injured face and pretty obvious desire to be anywhere else would be clear wherever the hell I went.

The images on the TVs caught my attention as I slipped through the crowd. News. Volume off and subtitles on.

The police were all over the pathway beside the river and the field next to the path. The reporter, a woman clad in a massive coat and scarf, spoke silently to the camera and the words scrolling below caught up with her while I slowed.

They'd identified the body; the family was being told and the police asked people not to speculate or panic.

They had a name. The dead girl who'd briefly had Ella's face had a name and her family now had years and years of agony.

Because of someone who knew my name.

Leaving the exposed spot and the TVs, I crossed through an open space surrounded by fruit machines and had to squeeze between someone's jutting chair and three young guys crowding the noisiest of the machines. Sweating, I moved closer to the bar and side-stepped a big man carrying a tray filled with pints of foaming lager. He paid me no attention despite almost knocking a fat shoulder into my chest, and joined his mates at a table. All of them, clocking me staring at the guy with the tray, gave me the once over.

The black and yellow bruise covering my eye and the other markings staining my cheeks and chin felt huge as they stared, but I kept my gaze on them, waiting for the inevitable challenge. Men in their late thirties, drinking like they were eighteen and ready to take offence at the slightest challenge because that proved their mindset of the world being against them and they were decent geezers who didn't take any shit.

Fucking idiots, I shouted inside and turned away, angry at them and angry at myself for a judgement based on nothing at all.

Through the three or four deep crowd at the long bar, I held a tenner and shuffled forward. Eventually, a teenage girl, flustered and unsmiling, reached me.

I ordered a pint of lager; she poured without speaking, placed the glass on a sticky patch and took my money. Seconds later, she'd given me my change and moved on, forgetting the man with the face of a thousand colours existed.

Jostled by the impatient crowd, I sipped the lager, relishing the refreshing taste on a throat that felt much too dry. Shoved in the back and rapidly losing patience, I shouldered past the others and pretended I didn't notice the stares at my black eye.

The booths directly opposite the bar were all taken and while a couple of tables remained empty in the middle of the floor, I didn't fancy any of them. Too exposed and too much chance of seeing my reflection in the long mirror below all the spirits if the numbers waiting to be served decreased. Instead, I found a spot between a couple of ugly pot plants near the door that led to the toilets and sipped my beer while unable to look away from the TVs.

More panning shots of the lonely path and the still river where no swans or ducks swam; more shots of the massive playing field with the nice houses in the distance, and the implication clear: how could something so horrendous happen near this pleasant, middle-class part of a town not far from Oxford? Why not in some rough shithole like the Sprignall Estate?

Almost unconscious of doing so, I rubbed gentle fingers over the grazes on my cheeks and didn't dare touch my eye. Vision from it wasn't as bad I might have thought although I did have to squint against any light brighter than murk.

Not for the first time since waking, I considered calling my boss, Tom, and faking the shits or something to get the night off. Being on a deserted building site with nothing but a TV for company didn't exactly make me feel great. After only a moment, I rejected the idea. If I could make it out of the flat to this sodding pub to convince myself everything was normal and I had no need to hide, then I wasn't doing a sickie later. If nothing else, Tom had placed a chunky walking stick in a storage locker we had in one of the cabins. Two weeks before, and straight after the rumble between the council and the developers led to downed tools, several homeless men had broken into the site. We'd got the lot on CCTV: the drinking, the fight over a bottle of vodka, the smashed glass and the man stabbed in the arm with a long shard. Since then, the fence had been reinforced, the gate more securely locked and a twenty-four presence on site while the management tried to get work going again. And Tom's stick stashed in a locker 'just in case of any more shit'.

If it came to it, I wouldn't be defenceless.

Those rambling thoughts faded. In the quiet of my head, the same question from a moment before came back, happy to point out thinking about the stick and work was nothing but a distraction.

Eyes back on the TV and back on the scroll of the subtitles as they showed the reporter's silent voice.

. . . a crime that appears to have shocked even experienced officers and a crime they will doubtless be keen to solve as quickly as possible.

Maybe I could help with that. It was time to own up to running away.

I downed the last of my pint, slammed the glass on to a nearby ledge and turned towards the doors. Outside. That was what I needed. Outside to a quiet corner of St Michael's Road where I could call the police and tell them the little I knew.

Right by my side, a voice spoke. "Hello, Jimmy."

Chapter Seven

He sat in the total darkness, staring towards the metal table upon which he'd placed the girl a few moments before. She was yet to stir. The lack of oxygen in the boot of the car meant she'd been unconscious even as he brought her into the building, crunching over the uneven piles of broken brickwork, not paying any attention to the daylight. Now, nearly two hours after the business beside the pub was done, he needed to deal with her. The riverside path was done. The park was done. And the little alleyway between pub and estate agent was definitely done. He had a few moments to spare.

Laura Flint. Hello, Laura Flint. Nice to meet you. Or maybe you don't think so. I can appreciate that. Girls don't like me very much; I can appreciate why, too. But what you have to understand is nothing I do is personal. None of it is against you. It's a means to an end. The same with you as it was with Loui and Cheryl and...

For a moment, the third name wouldn't come. He pictured the jutting ankles and the splashes of dirty water staining her skin where her socks had ridden down. The dirty water; the smell of the rubbish in the bins slightly overshadowed by the winter air, and the image of St Michael's Road unfurling beyond his van, still half asleep at this hour.

Meg Freeman.

Yes. Meg. Loui and Cheryl and Meg and now Laura on the narrow table he rested his fingers against, not touching her. Not yet.

Stop it. Just stop it right now. You can do that. Stop it. Stop. Stop. I stopped, didn't I? You can do the same.

The man with his fingers held firm to the table sniggered at the voice and its lies and Laura stirred.

***

She came to full consciousness in less than two seconds and the memory of the man who'd lost his dog came back a second after that.

She screamed and a hand clamped over her mouth. Frozen palm. Long fingers. For a few insane seconds, a dance of images filled her head: the man approaching from Harrington Place, looking near tears as he called for his dog and cradled a dangling lead; the brief moment of dazzling sunshine that came out of nowhere as he drew closer and her trepidation kicked up a notch; the splayed fingers on her face and reality switching to memory as she remembered an old film she and three friends had watched on TV a month before—some alien thing with spidery, crawling creatures that came out of eggs and ate people's faces—and a dislocated part of her mind was sure one of those aliens had jumped at her from the dark.

"No need for screaming," the man told Laura. "No need at all. All you need to do for a bit is stay calm and wait for Jimmy. He'll get you out of here, okay?"

Still trapped under the ice-cold hand and surrounded by equally freezing air, Laura tried to buck the weight clear. It tightened. All the blur of thoughts from seconds ago were dead and buried. Every facet of focus was on what had happened and where she was and getting out. Through the terror, the purest form of hate she'd experienced pushed through, desperate to see the man's face so she could know who was doing this to her.

"Jimmy's coming although not just yet. He has some stuff to deal with first," the man said almost to himself. "He's got his part to play. Like me and you, Laura. Okay?"

Carrying her as if she weighed nothing, the man boosted Laura from the table, swung her over a shoulder and crossed the room without pause. Her will to scream broken in the sudden, spinning movement, Laura blindly reached down and dug nails into skin. The man's calves, she realised. Powered by the same unthinking hate from a moment before, Laura raked her long nails into his skin.

Above, he chuckled even as he cried out and Laura was not far gone enough to miss the clear difference in tone between the two sounds; one man amused, one man pained.

Swinging Laura again, he dropped her to a hard surface. The impact booted air from her lungs and sent a bright ball of pain blasting across her back and head. Trying to cough and inhale, she failed at both and reached a weak hand into the void above. Her fingers struck rough cloth that might have been a coat before he slapped her forearm.

"Listen, Laura," he said and she was finally able to cough. Spluttering, gasping, she fought for breath even as she twisted. For a wonderful second, her lower half rose free from the slab. Then he grabbed the sides of her head and slammed it down, hard.

The fresh pain made the impact from a few seconds before feel like a gentle tap. Laura's yell collapsed into more coughing while she tried to sob.

"Listen." He said it a second time in the same flat tone as the first. "I need to put a small mask on your face. Help you breathe. If you don't let me, you'll run out of oxygen in a few minutes. Five, tops."

Through the storm crashing inside Laura's head and through the panic and sheer terror, a new fear came to a dark life. The first coherent thought since hitting full consciousness said:

Run out of oxygen? Oh my God. Where am I? Mum, get me out of here. Please, Mum.

He took a handful of Laura's hair, pulled her head free from the slab and slipped the mask over her face. Taking a moment to relish the feel of her hair and to recall the memory of the first girl's hair all those years back, he smoothed the long strands down and gently let go.

"Breathe normally. No panting. No shouting. You don't want to dislodge it."

She felt him shifting something attached to the mask, heard a soft rustling, and the mask shifted position a fraction. The first register of the glacial chill struck Laura, the rapid spread of adrenaline coursing through her system unable to combat it. They could have been inside an industrial freezer. She still wore her coat and jeans but no gloves. The man had made no attempt to remove her clothing but she couldn't process that thought or take it further. All the horror in the world skulked a tiny distance beyond it.

"Here." He draped a heavy blanket over her body. It stunk and immediately made her skin itch and not only because the material was rough. It belonged to him, and it was a filthy piece of rotten waste she wanted nowhere near her.

But, God, this place was so cold.

"It might make you feel better to know I won't rape you. I have no interest in that sort of thing. Not like others. I'm not like others."

Laura tried to block the word as soon as it came out of his mouth. Keeping the horrific potential of it at arm's length was all she could manage. And whatever the hell he meant by others was of no importance.

"If you keep that mask on your face, it'll do everything you need until Jimmy comes."

Who? Oh, God. Get me out of here. Get me home, okay?

Laura knew she'd be no physical match for the man, whoever he might be. Unless he was smaller than her, and that wasn't likely, she wasn't going to win a fight, but she could still hurt him. Yes. She had nails, didn't she? Long nails. And teeth. Whatever it took to get away from this man and his soft, calm voice and this dark, terrible nothing place.

Shrieking behind the mask, Laura swung her right hand towards the sound of his voice.

A torch light exploded into life.

To show the wall right at the end of the slab she lay upon.

The wall of small doors, all closed.

Apart from the one beyond her feet.

"Get some rest, Laura," the man said and that could not be true, was not possible.

Because he had no face. Only a void every bit as blank as the gloom stretching fingers towards her through what felt like the white swirl of a blizzard.

He shoved on the slab and Laura screamed as the wall of little doors swallowed her. Inches from her head, metal connected with metal and she was buried alive in a glacial hole.

"Don't lose that mask, Laura," he called through the door. His torchlight made the faded metal gleam. He held it over the tiny hole he'd drilled into the door. The green tubing that emerging from the hole flew back and forth.

"Jimmy will be here." The man clicked his torch off and the shadows eagerly rushed in to fill all the spaces. "Eventually."

Leaving the tubing to shake in its mad dance and Laura's muffled pleas to be heard by nobody, the man returned to the outside world and all its wonderful possibilities.

Chapter Eight

The guy who'd spoke leaned in close; the stink of his beery breath made me wince, and the dull cast to his blue eyes told me he was one of those blokes who practically lived in the pub. Probably a bore when sober, and a pain in the arse when pissed. I didn't want anything to do with either.

"What happened to your face?"

This, I did not need. Not even at the best of times. Seconds from striding through the mass of flesh and noise to find somewhere I could make my call to the police and hopefully do some good about what was still on the wall of TVs wasn't close to the best of times.

My options were limited. Talk to him, ignore him or just walk.

"Hey. I said what happened to your face."

A slight suggestion of aggression, a note hinting at the violence that probably lived permanently below his surface. While he wasn't big or a hardman, I was willing to bet a pisshead like that would throw punches or pint glasses with equal disregard. I wasn't in the mood to be caught in his shit.

Shouldn't have come out.

The murmur of my thought almost made me laugh. Yeah. Standing in the pub with too many people, and now the local alky wanting to be my mate.

My flat and all its peace seemed much too distant.

"I had an accident," I told him.

"Yeah?"

He swayed. Just a little. Enough, though.

"What happened to the other guy?"

"What?" I said it too loudly. "There was nobody else. Just me."

"Fuck off," he scoffed. "You look like shit. Some foreign bastard, was it? Fucking loads of them round here."

At the swearing, the couple at the nearest table looked our way, the woman frowning, and the man checking us out like we were good mates telling dirty jokes way too loudly. It wasn't much of a stretch to picture the guy coming over and telling us to shut it if Dull Blue Eyes kept up with the bad language.

"No." I tried to back away and find an opening in the crowd, but a woman with three kids came from nowhere to block my escape. I'd dressed in a fleece and coat, ready for the wintry streets. The heating and so much flesh crowded together made that a bad idea which seemed about par for the course over the last few hours.

"Loads of them," he said, voice rising. "I tell you what. The other night, I was in here when this—"

Too much had happened. Everything hurt, and the sight of the dead girl's face morphing into Ella's while she stared up at me would not go away. I cut the drunk off.

"Look. Mate." A single breath wasn't much help. "I came out for a pint, not to talk to anyone."

He blinked, my words taking a second to make it to his brain. "What? You being a cunt?" he asked eventually.

I rose to it and my reply was a fraction under a shout. "No. You are."

The noise of the conversations and the kids were all a rolling ball in my head while the slightest movement sent more perspiration soaking into the thin material of my t-shirt. The woman with the three kids pulled them close, all backing away while the man at the table shifted to rise and I took in all of it from Dull Blue Eyes' rapid panting to the kids on their forced retreat to the gleam of the lights over the bar, turned too bright somehow, made ugly because of their fierce shine.

The pisshead blinked a few times and backed away. Seconds later, he'd vanished into the crowd, a slightly stumbling shape known to most people, it seemed. They watched him go with either annoyance or resignation.

All at once, my insides flattened. People watched me from the corners of their eyes and I saw myself as they did: a guy who clearly hadn't slept much, half his face turned yellow and purple and one eye stained with a giant bruise. They saw trouble. They saw someone who'd been seconds away from kicking off with a drunk for no good reason.

What are you trying to prove by coming out here?

On all rational levels, I knew the most I was guilty of was not reporting the murder to the police. While that would probably get me in the shit, it wasn't murder. Staying in my flat wouldn't have been hiding there, no matter how much a worm of guilt said otherwise. And lurking in a busy pub with a marked face would make no difference. All it proved was that I wasn't one for crowds.

Inwardly, I laughed at myself. Crowds? I wasn't one for anybody. Let the world go; that was the thought that came most often in the silence while I tried to read my book and occasionally checked the few monitors which showed the hospital grounds.

Let the world go.

Let the world burn.

Old thoughts, both of them, and both I'd always wanted to believe were shared by Ella. That was a lie and I knew it. No baseless teenage angst for her, no sneering judgement of adults who seemingly knew nothing. She'd liked people despite being shy; she'd been interested in just about everybody and it was only afterwards that I realised that had been down to seeing people as subjects to draw.

She'd loved to draw, to paint.

Let the world go.

My thought alone, the memory storming out of the past where it should have rotted and died; an instruction from deep inside I'd followed without any debate or argument, and done so to the point that had got me my quiet flat and my meaningless jobs and nothing else.

What are you going to do?

I'd proved whatever stupid point I was trying to make to myself. I'd not hidden away. I was out in the noise and life of the town. I was on the receiving end of curious looks and probably speculation on what fight I'd got into the night before. If there was a lesson to be learned from any of it, I didn't know what the hell it was.

Face flushing and body much too hot, I refused to meet anyone's eye as I pushed my way back to the doors and the welcome chill of outside. A bouncer stood aside, studying me with the same degree of unconscious curiosity as anyone drinking in the pub. Luckily for me, I had enough self-control not to challenge him and stood at the edge of the pavement, breathing, trying to feel cooler and less constricted. A taxi passed, a couple of blokes left the pub to light up and I felt them and the doorman giving my back the once over.

Okay. So, you've come out and shown the world you're not a nutcase, right? Now get out of here, call the police and deal with what happened.

While the plan meant trouble, it was also oddly welcome. It meant control and order. Neither had been in my grasp since walking into that scene beside the river.

Hands in my coat pockets, I strode past the front of the pub, thinking of the best place to call the police. I made it level with the little alleyway between the pub and the building next door before a hand brushed my shoulder.

It was Dull Blue Eyes, come from the pub by another set of doors. Over his shoulder, the smokers were talking to the doorman and none paid any attention to whatever was about to happen between me and my new friend. They might as well have been in another town.

"You." He said it while swaying.

"Yeah. Me. What do you want?"

He stopped swaying. And grinned. "Talk to me like I'm a cunt."

He came at me, moving much faster than anyone would have expected. A weak punch struck my chest; another flew at my chin but missed. Before I had chance to react, he chucked his body at me. We stumbled together, swallowed by the gloom in the alley, my boots kicking through slush, puddles and scattered litter. Raging, swearing, the drunk managed to land a punch on my chin. I went further backwards, dirty water soaking into the ankles of my jeans.

The anger was more than anger, more than rage. It ate everything behind my eyes, and turned rational thought into a big, fat joke.

Screaming, I decked Dull Blue Eyes in the cheek, again and again even as agony bellowed in my fist and hot blood splattered from his nose to coat my face, coat and arm. Again. Again, until the murk lit with the white square opening back to the street turned into a starless night. Again, until the alley and the road and pub were all gone and I stood on the path with the Evenham a still sheet like oil and the old trees like a watching audience.

Again, until the drunk collapsed with his face a shifting blur and his body shrinking to a much smaller form, a child, a girl reaching for me while her face came back into view and sheets of blood poured from her head and she reached, she reached, she reached.

Ella screeched from the ground as the blood drowned her face, her eyes and I could only scream back.

"Mate?"

Everything vanished. It was like a TV switching off to leave a blank screen. An instant later, the wall of the pub and the estate agent returned, bringing back the unpleasant present, the dampness soaking into my jeans and the stink of the rubbish in the bins at my back.

"Mate?" The voice again, the question concerned and also nervous. "You all right?"

It was the doorman in the white square that opened to the pavement. No river or path. And no sign of my sister.

Panting and convinced the drunk would be dead at my feet, I leaned to him. He rolled over, revealing an unmarked face apart from splashes of puddle water. No blood. No indication I'd pounded him into the ground.

"Bill, you pain in the arse." The doorman approached and pulled the drunk upright. The man protested but only weakly. He wouldn't meet my eye.

"He's all right most of the time," the doorman told me and winked to show no harm was done or meant. In the perfect smoothness of his build, his heavy coat, his shaved head and sculpted goatee, everything probably was all right.

"Yeah," I said and it emerged as a croak.

At the opening, the smokers and a few others had crowded round, all eager to see a rumble. The doorman told them to move aside as he forcibly led Bill to the street, the drunk walking with his head down and not making a sound.

I followed for a single step.

My boot hit a patch of ice. A second later, I hit the filthy ground.

Legs splayed, arse throbbing much like my face, I sat in the melting frost, making no attempt to pretend I'd done anything but tripped as the men on the pavement giggled and one gave me a mocking cheer.

"Fuck this," I whispered.

"You're not having a good day, are you?" the doorman said and sounded genuinely sorry for me.

"Not in the least."

I shifted to rise, hands squelching on something I could only hope was mud, the cold already stealing through the seat of my jeans and coat. A look at the doorman made me stop.

He was looking behind me. To the great bulk of the bin.

Turning my head took forever.

Jutting from the underside of the bin, the white of a bare ankle shone, and the marble flesh was a million miles from the coal-black of the dead girl's blood a few hours before.

Chapter Nine

As a makeshift cover, the plastic sheeting supplied by scaffolders working on a building further along St Michael's Road wasn't perfect but it was better than nothing when it came to protecting the alleyway from sight.

A few officers stood in a tight line on the pavement, hands folded, and their bodies forming a wall. They gazed straight ahead, not talking and giving the impression of unseeing the people crowding on the other side of the road—the crowd kept all the way back to Church Walk by tape. The pub had been emptied within minutes of the police's arrival, most agreeing to leave their lunches and drinks without too much complaint when they realised the police were telling rather than asking. Several men protested with varying degrees of volume; a quick offer of a few free drinks from the pub's duty manager placated most of them. The rest were led to the doors and the street by officers not in the mood to take any trouble. At the same time, the staff in the adjoining estate agents were told to leave their building. They stood in a small group outside a nearby Starbucks. While some suggested they go inside, others were content to vape. They kept all their attention on the police and anonymous figures in their white suits passing beyond the officers and sheeting into the mouth of the alleyway.

In a long convoy, vans and cars covered the opposite side of the road. Officers stood near them, either silent or on their phones. Above, the sky remained clear of a helicopter. The rumour had spread through the assembled watchers that it wasn't available while others maintained it was already in use over the river a couple of miles away. No noise came from above and the sun refused to break through the featureless sky. More rumours spread: the body beside the pub was a homeless man, frozen to death overnight; the body was a stab victim, left to die after being mugged.

The body was another girl.

The opinions and views flowed from person to person, shared, scoffed at, elaborated and passed on to stream with the wind and be shared on text, email and online. Less than ten minutes after the first of the police vans had sped into St Michael's Road, lights a spinning dance of colours and sirens a non-stop howl, a new rumour came to life in the watching crowd.

There was another murder scene a few miles away in a park. Another dead girl, and that made three if the one in the alley was a girl.

Standing at the front of the crowd and jostled by bodies, the young man dressed in a heavy coat and faded jeans heard the rumours and gazed blandly at the surrounding figures while studying the police.

Bill Lister stood flanked by two officers, hugging himself, face miserable but still. He muttered something—the watching man had no way of knowing what but he guessed it was a case of outlining the brief fight that had uncovered the dead girl—while one of the officers wrote on his pad. Bill seemed smaller and scrawnier than usual, certainly more so than their conversation in the van earlier that morning. While never a big guy, he now appeared diminished. It was as if the years of drinking and barely eating had caught up with him in the space of a few hours, turning him into a stunted figure in his sixties rather than forties.

The young man in the crowd had no worry or fear his part in what was happening would reach the police. Bill knew the score if he wanted his drink and his money. Tell them what happens, Bill had been told by the guy driving the van earlier in the morning. Tell them what you saw and then come to me for your reward. You can do that.

Bill could do that. Bill wanted his reward.

Still watching, the man brushed loose hair back from his forehead, the strands hanging towards unlined eyes, and scanned the other figures further up the road. Behind, a few shouts broke out as people demanded to know what was happening, who the body was. The man caught a moment of a voice to his left from a woman clutching the hand of a fat man.

"We need to get up there, Colin. I want to know who it is."

The young man brushed hair back again and rolled his eyes. Get closer to the pub? No chance. Even as the demands for answer grew in volume and frequency, several officers drew closer, one readying himself to tell the people to move further back.

Without seeming to make a move, the watching man crept away from the front. He kept himself close enough to see—three bodies ahead—and caught the eye of a teenage girl at his side.

She smiled and quickly looked away.

He also smiled.

Coming from the pub, walking with three officers, Jimmy Marshall was led to one of the cars where more officers shielded him from direct view. It wasn't much of a guess to know they'd taken Jimmy's first statement and were readying him to transport to the station for a more detailed questioning. Don't let the public see, though. Don't make Jimmy a suspect—at least, not in full view of the masses.

Where the road turned into Carling Way, several vehicles halted. Seconds later, the first of the TV crews speedily approached barrier of officers and tape, their cameras recording, the reporters racing through the basics of their reports due to go live within minutes.

At the same time, police ordered them to move back and to get their vehicles off the Way; it was a no-parking area and they needed to move right now. The cameras swallowed the images and the raised voices while the Saturday afternoon dragged on and the sheeting blocking the dead girl from the hungry eyes flapped at its edges.

In the crowd, the watching man with the pleasant good looks and the loose hair was gone. The girl who'd smiled at him a moment before took a quick look around before dismissing him from her thoughts with some regret that a guy just a couple of years older than her had moved on before she'd had chance to say anything.

He was not sad to lose a chance with her.

At sixteen or seventeen, she was too old for his needs.

Chapter Ten

They brought me to an office rather than any kind of interrogation room. As the officers outside The Boar said again and again during my long questioning, I wasn't under arrest; they needed my help and as much information as I could offer. I had no urge to get a solicitor involved especially as it felt like they would delay everything and make it all so much more real. Maybe a stupid way of thinking but at that point, I didn't give a shit. If it meant getting away from the police and people back to my flat, I'd do just about anything.

"Have a seat, Mr Marshall."

The officer gestured to a seat beside a desk piled with papers and a computer. He'd shut the door behind us, blanketing the sound of ringing phones, voices and footsteps. I'd never been into Lawfield's police station and hadn't known what to expect. At a wide reception area, pleasant and clean, the four officers who'd brought me from the surreal scenes outside the pub led the way to a door locked by key code. We went from there to a corridor lined with bright white walls, passing offices that could have been part of any modern company and ended in the room I suspected was more of a free for all space rather than the officer—his name was King—used exclusively.

He sat; I took a few quiet breaths. A window opposite showed a wide wave of green that ended at the road. Beyond the road, a huge golf course grew towards Netherton Woods. Out there, in the gloom between the trees and crunching through the deep piles of rotting leaves and dead twigs, all the shit of the dead girls and whatever the hell was happening would be far out of reach. Not for me, though. Not while King studied my beaten face without making an attempt to hide his appraisal.

"That looks bloody painful."

I touched my eye with gentle fingers. "Yep."

"Coffee? Tea?"

"No, thanks."

"Sure?" He sounded surprised. "It's decent stuff. None of that vending machine rubbish here."

He smiled. I didn't.

"No, thanks. I'm fine."

Nodding, King said: "You told my colleagues you were beaten last night. That right?"

"Yes. Down Mansfield Road. This morning, actually. Not last night."

"An attempted mugging?"

"Well, they went for my phone." I tapped my front pocket. "I managed to hit them a couple of times. It was only a kid. I don't think they thought I'd fight back so they legged it."

"A kid did that?"

All the smiles were gone.

"No. Not all of it. The ground did most when I tripped. He got a boot into my face which was this." Again, with the soft touch to my eye.

"And you didn't call us? Didn't want to tell the police?"

"To be honest, there didn't seem much point. It was still pitch-black. I got no look at him at all. Couldn't tell you where he ran; couldn't give a description and he got nothing off me. I just wanted to get home and sleep after my shift."

"Fair enough."

King leaned forward, hands on the desk. While not built, he had a presence that didn't come purely from physicality. Maybe it was the calm brown of his eyes. He wouldn't get results from bashing heads; he was a guy with a shitty job that involved shitty people.

"Can we go over everything that happened from the moment you got to the pub, Mr Marshall?"

It occurred to me to tell him he could call me Jimmy. I didn't. We were police officer and person of interest, not mates.

Looking King straight in the eye, I repeated the stuff I'd told the other police while we stood in the wind I didn't really feel, obviously missing out the trippy headfuck of being taken back a few hours before or Ella's blood-soaked face right at my feet. A few other pieces occurred as I spoke—how quick our little fight really had been, the smell in the alley that I'd put down to rubbish but was clearly something much worse. . .and the creeping surety the drunk had wanted me to get into the alley.

That last bit came out before I could stop it, and it was more than idle wondering. It was close to an accusation my drunk friend knew something.

"You think he deliberately started the fight at that point so you'd end up in the alley?" King asked.

"It's possible." A politician's answer.

"We'll bear that in mind." A politician's reply. I held a grim smile inside. King went on while the outside sounds of the station were beyond the closed door and stuck on the far side of Lawfield at the same time. Maybe out there in the polar wind blowing through the quiet of Netherton Woods, or down the long pathway next to the Evenham where a dead girl's bloodstains still marked the ground.

"For what it's worth, I don't think you're hiding anything, Mr Marshall. I think you were unlucky this morning. . .or maybe not. We would have found the body at some point. Your altercation with Mr Lister means we found it much sooner." He tapped a longer finger on the desk. "You heard about the events out by the river, I take it?"

"I heard."

"It's far too early to put any connection between that and the scene next to the pub. Far too early." He looked away, barely for a second. Long enough, though.

"There's an ongoing investigation. Detective Superintendent Clyde Fulcher is in charge. He's out there, now—"

I interrupted. "At the river?"

King shook his head. "We had reports of an attack in a park. He's attending that event now."

"A third one? Jesus Christ."

King was quick to shake his head again. "Not necessarily. It's far too early to say." A second later, he changed the subject. "Your face looks like more of a sustained beating."

"What?"

He said nothing. I realised the switch was designed to confuse me. Start with a bit of connected information, make it sound like he was sharing and then trip me up with an insinuation. In the silence of his appraisal, I realised a second issue: ordinarily, there was no way they'd have told me anything about another body, but he had. That was another part of his style. King suspected I was involved and the bit of information was designed to get a reaction from me. Of course, I had nothing but dismay.

And a creeping sense of familiarity.

"You look like you got the shit kicked out of you." King jabbed a finger at my face. "That is not a quick kick in the face from a kid after your phone."

Desperately hoping the sweat forming under my hair would not trickle down my forehead and the flush discolouring my cheeks could be put down to the warmth of King's office, I said: "Are you accusing me of something?"

"No." Any friendliness had left the room. I was with a police officer and all the weight of law sat on my shoulders. "You're scared, Mr Marshall. Other officers might think you're a liar. I think you're keeping something to yourself." He lowered his voice as if we might be overheard. "We have two dead children. We might have a third. If you can help us, I will appreciate it."

It was only through luck that my hand remained steady as I gestured to his pad. "You've got everything I know there. I told your colleagues the same outside the pub."

King leaned back. "You work the nightshift at the hospital site?"

"That's right."

"We can check that."

"Please do." I rattled off a number. "That's my boss, Tom Hemmings. You want to know where I was at any point, you ask him."

King made no effort to write down the number. Instead, he met my eyes. "Do you really think Bill Lister directed you to that alley?"

The answer came with no bullshit. No finesse. "Yes."

"We'll see what we can find out from him. You're not planning on going away anywhere?"

"No."

"Good."

King rose, crossed to the door and opened it. "I'll see you out."

Without another word, I walked with King back down the corridor, watched from the offices, to the reception and out through the heavy doors to the steps and the wind coming off the golf course in an unbroken flow. There were no players in sight and probably wouldn't be for another couple of months. Four in the afternoon had come (which felt nuts seeing as my walk to the Boar could have happened minutes earlier) and shadows crept in from the treeline to blacken the road and pavement. It would be a long walk back home. Probably dark by the time I made it.

"Thank you for your time, Mr Marshall," King said and left me.

I studied the damp green where nobody walked or played. In the distance, a few birds rose from the trees, each one a darting speck against the grey. Puddles pooled over the station car-park, the remnants of melted frost. I thought about the patches of ice close to invisible on the path that morning and I thought about the damp crawling up and down the walls in the alley.

I thought about Ella's face stained red as all the blood in the world rained through her eyes and down to the slash of her mouth.

Chapter Eleven

Unable to see the time on the cracked face of his watch, Bill Lister took a guess it was gone eight and approached the rear of the shops. On the outskirts of the Sprignall Estate, Middleton Place could have been removed from the rest of Lawfield and dumped in some deep hole. Bill hadn't seen anybody for at least twenty minutes. He didn't think it was all simply down to the low temperature or the night come down fast. There'd been a heavy police presence in the estate for much of the day, most of it focused in and around Artindale Square where the girl—the first girl—had lived with her parents and uncle.

But Bill didn't want to think about it so he would not.

Despite the almost crippling desire to get into the rear of the derelict shop where he'd been told his reward waited, he took a moment to double check the area. A car turned into a street a good fifty feet away, its light spearing the murk but not coming anywhere near him. A thin mist hung low to the ground; the car's lights became weak and ghostly beyond the white. In seconds, its movement faded to silence. Few lights shone in the windows of the houses at Bill's back. Between him and the squat terraces, an ugly patch of grassland was a churned mess of frozen mud. Two bins stood at its perimeters, both scorched and melted by recent fires. The council would replace them and the same would happen again. In the meantime, waste grew in the messy tangle of bushes at the far end of the green. Crisp packets, crumpled cans of soft drinks and strong lager jutted from the shrubs like plants. Further inside, flattened condoms and a few needles lay buried below the earth hard like rock. Moisture dripped inside the bushes where the ground took it and more ice formed.

In front of Bill, the few shops were silent. While he hadn't been this way in months, he had an idea only one of the buildings still functioned as a business, and that was a mini supermarket down the other end. Over the last couple of years, the florists, Chinese takeaway and launderette had closed, leaving the precinct to the kids who hung around at night, to the occasional dealer and to people like the young man Bill had come to see. While the police spent a lot of time in Sprignall, this patch had been left to rot. Too far out. Too close to the edge of the town with nothing beyond but the parkway and miles of fields. This was the forgotten corner of the estate and Bill could not wait to get the fuck out of it.

He grasped the metal at the centre of the gates, aware the terrible sting sank into his thin gloves and not caring.

This was a bad idea. This whole thing from the moment the man had approached him while he drank in Tirrington Park to whatever the hell had gone down this morning to the fight with that guy outside the pub to right now was a bad idea, and all he had to do was turn around and walk as fast as he could. Get out of the estate, get out of Lawfield if need be. There were plenty of roads, plenty of secret ways into the surrounding cities. He could walk all the way to Oxford if he wanted do. He could be a waste of a man there as easily as he could in Lawfield.

Close to tears for reasons he did not want to consider, Bill pushed on the gates. As promised, they were unlocked and swung open with a resounding squeal. There'd been no oil applied to the hinges in years. Decades, maybe.

He stared into the nothing visible at the back of the shop and slid his hands into his armpits. The stink of his unwashed body and filthy clothes had long since stopped bothering him, and while nearly all scents were close to destroyed by the cold, he caught a breath of something animalistic and savage. It vanished to be replaced by the sharp tang of a mix of spirits.

Bill's mouth watered; his throat begged for a drink. He stepped into the gloom.

Chapter Twelve

"Have you got it?"

The question came to life before Bill had chance to stop it. Immediately, his face flamed, the heat of his cheeks untouched while the rest of his body felt like he'd stepped into a freezer, not the storage area of a shop.

"Don't worry about it," the man replied and not for the first time, Bill felt man wasn't right. His strange, frightening acquaintance was barely out of his teens; he was still a kid, really. Probably born while Bill's life was already lurching to its drawn-out end of being claimed by the bottle.

I'm scared of a boy. He's not even twenty-five.

If there was anything to come after his dismayed thought, Bill couldn't find it.

The younger man held a torch, the strong beam exposing a floor thick with dust and dirt, and the lower half of a wall draped in cobwebs. For a moment, he flashed the light over his face, revealing a pale face although Bill didn't think the paleness was down to anything unhealthy. The youth's face was naturally that shade, made more obvious by the thick weight of dark hair and eyes as green as a cat's.

"I never told you my name."

"That's okay," Bill replied and his thought was a speeding rat in his head. Shouldn't have come here, shouldn't have come here.

"It's Robert."

"Okay."

The torch light traced a pattern over the dirt. Bill couldn't help but look while his mind begged him to get out, get away through the rat runs of alleys all over the estate. The police would still be on Artindale Square and that couldn't be more than a mile from the shop and the torchlight and the strange kid.

"You did well outside the pub." He ran the beam from the torch over the opposite wall. A tall shelving unit jutted from it, the shelves empty, most hanging loose due to the rotting wood. Bill tried to remember when the place was last in use even as he wondered where the nearest other person might be and if they were within hearing distance.

"Did you tell the police anything?"

Despite his fear, anger rose inside Bill. He'd had a job to do and he'd done it. Being questioned by this little shit was bang out of order.

"No. They asked a lot of questions; I told them what happened with me and that guy. We had a fight. End of."

Keeping the anger from his voice was difficult; he managed to do so, holding it in check through the promise of a drink. Of a lot of drinks.

What about the dead kid? Who put her there under that bin?

The same question the law asked while they implied he knew so much more than he said, but he could not think about either even though the answer was obvious.

Couldn't think about it, though. Not here with the mould and the quiet.

"Good." The torchlight struck a hold all on the ground. In the poor light, Bill hadn't noticed it all. "They'll want to speak to you again soon. You just tell them the same stuff next time, all right?"

"Yeah." Bill's focus became laser sharp, a pinpoint on the bag. Its zip glinted and the smooth material of its side suggested it was brand new. Not that he'd have given a shit if the lad presented him with a bin bag as long as he got his reward.

"All yours." The youth nudged the bag with one foot. Its contents tinkled and the insides of Bill's cheeks turned as dry as the cracks in the pavements and in the frozen mud surrounding the old buildings. Keeping an eye on the kid, he grabbed the bag's handles, slid it close which caused more soft tinkling, and tugged on the zip. Although there wasn't enough light shining in his direction to be sure, he thought he saw at least three bottles of good Scotch, two vodkas and a litre of gin. And wedged between each bottle, a bundle of notes. Five hundred quid if the boy—no, the man—had told the truth.

"What do you think about the dead girl?"

The question came out of nowhere. Bill looked up, licking his lips and not aware of doing so. He registered the bottle held in a small, clean hand and had time to think: it came from nowhere.

"The dead girl? Beside the pub? Her name was Meg Freeman."

Bill's gaze dropped to the bag with his drink and his cash.

The bottle swung through the air without a sound.

Glass smashed into the side of Bill's head, turning his universe into a supernova. Collapsing into the shards and the rich aroma of Scotch, he lay splayed like a dying fish, mouth opening, closing, blood filling it and coughed out to spray up and rain back to his face in droplets. Half his vision had been destroyed; hearing had been almost banished apart from the thunderstorm echoing through his skull.

The younger man crouched over Bill, ignoring the shattered glass and the stink of alcohol. The stench sank into the dirty floor, was taken by the mould and damp crawling over the walls, was consumed by the hungry dark. Briefly, a sliver of moonlight slid in through the still open rear doors, joined the beam from the torch and revealed more of the derelict shop. Its floor met a security door at the far end which in turn opened to the empty front and the windows sealed behind heavy shutters.

The shadows crept away from the light. Clouds passed back over the moon, turning the interior again into an almost void.

Still crouched over Bill, the youth took the bottle of gin from the back, unscrewed the cap and upended the contents directly over Bill's face.

Spluttering, choking, Bill fell into a lake of fire as the alcohol soaked into the streaming wound at the side of his head and flowed through the blood in his mouth. He inhaled, choked and tried to breathe again. All thoughts had been destroyed; he had nothing beyond the screeching need to get away. Bucking his middle did no good; his attacker rode him like a horse and continued to empty the last of the gin while all Bill could manage was a high-pitched whine.

"Loui Cameron," the boy said in a light tone. "Meg Freeman. Cheryl Temple. Laura Flint. All the girls, Bill. All them and more. So many more of them."

The last of the spirit ran over Bill's face. He thrashed his head from side to side. Blood and alcohol splattered the floor. Neither touched the boy's arms or clothing.

"All the girls I want, Bill."

Another bottle grabbed from the bag. Vodka.

"I tell you, Bill. I never feel as alive as I do at times like this."

A resounding smash as the lower half of the bottle struck the floor, leaving the top half as a jagged chunk of glass.

Through his torment, Bill heard someone else speak and that made no sense because he and the little bastard who'd hurt him were the only people in the shop. All the same, a new voice, sad and regretful, spoke to him. "I tell you a secret, Bill."

For a second, Bill heard nothing beyond the crackle of the fire.

"This thing scares me. It won't listen to me; it won't ever stop. I've done bad things. I know that, I admit it, but this thing?" The new speaker sighed and there was a mix of exhaustion and self-pity in the breath. Whoever the new person was, they were of no help to him. The few words were enough for Bill to know the speaker's focus was all on himself, not on helping anyone else.

"This thing is much worse than me. This is as bad as it gets. And I can't stop it."

The new person was gone without another sound, leaving Bill to try to suck in clean air that didn't burn, to fail utterly.

Then the man barely out of his teens ground the broken bottle into Bill's face.

Chapter Thirteen

Feeling like I'd been awake for days, I fumbled with the key and rested my forehead against the door. A jumble of thoughts competed with the ache in my feet and legs for attention. Trying not to give a shit about either, I finally managed to connect key with lock and slipped inside.

The place was almost completely devoid of light. The only illumination came through a gap in the curtains on the far side of the living room. Silver daggers of moonlight pierced the gloom. I hit the light switch harder than I meant to, and ignored the thud in my hand.

It was after six. The long walk from the police station and King had been a slow one, my energy levels bottoming out due to the stress and too little sleep. By the time I'd hit the main area of shops, they'd all been closing up, staff eager to get rid of the last stragglers. The pubs had been about as busy as I'd expected: people out of the wind and the gloom to have their dinner before heading home to Saturday night TV.

Then the Saturday drinkers would be out and Lawfield would become a bustle of noise, bodies and taxis.

Slipping off my coat and chucking it at the stand by the phone, I checked my mobile. No missed calls or texts. If King or any other copper had anything more to ask, they were keeping quiet. And I had to wonder how quiet they'd be once they dug out my real surname. It was a matter of time. While they didn't know I had any connection to the first murder scene, I couldn't get away from being the guy who'd discovered the dead girl next to the pub. They'd be looking into me even if it was only a cursory search, and that would search would lead beyond the name Marshall.

I took a long shower, gave my multi-coloured face a once over in the steamy mirror, dressed in fresh clothes and cooked a chilli. Avoiding the news while I ate, I tried to let the shitty day go and couldn't quite manage it. For years—probably since being a kid—I'd lived with self-control and been in charge of my life. No relationships to get in the way and make things messy or complicated; no career, only a series of jobs which suited me. In the space of less than twenty-four hours, control had been chucked out of the window.

I finished the meal and planned the rest of the evening (I'd called Tom on the walk home to outline the whole thing with the police and beg for a night off. Tom, being a good guy, had been only too quick to give it). I saw myself polishing off a bottle of decent whisky Tom gave me for my birthday two months before and watching a couple of films. Maybe even getting pissed and sleeping the sleep of the drunk.

Content to stay where I was for a while, I remained on the sofa and time passed. I thought of little, paid less attention to the TV and kept still to lessen the chance of my bruised face waking up.

In the hallway, the phone rang, its shrill noise making me jerk back and hiss. Confusion and a strange panic came at the same time as I checked the time. Close to half nine. It'd been well over a year since someone called my landline; keeping it plugged in was simple habit. And after the afternoon of telling the police on the street outside the pub what had gone down, then the conversation with King, the last thing I wanted to do was talk to some fucker about an accident I hadn't had in the last year.

Silencing the phone by yanking it off its little table was so welcome, I almost didn't want to destroy the quiet by speaking.

"Hello." I said it as a statement, not a welcoming question.

Down the line, hush came back. Except not total hush. The wind whispered monotonously, and in the background, traffic. Whoever was calling me, they were doing so from a public phone.

"Yes?" I said too loudly, seconds from disconnecting the call before grabbing that bottle of Scotch from the cupboard and not moving off the sofa until nature called.

"I know what you did."

The speaker whispered it; each word delivered with a soft, plosive hiss. There was anger in his voice. A lot of it held in check. Barely.

It's him.

I told myself that was shit but couldn't believe it. He knew my name, after all. Not much to assume he somehow knew my phone number.

Despite the comforting weight of a heavy fleece and the radiators all red hot, a new thought froze me all over.

If he knows your name and your phone number, then he knows where you live.

As much as I wanted to believe that was just paranoia, it felt legit. My landline. That was the thing. The number I'd given to exactly one person in the last year and that was Tom Hemmings. If he ever called, it was on my mobile. The landline was a relic, something to be forgotten about and something to be used by a person who couldn't get my mobile number, but could track me down the old-fashioned way.

"I know what you did."

The background sounds were little help; trying to place the location and failing, all I could be sure of was traffic moving rather than stopping and starting.

"Who the fuck is this?" I shouted.

"Fuck you." I'd angered them, whoever they were. They didn't like to be challenged. But fear also mixed with their anger. Panic, maybe.

"You bastard. I know it. I fucking know what you did."

It wasn't panic, I realised. It was grief. A cold flame lit inside; the fire fuelled by memory.

"Where they found her. That path." The caller took a few breaths; the line hissed. "You meet me on that path in an hour. That field behind Water View. That path that goes across it and comes out at the river."

I knew it. Knew it well. After all, I'd washed my bloody hands in the freezing water not far from it that morning. It was too close to where I'd walked into the girl being beaten to death. No way was I going back down there.

"You meet me there or I tell the police what you did."

"I didn't do a fucking thing." Not raising my voice was something of a miracle. "Who the fuck are you? Huh? What's your name?"

"Fuck you, Jimmy."

Somewhere down the corridor, a door slammed and the sound was the only proof there were other people in the world beyond me and the man who knew my name. The killer.

"Who are you?" I whispered. And then a second question: "Why did you do it?"

They inhaled a sharp breath, maybe wishing for the warmth of a house instead of the ice-box of the public phone they'd taken over somewhere out in Lawfield's Saturday night.

"Me? Don't fuck with me, Jimmy."

"What are—"

"You meet me there." He screeched it. "An hour."

He was gone.

Gently, I put the phone down and tried to get a hold of everything spinning and shaking inside. For the first time, my flat no longer felt safe. It had become as exposed as the streets below or the black clinging to the fields and the surface of the river while I stood over the dead girl. While she looked at me and wore another child's face.

My fear and confusion and anger were swallowed by a sort of auto-pilot. It wasn't like switching off after work and walking home through the quiet and emptiness of a still sleeping town. It was survival taking over, and survival said it'd had enough of not understanding the threat to my peace, my secure world.

I grabbed my coat and headed out. But before I left, I took a knife from the kitchen.

Chapter Fourteen

Even with the hundreds of people out for the drinking and socialising as Jimmy had pictured, Lawfield hid itself from the surface of things.

On that surface, the day's events were exposed to full view and nobody out for a laugh or to get pissed wanted to look at the image of the dead girls in any detail. On the surface, a rumour had spread within seconds on Facebook that the police had arrested three Syrian refugees and they were being held under armed guard. On the surface, two men from Afghanistan had been beaten outside a café near the river after their attackers accused them of knowing who'd killed the girls. And on the surface, the night had come down much harder and quicker than at any other point of the winter. A sunset bleeding through grey to be swallowed by the first of the stars. A burst of needling wind throwing itself off the river and blasting straight down Albion Way where police had parked their vans and cars and stood on corners to keep the peace. A threat of snow that refused to fall while the people drank and laughed with friends; they ate in their favourite restaurants, and very few were able to put the murders far from their thoughts.

The pub Jimmy had visited at lunch remained closed, and the investigation in the alleyway at its side continued. Officers kept the road clear while their lights shone on the alley's opening. Hours before, the body had been removed and Cheryl's family notified. Her mother, Sheila, lay on her bed, staring at the wall and seeing nothing but her daughter's face. Her father, Bryan, hadn't gone more than a few feet from the conservatory since the afternoon. A sea of crushed lager cans surrounded his feet while he gazed at the night-filled yard and thought about his wife's Valium mixed with the pills leftover from his appendectomy before Christmas. Cheryl's younger sister, Kath, sat on the sofa, held in her grandmother's arms while both wept.

In Lawfield's spacious suburbs, parents told their teenage children to stay in, to talk to their mates online but not in person, and the parents occasionally looked from kitchen windows out to their empty gardens while the kettle boiled. In those windows, all they saw were the lines of worry on their watchful faces.

Along a narrow path that fed from a block of flats to Tirrington Park, four boys, all fifteen, biked slowly, faces and hands covered. They'd promised their parents they were going no further than each other's houses—the homes all at most three minutes' walk apart—and they'd be home by eleven. From that lie to the dozing streets with conversation muted and lips like ice flakes behind their scarves, they'd made it to the edge of the park where the white of the tent swallowed the grass. Around it, a wide cordon marked by tape was a clear barrier, and the boys, despite their bravado of twenty minutes earlier, had no urge to get any closer. It wasn't the sight of a few cops beside the tent or the non-stop tremble of the tape. It was something colder than the winter, more final than the sun setting during the afternoon. After a few minutes' worth of forced humour and debate about trying to get some shots of the tent, they left, promising each other they'd make it closer next time.

D/Supt Fulcher's son was not one of the boys on their bikes. Will Fulcher knew his dad well enough to know the sort of shit he'd be in if he left the house, so while other boys retreated from the sad scene of Cheryl Temple's murder, Will stayed in his room, iPad in hand, the boy hopping between his social media accounts and the chat with four of his friends.

In the family living room, Fulcher's daughter Jo sat near her mother, phone on her lap and most of her attention focused on the TV. They'd gone over every angle of the murders before Clyde arrived home twenty minutes earlier, Jo more than happy to stay in, and Barbara Fulcher secretly relieved to the point of tears that was the case. Mother and daughter watched Gogglebox in companionable silence, neither verbalising how close to home the murders felt due to the work of their husband and father.

Aware of how his family saw him—the man who could not help but to bring the horrors of his job closer to his loved ones—Fulcher stood in the rear garden, door open a crack while his dog Tommy sniffed at the flowerbed, apparently not bothered by the night's freeze turning his master's nose red.

Fulcher hissed at the dog to get a move on although he paid the animal little attention while his thoughts were consumed by what had happened at the press conference with Loui Cameron's mother. As the

Dobermann wandered across the grass towards a tree and cocked a leg, Fulcher checked his phone. Twenty minutes home, forty minutes from the incident room and its stress and noise and there was nothing new for him. No sudden calls or texts, no breakthroughs come out of nowhere as they did in the films and so rarely in real life. Not a fucking thing to end this shit. All he had was Erica Cameron's insane shrieks to the cameras, her agony exposed for all to see.

Watching Tommy grin his doggy grin while he urinated and steam flowed upwards, Fulcher kept a hand on his phone. He saw his dog but his mind was not on the animal. It lived inside the words he knew he'd say to his wife before long—I'm going back out, love.

Away to Lawfield's north and several miles from Fulcher standing in his garden, the Sprignall Estate was much quieter than the police had expected during their urgent planning for the hours ahead. With the trouble involving the Syrians and the great speed with which rumours spread out with the first murdered girl being one of the estate's own, officers expected hours of calls to Sprignall, drunken trouble and vans filling with men and their fists all eager to hurt whoever hurt children. For the most part, Sprignall existed in a state of uneasy peace with only the occasional loud voice falling out of open windows or squeal of brakes as cars took corners too quickly, the estate appeared much as it did on any normal night.

Except for all the lights streaming from the windows in Loui Cameron's home or the police cars parked throughout Artindale Square. Except for Loui's mother Erica shrieking as she threw mug after mug at the kitchen wall while her husband stayed in the living room, drinking strong lager, the man not giving a shit about the noise of screams or pleas from the officers who'd been in the house all day for Erica to calm down. His baby girl was dead, his wife was a basket case; his brother had left the house an hour before without a word, and the law was in his business like never before. He'd drink and drink and drink and there would not be a single shit given.

Sprignall was completely removed from normal as time passed. While not a soul had said the word, it remained haunted by the day's events.

A fact known well by the person watching in the woodland running through the square's rear, apparently unbothered by January shoving its needles into the air or the steady push of the wind.

And from the old trees bordering Tirrington Park.

And on the narrow path running alongside the Evenham where someone waited for Jimmy Marshall.

Chapter Fifteen

Killing the engine and listening to its steady ticking, I studied the car park. Nobody about, and only five cars visible. That was pretty normal; there were few businesses around and the shops and restaurants of Albion Way were a good five minutes' walk away. A while back, a cluster of office buildings stood on the other side of the road, but they were all marked for demolition to be replaced by new housing. Until that happened, the car park was forgotten or ignored by a lot of people.

My phone read just before ten thirty. If I wanted to meet my caller at the right spot, I had ten minutes to walk about half a mile.

I remained in the car.

The guy on the phone hadn't been the same person from that morning, and nothing he'd said made sense. No. I was dealing with someone new. A person who thought I had something to do with at least one murder and probably the others.

Calling the police wasn't an option I let myself have. Too much had happened; too much shit out of my control. Whatever the hell was going on, I would take that control back.

Out the car and striding across the smooth ground, the weather closed in fast. Coat zipped to my neck, hands in pockets and only one of them gloved. The other clasped the handle of the knife from the kitchen, the metal stinging my skin.

Breathing as normally as possible and hoping the sweat below my fleece and coat wouldn't worsen, I crept up a crumbling embankment covered in tatty grass and staggered down the other side to the pathway.

Fingers still wrapped around the knife's handle, I walked. Unlike the usual journey home, there was no autopilot; there was total focus, my senses keyed up in a way they hadn't been in years. The slightest rustle in the undergrowth as a nocturnal animal passed; the occasional crunch as I stepped on small pieces of broken twigs; my own sniffing as the moisture in my nose threatened to spill. So many sounds flying in on the wind, so many places to look in case he came out of nowhere, so many questions the police would have if they caught me heading in the direction of a murder scene.

Refusing to rush despite the apparent lack of time, I drew close to the cut through the trees my caller had specified. Still at least a hundred steps away, I edged towards the riverbank and slowed, each tread of my boots as light as possible. Loui Cameron's patch of land remained another ten minutes further down the path; there was nobody in sight—police or crazy fucker on my phone.

Nearer the riverbank than the tree side, I stopped with another twenty odd steps to go and kept my hands in my coat.

Movement close by.

It came from the narrow path, a lumbering thing all in black, one of its arms ending in a thin, tapering point.

That point rose, aimed straight at me and the shape's wavering cry was all the agony and grief in the world. Worse, that grief was like having a mirror held up to my own.

"I know what you did, Jimmy."

Chapter Sixteen

She'd prepared herself. There'd be time to do so while he'd left her, buried alive in what could have been a freezer but what she thought might not be. Gradually, the fear had faded because animal survival had no use for it. Desperate cries achieved nothing and she'd fallen silent behind the oxygen mask. The need for food had passed quickly, forgotten in the face of her possible death and the sensation of the walls closing in. The stinging, aching demand for water had sunk its claws into her throat, and the awful cold, weighted all over her body despite his blanket, had slowed her heart rate and thoughts to a crawl. Even so, she'd made herself ready. When she heard the approaching steps, she tensed her muscles, stared straight up, gripped the waking terror and snapped it in half.

The second her drawer was fully open, Laura wasted no time.

She shoved a fist up, connected with his jacket and wrapped the fingers she could barely feel around the material. Anchoring herself to him, she swung her other fist with all of her dying strength. By pure luck, she hit his chin and heard a soft grunt. The impact was nothing; the grunt was the entire world. Food, water, heat were meaningless compared to the knowledge she'd managed to cause him some tiny degree of pain and surprise.

With gentle care, the man removed Laura's hand from his coat, grasped both her wrists and forced them down to her sides.

"You done?"

He sounded amused. With that, Laura's anger, trapped for so many long, silent hours behind ordering herself to stay calm, roared back to life. She screamed, the sound croaking and cracked through her dry throat. The oxygen mask fell loose and a wall of sub-zero air crashed into her face. As she thrashed on the sliding table, the man placed a soft hand over her mouth and nose, muffling her noise and cutting off her breath.

Laura's fury collapsed to be replaced by unthinking panic. Heart pounding in her ears, she grabbed his hand, but it was like trying to dislodge a frozen rock. He waited another few seconds, then slid off her.

"I have water."

Choking, licking the insides of her cheeks for any saliva she might have missed, Laura sucked in air, almost weeping with gratitude at the word water, and surely nothing could be worse. Reliant on him to keep her alive, desperate for fluid—even more so than food despite not being able to recall when she'd last eaten—and tongue like a rug hanging loose, but God, she'd never been so thirsty. Not even during the previous summer when a heatwave all through July had turned the country into an oven. This was a dry hell and the man was the devil.

She heard a cap unscrewing from a bottle; a moment later, water splashed over her face, droplets running through the muck and sweat staining her neck. She swallowed like a machine, thoughts of the devil and what might happen after the water all distant. Nothing mattered but water. Not slowly freezing to death, not the fact she couldn't feel her fingers or much below her waist; not the fear, not the mental hallucinations breaking through into the coffin he'd buried her in, and not the constant struggle to keep still in case the mask fell off and she suffocated in a void and the arctic chill.

None of it.

The water stopped and Laura managed a weak cry for more. It was the sound of a baby bird calling for its mother's food.

"You'll puke," he told her. "More in a minute. First, I wanted to talk."

She sensed him crouching without sitting. Before he spoke again, Laura's thought processes, kicked up several levels by being slightly hydrated, sought escape. She could roll to the right, drop to the floor and run. By the sounds of his approach, the door was in a straight line on the other side of the room. Even if he came for her, he was as much in the dark as she was. They both had their equal chances: escape or recapture.

He placed a firm hand on her stomach. While he didn't punch or use a firm hold, it made any movement Laura might make impossible.

Wait, she told herself. Just keep calm and wait.

"I know this is horrible. I really do. The things I did. . .I. . ." He sighed. Even in her dread, Laura was able to pick up on a new tone. The man no longer sounded the same as earlier. She couldn't say gentle or soft and definitely not friendly, but something had changed.

He sounds more human.

It was an adult thought and all the more terrible for it.

"Hurting people. . .it's not what I do any more. It's not, but this is. . ." He sighed again, sounding close to tears.

Then he moved.

The hand on Laura's stomach lunged for her face. She had no time to react before he shoved her back down, the mask falling free and the rough skin of his fingers like sandpaper on her cheeks.

"You'll stay here. You'll stay here. You'll stay here." He raved it, spittle striking her lips and nose. Laura closed her eyes involuntarily. The idea of escape had been snapped in two and all adult rationality was gone. She was a child again and at the mercy of a monster.

Unable to fight against him, she wept as he shoved the mask back over her face, grabbed the trolley and pushed.

Metal on metal howled. As the darkness took her again, the man's hisses coming through the little door and the tiny hole he'd made for her tubing might as well have come from the moon.

"Don't believe that piece of shit, Laura. He lies. He always did and now he lies to himself. He loved what he did. He didn't care about hurting children or what it did to their families. All he cared about was what he wanted and what he could take. Men like him only ever care about what they can take and they pretend to themselves they'll stop doing it, but they're liars."

Laura screwed her eyes shut, tears leaking through, and prayed for one of the few times in her life, begging a faceless god for help. The monster who'd trapped her here, his words were only meaningless rants and she cared nothing about them.

Lower, softer: "Jimmy will come for you, but he's going to be too late. You'll be dead by the time he gets here."

There was nothing more, no sound of his departure, no banging door. The man might as well have simply vanished.

Still sobbing, Laura clenched her dirty hands into fists, closed her eyes and pretended she was a statue. Statues didn't move or feel the cold. They were not afraid. They had no reason to fear the dark or being buried alive or know they were going to freeze to death before any help came.

Statues didn't wait for the return of the scratches on the other side of the door from things eager to meet her once the air ran out.

Chapter Seventeen

The black moved again, a slow step crushing dead twigs.

A man. A baseball bat in his hands.

Dressed in a knee-length coat and with a balaclava pulled over his face, I had nothing to go on for his appearance but I could see enough to know he was not the killer. Shorter and much scrawnier. Thin or not, though, he held the bat like he knew what to do with it.

"Jimmy Marshall."

There was no whispering as he'd done on the phone, no attempt to keep our business secret from anyone passing by, and that's what made everything real. He knew nobody would disturb us, not on such a shitty night when the nearest house was all the way across the field and our voices would only be heard by mice or hedgehogs.

"You want to talk?" I kept everything as soft as possible even though soft felt like an alien idea. Steam blew from my mouth. The thick scarf around my neck and wedged into my coat helped block the weather but not enough. And on all sides, the image of the dead girls crept closer along with their names.

Loui. Cheryl. Meg.

All dead. All murdered by a man who knew my name.

"Talk?" He sounded like he wanted to spit at me. "Fuck talking, you cunt. You ain't worth talking."

"Look. I'm not who you think I am. I haven't done anything. Okay? I found a body, that's all."

Loui's small, hurt form could have been right at my feet. With my dead sister's face. I swallowed and forced the rest out.

"By The Black Boar. This afternoon. I found her, all right, but I didn't do anything. Jesus. They found another girl at the same time. How could I have been in two places at once?"

With his free hand, he pulled the balaclava up. He spat. It hit the ground with a healthy smack.

"I know, you fucker. I saw it. On TV. I see you right there with the filth, talking to them."

Filth. I marvelled at the archaic word. It was like something from The Professionals or The Sweeney.

He drew closer, bat raised and ready. I was seconds from pulling my knife but kept it hidden. Freeing it would mean admitting talking to the nutcase wasn't going to help.

"How did you get my number?"

He laughed, a grunting, pained sound. With it, I got a smell off him. Beer. Cheap stuff. Shitty cans of cheap lager that were only ever sold in corner shops where the guy behind the counter didn't care who he served or at what time. The drink of drunks at eight in the morning.

The stink tried to take me back in memory to my teenage years; I refused to go.

"It ain't hard to track someone down. Not these days. Jimmy."

Another step closer towards me and my fingers dug into the knife's handle.

"Jimmy." He crooned my name, narrow lips parting into a leer, bat raised further.

I understood. Talking had ended. Soft had failed. And control was totally out of my hands.

I went on the verbal attack.

"Who the fuck are you?"

He didn't answer the question. "I know exactly what you did."

"I didn't do a thing. Now you tell me who you are or we're done."

"You want me to go the police?" He shrieked it and I didn't know whether or not to hope someone was coming towards us. A guy walking his dog. A couple of kids on their way to the park, probably carrying bags of tins or with a few rolled joints in their pockets. Nothing came. Not a single step. Not a single rustle in the greenery or through the riverbank.

"Work at the hospital, don't you?"

I kept quiet.

"Yeah, you do. I asked around. People remember you, Jimmy. Nobody's seen you for years, but they remember you. Weird Jimmy."

Madly, the nickname was like a physical blow, forcing me back a couple of paces. Weird Jimmy hadn't existed to anyone in best part of fifteen years, not since leaving school. Weird Jimmy. The name as matter of fact as any description might have been. I could have been Skinny Jimmy or Tall Jimmy, but no. I'd been Weird Jimmy since the age of fifteen. Pretty much all of the last years of my school life, and while it had rarely been used as an insult even by the nastier kids or those who just didn't think, it still felt the man had smashed me in the stomach. My centre became a hot ball and that same heat baked my cheeks, cooking me from head to toe and turning my body into a shrivelled, weak stump. I was a boy, again; small for my age, scrawny, nothing but dangling arms and stumpy legs, and there was no strength in me to right any wrongs, to fix all the broken things life had given to my family.

Weird Jimmy. Weird fucking Jimmy. Hey, Jimmy. Coming down to school later? We got some tins off Paul's brother. Zoe and Fiona said they were coming, yeah? Round the back of the sports hall. Nobody'll see a thing round there, yeah? You coming or what?

And inside, the answer I'd given, I'd always given because it meant I could get away from people and voices and noise.

No, thanks.

"Weird Jimmy." I whispered my old name quietly enough to barely hear myself.

"What are you? Like a security guard for the hospital?" The guy went on before I could answer. "Good job for you, right? Plenty of time to keep yourself secret? Time to plan what you do with the girls?"

I'd had enough. The past fourteen hours had been a dream that made no sense and it was all only getting worse with the man and his bat and his fucked-up words and the name out of the past come to poke and needle again.

Pulling my hand free, I turned my wrist so the moonlight caught the blade.

"Put that bat down. Right now."

"Fuck you, Jimmy." He shook and while I wanted to believe he was scared, that wasn't true. It was all rage.

"You killed her. Beat her. Fucking beat her with a hammer." He sobbed, trembling below his big coat and his balaclava. I had to hope his line of sight would be next to nothing with his tears and the material blocking his eyes. The bat shook even though his grip remained strong and I finally registered the speeding thrum of my heart and the sour, hot taste of my spit.

"Put it down," I shouted.

Bellowing, he came at me.

It was only afterwards that I saw how it happened. In the moment, there was nothing but reaction.

The man covered the space between us in no more than three seconds; the bat swung and the air around it hissed. I jerked back and tried to lunge to the side at the same, my movement awkward and jarring from feet to chest. His makeshift weapon missed and his own momentum sent him spinning round. Managing to grab a handful of coat, I threw a wild punch and went for the handle of the bat at the same time.

My punch missed, but I got the bat and pulled as hard as I could. It slipped from his hands as he cried out and tripped. Dropping my knife and fumbling with the bat, I tried to get my boot down on the blade and had no idea if I managed it. Still crying, Balaclava Man threw himself at me and it was only his slight build that worked in my favour.

I shoved and down he went, right at my feet.

The bat moved in my arms, my hands and I later wondered if I'd really wanted to do so or if the movement just came from my need to survive.

Either way, I hit him in the side of the head and he pitched over.

I stood on the spot, panting, sure I was about to vomit. It took a few seconds for my heart to stop thundering in my ears and when it did, the first new sound in those horrible minutes reached me.

The crunch of mouldering twigs and the loud rustle of leaves crisp in the winter.

I tried to look in all directions but it did no good.

Whoever had watched our conversation and fight was already running from the bushes beside the river.

Chapter Eighteen

In the warmth of the stolen car, the man took a moment to study the surrounding area. Other than a couple walking a dog on the far pavement and rounding the bend in Water View, nobody was about. Not surprising. Around here, people would go only as far as their neighbours and home by ten for bed at half past. Maybe eleven if they didn't have much on the next day. Their expensive cars filled driveways or stayed secure behind locked garage doors, and despite the weather, their gardens were well-tended and tidy. He knew the car and its presence would be noticed, but it—and he—were safe for now. And even if anyone noticed a strange vehicle parked between the old trees on the pavement, he could be away in seconds.

Satisfied he wasn't going to be challenged or disturbed, he thumbed the screen on his phone and adjusted the volume. Within seconds, the broadcast came to life. The clip had been uploaded to YouTube, but not taken from the BBC or Sky or any mainstream channel. No way were they going to play the next couple of minutes in their entirety. Their reports of the press conference had cut back to the studio a few seconds before it all went nuts.

The room with its plain backdrop. The long table with its three jugs of water and the glasses all filled, all untouched as they remained untouched for the next few minutes until the fun began. The man in the car, seen only by a cat keeping low to the frost and grass as it slipped over a garden, witnessed dozens of press conferences over the years. Idly, he wondered if there was some guide that the police had to stick to. Same room, same minimal furnishings, same anonymous setting, same unfriendly place. He could be watching the unfolding scene ten years ago or back in the mid-nineties or further into the eighties.

Seventies.

Further.

"Good afternoon." The man in charge spoke to the camera. The officer the man saw outside the pub in the early afternoon while the pretty girl had offered him a smile and he'd vanished before she had chance to do more. On screen, the officer looked more like TV police than he did in the flesh. He had the look and build of a character actor, one who spent his career playing private detectives or long-serving cops probably one week from retirement.

For the first time in much longer than the man in the car could remember, he found a thought amusing. He sniggered, the sound breaking the silence in the car.

"I am Detective Superintendent Fulcher and I am leading the investigation into the events that have transpired over the last few hours. It goes without saying that these events. . ." Fulcher paused, either with genuine sadness or the required professionalism of someone in his role and with his experience of terrible events. Either was more than possible, the man knew.

He studied Fulcher's face, marking each line around the eyes, and the bags under them. The image was stored far below, its implications noted. The cop was not to be underestimated, the man realised. Not at all.

Fulcher cleared his throat and the shot pulled back a fraction. Two other officers sat at the long table. Between them, a fat woman the man in the car instantly loathed. Fulcher went on, managing to outline very little of the three murder scenes without sounding as if he was hiding anything. All the while, the man studied the fat woman. Thirty-nine, but looked more than ten years older. Dirty blonde hair yanked back, no make-up and blotchy, swollen cheeks and eyes. All to be expected given what has happened to her daughter. The woman was someone who slept little and woke late, a state of affairs ready to grow. Watching her sniff and dab at her eyes, the man guessed she would be lucky to get more than few hours sleeps a night in the long years ahead, and the rest would be poor. Her dreams waited, and in those dreams, her daughter was not rotting meat.

An ugly chain around her neck hung low between saggy tits; four, five, six rings clung to sausage fingers and in her face, he saw a woman who did nothing for anyone and expected everything done for her.

Fulcher took another breath. Watching on his phone, the man refocused on the cop.

"Now, we do believe at this time that the acts of violence are all the work of one individual. You'll appreciate that I am not able or willing to offer any motive but I will point out the main similarity between the young ladies. All were dark-haired and while we do not believe that this is the sole connection between them or that another young person of the same age as the victims have any reason or cause to worry, we would ask parents, teachers, friends to exercise care and caution at this time."

He could be reading from a script, the man thought before realising Fulcher more than likely was. One prepared moments before he came out to the glare and unblinking eyes of all the cameras.

"We would also ask people to avoid isolated areas over the rest of the weekend. While we cannot stop people from going where they want, we politely request that, if at all possible, you avoid the quieter parts of the town."

A slight murmur greeted that and he knew the question given life was what, exactly, did Fulcher mean by quieter parts. The river? The parks?

"I will take a few questions in a moment." Fulcher gestured with a beefy hand to his left. "I have with me Mrs Erica Cameron, Loui Cameron's mother."

No pause there, the man noted. No emphasis on the dead girl's name or her relationship to the fat bitch at the table.

"Mrs Cameron will say a few words and only a few." Fulcher somehow managed to look as if he was eyeing the assembled reporters and journalists individually. "I would ask you to hold on to all questions for me to answer if I can when Mrs Cameron is finished. Thank you."

Fulcher remained in place, resting his hands on the table beside his glass, looking ahead. Gazing at his phone, the man studied the woman for another moment, aware there were a good thirty seconds of nothing before she got it together enough to speak. In the quiet, he scrolled quickly through the comments, noting the number more than the meaningless content. Almost five thousand, and more coming with each passing moment.

"My daughter." She got no further before having to take a breath. "My daughter was Loui." She broke into sobs. Dozens of flashes turned her face and the backdrop white and the clicking of the cameras comes through crystal clear on the man's phone. Even with the tears, the fat woman didn't lower her head. Voice low and rough, she sounded like someone with a bad case of flu. "Loui. Loui Cameron. She was thirteen and... . she was. . .she was the world to me and her dad."

That did it. Erica bent her head. The cameras were white explosions on all sides. One of the female police leaned in close, whispering and sliding a bundle of tissues into Erica's hand. Without using them, the fat woman looked into the nearest camera. As luck had it, the camera was right beside the one broadcasting to the BBC so in the peace and secrecy of his car, he could almost look her straight in the eye.

Here it came. The moment the mainstream news cut their broadcast.

The man's face grew still. Once upon a time, he might have laughed or least taken some mild pleasure from knowing his actions had such a huge impact. Not now, though. Too much was different. He was different.

As if in agreement, a voice tried to yell at him from somewhere that felt like the backs of his ears. Far away and weak and pointless and still pretending to itself it was honestly remorseful. The protests were nothing. Same with the pleading and the desperate wish to be left alone.

Not for you. Not today, Robert.

Straight to the camera, Erica went on. "I know the man who did this, you. . .you're angry. I know that. But you can do . . .good." For the first time, the volume and pitch altered. Erica's tone became quieter and faster at the same time. "You can talk to the police. That's all that they want right now. You just give them a ring. You. . ." She lowered her head, inhaled deeply and the sound was nothing but snot and tears. Then she was up before anyone could react. Even the police right by her side weren't fast enough.

Glasses, jugs of water and her section of the table tipped over, crashed and broke with a storm of noise. On all sides, chaos broke out and the camera saw it all; the dozens of flashes turned the conference into a non-stop explosion of white.

Erica was up, booting aside a snapped chunk of table as the two female police attempted to pull her away. Her much greater bulk made that impossible. A mother's furious grief made her unstoppable.

"You son of a bitch, you fuck. I'll fucking kill you. I'll cut your fucking heart out. I'll—" She was jerked backwards for a moment and threw a fist that caught one of the officers on the cheek. "Fuck off me, you bitch. Fucking get off me."

The woman stumbled and came for Erica again, face already reddening. Rubbing his chin where Laura had landed a weak but lucky blow, the man watched Fulcher grab Erica's arms, pinning them to her sides, but not before the woman managed another insane shriek of her pain right at the camera.

"Fucking cut you open, fucking cut you for what you did to my little girl. Fucking cut—"

The recording ceased and the comments kept coming below the frozen image of the woman's snarling hole of a mouth.

Tracing a finger over the screen, the man took as much as he was able from the shot. Erica's broken heart, Fulcher's desperation to keep order, the thousands of watching eyes all seeing the same as he did. And all of it down to the simple action of killing a child. The same impact, the same grief festered in the houses of Cheryl Temple's family, and Meg Freeman's. He'd seen into those houses simply by letting the wind take his sight through windows and sealed doors. Parents and siblings shocked into silence, their thoughts spiralling downward, further and further towards whatever might be waiting for them at the bottom. The madness of deep mourning; the need to drink until unconsciousness took them faraway; the image of painkillers in the bathroom cupboard, almost forgotten behind old bottles of aftershave.

Lives had become ash, rooms were far too quiet, houses now haunted by the absence of children, and all of it a means to an end exactly as he'd told Laura. Nothing personal here, no harm meant, but still a job to be done. And once that job was done, he might return to the families and see about ending their suffering. Sending the parents and siblings into the dark after their daughters and sisters would be as easy as the flick of a knife or the quick thud of a hammer into skull. There was nothing personal about any of it. Whether or not Laura could understand that, he had no idea. Doubtful. She was only a child, after all.

But Jimmy was not. Jimmy understood the power of murder, the never-ending days that came after it and sank into the future. Jimmy could get behind that even if Laura could not.

Another distant protest tickled the man's ears, the faraway shout falling apart into weeping. Irritated, the man took his thoughts from the present back several hours: path and fields coloured like thick soot because the night didn't want to let go; the only sound the rustle of the long grasses, and the warm, pulsing blood born from the hole in Loui's face.

Nothing before that, though. Or at least, nothing he could see. He had a slight impression of driving along mostly empty A-roads and utterly deserted B-roads, everything ahead a straight line, and behind little more than imagination.

Whatever lived in the past, it was none of his concern. Today mattered. Today and the next few.

By dawn on Tuesday morning, all of it would be over. Or beginning.

He started the car and met his own gaze in the mirror.

A boy to older people who'd forgotten much of their own youth; a man to teenagers because he was beyond them. Smooth skin, eyes a gleaming green, lush hair hanging in waves. A boy and a man who might walk beside a younger girl and make her feel special, make her wonder if a secret kiss would be as great as her imagination played over and over.

And then his face vanished, so absence filled the mirror. Inky nothing consumed the world and beyond, and in that space, things walked.

Things of the cold and dirt, eternally on the hunt for a way back to warm life, to hurt that life as they'd done when they'd been flesh and blood; coming closer, their hands opening and the doors between them and the man in the car parting a tiny fraction.

A growl of the car's engine broke the road's silence. It left the detached houses behind with their curtains securely closed, lights beaming in no more than half a dozen.

Where the pavement turned towards a public footpath, then the massive sheet of playing fields, no living thing walked.

On the far side of the grass, Jimmy stood over an unconscious man and the night stood over Jimmy.

Chapter Nineteen

The splash of the man's bat hitting the water seemed way too loud. I could only hope if there was anyone on the far bank, they'd think it was a tree branch coming loose.

Knife back in my pocket, I grabbed the guy by the arm, slung it over my shoulder and gripped him in an awkward side hug. Leaving him on the path felt tempting although only for a moment. Someone had overheard our confrontation, and even if they'd had nothing to do with the murders, my attacker thought I did.

The guy didn't weigh much, but it was still like dragging a bag of rocks. Within minutes, every muscle in my upper half begged for relief and sweat stung my lips. I kept going, the man's trainers dragging on the path, creating a non-stop scraping sound. He muttered nonsense, head still hanging limp. We passed beyond the trees, a low run of bushes taking their place. One step. Another step. Another. The whisper of the wind, sharp and nasty as always, through the weeds on the riverbank. The occasional hoot of an owl. The fire in my lower back. The t-shirt stuck to my chest and the mad urge to drop the man and rip my coat, fleece and shirt away so the winter could shove itself all over my baking body.

We kept going. Somehow. Long minutes after he came at me with the bat, we made it to the embankment that dropped on the other side to the car park.

"Up we go."

He mumbled gibberish. Knowing the incline would be far worse than the level ground of the path, I pulled him, both of us crushing frost and grass, him still trying to speak and me panting like an old dog.

We made it. Shaking, sure I was about to pass out, I took the man to the car park and all but collapsed as we reached my car. He slumped on the side, supported by it as I fumbled with the keys and bundled him to the back seats.

Taking a quick look to the unlit corners and at the three other cars, I slid into the other side, took my knife out and held it low and out of sight.

As much as I wanted a moment to catch my breath and let my aching body and still throbbing face relax, there wasn't time. I had too many questions and no answers.

"Hey. You awake?"

He grunted, but didn't lift his head. His chin rested almost on his narrow chest.

"Hey." I reached for his shoulder.

He moved at once, hands going for mine, his war cry deafening in the confines of the car. Shoving hard, I managed to get a hand on his face, and pushed. The back of his head hit the window. He cried out and I couldn't deny the burst of savage happiness. Two blows to the skull within twenty minutes couldn't have done him much good. Problem was he seemed the kind of guy who was too dense to know when to stop despite my free hand grabbing his throat and my other bringing the knife into his line of sight.

"Shut up," I said as calmly as I could manage which took some doing.

He saw the knife and was still. Enough moonlight shone on his face to show the rage in his eyes. No real fear, though. Anger didn't have time for fear.

"Now. You're awake and you're not an idiot," I told him. "Probably been awake for the last ten minutes while I dragged you here, right?"

He grinned at that, revealing teeth too white and too perfect to be real. He wore a couple of rings which, to my untrained eye, looked like they might be worth a few quid.

"Fucking hit me," he muttered.

"I know. You're lucky that's all I did. Now, who are you?"

Bravado seemed like the best way to go. If nothing else, it helped to hide how knackered I was from carrying him to the car. The adrenaline from our fight had faded, leaving me shaky with a cramping stomach.

It seemed he wouldn't answer for a while, doing so to make me repeat the question and start to lose control. Realising I knew his game, he said:

"Carl Cameron." The man coughed, then winced. He touched the side of his head where I'd decked him and checked his fingers for blood. Seeing some red, he swore and shifted his gaze from my face to the knife. Apparently deciding he wasn't fast enough, he pressed his head and back on the door and watched me play place the name.

Carl Cameron. A name I hadn't heard of or thought about since school. There'd been a whole big family of them. Four brothers, if I remembered correctly, and a couple of sisters. Not to mention various aunts and uncles and all of them people nobody wanted to have anything to do with. We'd all known they were into low-level crime. Shoplifting, a bit of dealing, intimidation. There'd been a few rumours I'd caught without being told directly—that the older members of the family (mainly Carl's dad and two uncles) knew some really dodgy bastards in London, but if anything ever came of that, I hadn't heard.

In any case, I'd had nothing to do with Carl Cameron or his shitty family, hadn't heard anything about them since leaving school. And neither point was the main one right at that moment while my stomach squirmed and the sweat on my head and neck dried to icy pellets.

No way was this runty figure Carl Cameron. Carl had been tall and broad and handy even at seventeen or eighteen. Mr Baseball Bat stood, at most, five eight and probably weighed about ten stone.

"Bollocks," I replied and he grinned again.

"Carl Cameron's my brother. You remember him. You won't remember me. Steve."

Despite his surety, the name rang a bell. If I was right, Steve had been two years below us. As little as I'd had to do with Carl, I'd had even less of a connection with his younger brother.

I leaned closer, knife raised.

"Who was that in the bushes? Carl? Brought your family along for the fun?"

"What?"

He didn't need to say anything else for me to know he had no idea what I meant. Honest confusion came with his question; not over the top denial or threats. For the first time, he looked like relatively normal—like someone I might work with. Andy or Tom, maybe. Even though it lasted only a few seconds, I saw no lie or bullshit on his face.

So, if that wasn't Carl Cameron, who was it?

I didn't want to think about the question let alone answer it. Of course, that didn't stop my mind hissing that best case, it'd been a stranger who already had the police on their way; worst case, it'd been the boy attacking Loui Cameron that morning.

Licking sweat off my lips and pretending I wasn't breathing too fast, I went on.

"All right. Let's try this one. Why the hell are you coming at me with a bat? Why are you calling me and telling me to meet you out there? What the fuck is going on?"

"You killed her," Steve whispered.

"What? Who?"

He shook as if the soft breeze had found a way in. While the car was barely warmer than the outside, it wasn't the night that made him shake. Fresh tears fell and there was something pathetic about the skinny shape of a man, sobbing like a child. Not wanting to admit to my disgust, I pulled back but kept the knife raised.

"Loui," Steve replied eventually, voice flat as the tears stopped. "You killed her."

My mind tried to shout Ella's name with a mad glee and I stopped it by focusing on Steve. "I didn't kill her. I didn't kill any of them. Why do you think I did?"

"I saw you." Abruptly, he slid closer, face only an inch or two from the knife. "I saw you on the news. Outside the pub where they found the other girl. I saw the police talking to you so you tell me why the fuck you were there, Jimmy. Tell me why the fuck the police were talking to you."

He moved fast, both hands coming for the knife and my wrist. I threw myself backwards, hit the door and got my boot up. It wasn't by much but pressing the sole against Steve's stomach gave me another second. I shoved my hand at his face in a clumsy cross between a punch and a grab, and raked his cheek. He pounded my forearm, hitting blindly as the knife dropped to the darkness below the front seats.

Swearing, screaming, Steve landed a slap on my bruised cheek. Fire flooded my face and head. Furious and sickened by my non-stop fear, I shoved my greater weight right at him.

Both of us struck the opposite window. The car rocking and filled with our mad threats, I got a wrist up to his neck and smacked his head on the glass over and over until his grasping hands fell from my jacket.

Spluttering, Steve spat at my face and chest. I eased the pressure slightly and tried to breathe normally.

"Stop it. Just stop it." I kept saying it until he stilled, and pulled myself away, both hands ready.

Coughing, gasping through a throat that had to hurt more than his head, Steve bent double and sucked in deep breaths.

"Fucker," he managed.

"Listen to me." Like him a moment before, I shook. "I didn't kill anyone. I was in that pub. I went outside and found a body." Missing out that whole surreal fight with the drunk nutcase seemed easier than explaining it. "The police wanted to know everything I saw. The TV people turned up at the same time; I left with the police and spent a while talking to them. Next thing I know, you're phoning me to tell me you know what I did and that I killed your. . ." I had to stop there, unable to bring myself to say daughter. It was just too horrendous.

"Niece," Steve hissed and peered at me.

"Niece," I repeated. "Not her or any other girls. For Christ's sake, they found that girl at the park the same time I was in the pub. How the hell could I have done any of it? I did nothing. Not a fucking thing so you tell me why you think you did."

For a long time, we sat without speaking. Steve's breathing eased although it still held a nasty, rasping sound. The growing sharpness sank below our clothes and the minutes crept closer to midnight.

"Weird Jimmy." Steve said it without making a move. "Weird fucking Jimmy. You always was an odd cunt. Even at school. Everyone knew it. Never said shit to no-one. Never wanted to be a part of anything. Always walking around like your shit didn't stink." He sniffed and held a hand to the side of his head. While I couldn't be sure, it looked like he was bleeding more. "I remembered you. You stood out. Weird Jimmy." Steve laughed and it sounded painful. "I'm at home. My brother's there. His wife Erica, she's screaming. She's screaming without taking a breath. The police keep coming and going and the neighbours come and go and I'm just sitting on the sofa with my brother, neither of us saying a word because we can't. It's like we've forgotten how to speak."

Although I had no idea where Steve or his extended family lived, I saw the living room. I saw the massive TV screwed to the wall. I saw the lack of books. I saw the photos on display, all glossy and professional shots, where the family didn't look like a bunch of rough bastards. I saw the two men slumped on the black leather sofa and their booted feet resting on the thick white of the carpet. I saw the milling shadows dancing over the doorway and the wall beyond as people tried to console the ruined family while outside, there were at least two police cars that people took sneaky looks at from the gaps in their curtains.

"The news comes on." For Steve, I was equally there and not there. He was back with his brother in the house of noise and agonised grief, and he was right with me at the same time because, for him, it was all about me.

"The news comes on and I know where it's at straight off. The Boar. I drink there sometimes, only when I do, there ain't loads of the police right outside the doors and the news ain't saying they found another dead girl like the one beside the river. Like Loui."

Steve took his hand off his head. I was right. Fresh blood stained his fingers. Seemingly unconcerned, he wiped the red on the sleeve of his jacket, fingers rasping on the material.

"You think I killed those girls. . .because you saw me on the news?" I couldn't get my mind around that sort of logic. "Because I'm Weird Jimmy?"

"If anyone was going to do it, it'd be you."

He didn't need logic. I saw that. He had an idea in his head and that was enough. Proof? Who needed proof or even sense when you were pissed out of your head and crippled by grief?

"So, I see you on the TV and I called a few mates. Turns out nobody seen you for years but someone heard you was working at the hospital. Like security. I put two and two together and I figure it's you."

"Christ."

There wasn't any point in arguing. It would have been like arguing with a true believer about their religion. He'd seen someone to blame and that was all he needed.

"I get your number online; I call you and now this." He looked around the dimness of my car as if seeing it for the first time.

"Look, Steve. I don't know what's going on here. I don't have a clue, but I did not kill your niece or the girl at the pub or the girl in the park. All right?"

Less than a foot apart, we stared at each other. I waited for the man to at least look like he believed me or for him to state my guilt like it was an indisputable fact. He blinked a few times, mouth hanging open to give him the look of a total moron. It wasn't stupidity that powered him. Not being uneducated. Not being part of a dodgy family. Not fear.

It was rage.

It was grief.

The man wanted to believe me. Maybe he actually did so, deep underneath all the surface things of real life, of paranoia and a lifetime of knowing who to call when you wanted something done off the books. Maybe down there, he knew me being a murderer was ridiculous. Still, the fire of his grief cooked thoughts that made sense.

"You—" Steve got that far before lowering his head and sobbing. I made no move to comfort him; my hands remained ready to grab his fists if they started flying again. Likewise, he kept still while snot and tears dripped to his chest and lap. He tried again after a few seconds, murmuring my name before the word fell away into fresh weeping. Moments passed. Steve took a few breaths that shook in his throat and chest before lifting his head and wiping his eyes.

"Shit," he whispered.

"I'm telling the truth, Steve."

"Weird fucking Jimmy." He said it almost like he wanted to laugh but had forgotten how.

"You want me to take you to a hospital? For your head."

"Nah." He inhaled again, seemingly back under control. I kept my hands ready all the same.

"Home?" I asked.

"Sprignall? You been there in the last fifteen years, you fucker?"

"No," I said truthfully. Lawfield was, for the most part, a decent place, but its estate had a reputation as an area it was wise to avoid unless you knew the locals.

He laughed bitterly. "Yeah. Come over. See my brother. See his wife. See the house full of coppers and... . shit."

"Steve?"

While he wasn't stone cold sober, the appraisal he gave me at that moment was the closest he'd been during our confrontation and conversation.

"Yeah?"

"You know I didn't hurt anyone, don't you?"

When his head jerked to the side and the whites of his eyes were abruptly huge and shining, I pulled back, thinking he was coming for me, again.

A second later, I understood.

He was staring right behind me to the empty car park.

Lunging for the front seat and trying to yank the keys free at the same time, my boot caught Steve in the leg. Trying to pull clear, he hit the side door with a heavy thud. I clambered into the driver's seat, keys sharp and jagged in my hand.

I didn't dare check to see who Steve was staring at as we sped away.

***

The lights from the rear of Jimmy's car slipped around the curving section of road running out of the car park, leaving only the squeal of tires before that faded along with the ghost of the lights.

Silence swallowed the car park.

In the slivers of night that fell from the high wall of bushes at the car park's edge, a particular thin section of shadow crept away.

The silence remained.

The eyes had gone.

Chapter Twenty

Carl Cameron held the final half inch of his last fag to the new one dangling from his lips, lit it and dropped the dying smoke. It fell to a thin layer of frost, dead before it landed. He took a few puffs. It was only after another minute passed that he realised he'd managed to complete the action despite the trembling in both hands that had nothing to do with being outside. A few moments after that realisation hit, another landed.

His reactions were several minutes behind the cause. Probably had been all day. Yeah. That sounded about right. He'd splashed coffee on his thumb at some point in the evening (time had stopped having any meaning a couple of minutes after the police knocked at the door), burned it and not been aware of the heat or the pain until one of the cops, one of the women, offered him a tissue.

Carl smoked, keeping still as he stared at the garden without taking in an inch of the level grass or patio area or decking. He'd been dressed in a pair of old jeans and a heavy fleece when the knock at the door came, and wore the same clothes hours later. Changing them seemed pointless. So did eating. Had he eaten? He didn't think so, and yet, no pain held his belly, no demands for sustenance filled his body. Coffee. Yeah. He'd drank coffee. Probably a lot. Smoked, too. He was smoking now. Yeah.

The house remained as quiet has it had for the last hour. Erica took a few pills earlier and now lay on the bed, covers a rumpled mess at her feet. All the rooms darkened, the law finally gone and Steve off somewhere. Carl hadn't noticed his brother leave and it was only the knowledge he stood alone in the garden that made Steve's absence a fact.

Not that it mattered.

Nothing mattered.

Not one fucking thing.

Carl smoked.

Time passed.

He did not think, at least he did not think in any way he knew as familiar. Thought processes were as disjointed as his sense of time or place, and while he was aware of this change, it mattered no more than his brother's whereabouts.

Calling a few contacts in London, that had been a thought earlier; a brief idea that fell apart without a sound much as his fag fell to the frost. Both dead before they hit the ground.

And what good would it do to call those men he'd had next to nothing to do with for the last five years? They'd come running to help, yes, even though he was out of their business and they out of his. They were not monsters. They were not the world's bad guys. They were men who knew what needed to be done and who did what needed to be done. That was all it had ever been in the old days before Erica made him put a stop to it and promise the rest of their life in Lawfield would be normal and safe and dull. And they had been.

Until today.

Carl had not called his contacts. Come running or not, Loui would remain dead, and there was nobody to punish for that crime.

Nobody.

Yet.

He puffed on the smoke, no more tasting the fag than he felt the increasing heat as the embers drew closer to his bare fingers or let the sharpness in the motionless air bother him.

"I would like to meet you," he said without making any effort to whisper. The words failed to reach his ears, and the new part of Carl brought to life in an instant when the law started speaking in their low, sorrowful voices was aware his hearing no longer worked as it should.

Whispering—despite the close proximity of their nearby houses with their sealed windows and the road that ran at the back of the houses—was not a fact to Carl while he took a last drag on the smoke and let it drop to the scattered pile of other dog ends. There were no facts for Carl other than what he told the night.

"I would like to meet you. I would like to have you right here in my house. I would like to cut your clothes off so there's nowhere for you to hide."

Carl's voice and tone remained steady. Years back, he had said similar about and to a select few men before hurting those men for their transgressions or threats. In his wilder days, there'd been no need to raise his voice and there was no need now. The promise was the same, the utter conviction behind his words was as much fact as the silence sitting on

Lawfield or the knowledge he and Erica would never get over what had been done to their little girl.

"I would save your eyes for last," Carl said to nobody and it was only then that he wept. Since the police arrived with their terrible news, a fire had cooked his barrel chest and made each breath feel like he lived inside an oven. It consumed his body, his heart. He fell to his knees, striking the frost and hard grass as his dog ends had over the last hour. Tipping to the side and curling into a ball, Carl Cameron sobbed and knew nothing but his soul baked into so much ash. His house, his garden, his wife and the seemingly never-ending winter belonged in another world, and he was no longer part of that world.

The figure standing utterly still and gazing at the garden fence from the other side of the road knew the pain unmanning Carl Cameron. It understood that pain.

It had known that pain for long years.

Chapter Twenty-One

King broke the silence as Fulcher had known he would. The man was good police but that wasn't the lone reason Fulcher had called him after leaving the house and telling Barbara he'd be back soon. No, King was an all-rounder. Fulcher had known a lot of officers over the years, too many to recall right then, and worked with some who'd started as grunts and made it up to much higher levels. While he'd prided himself on being able to open up to several, he had not shared a real link with many. King knew the score of being police and being as much of a civilian as the last of the stragglers heading home.

"What are we doing here, Clyde?"

They were the first words either man had spoken in a good ten minutes. Fulcher checked the time to be sure. Coming up for last orders in the pubs and clubs, and Lawfield's backstreets and main roads all slipping away into sleep. While the takeaways dotted around would do a decent trade for another couple of hours, things were not normal. Too few taxis passing behind him and King on Carling Way; only a handful of pedestrians down where the road met Church Walk, and almost none heading up towards the windows of The Black Boar or the heavy sheeting still sealing the alleyway where Meg Freeman's poor body had been found. In the last hour, Fulcher and King had seen three people—two women and a man all in their early twenties—pass, the three keeping to the far pavement. While they had stopped and clearly discussed what had gone on twelve or so hours before, they'd headed off and Fulcher had breathed a silent sigh of relief. Getting out of the car and ordering a bunch of pissed up kids to move on was not what he fancied right now. No sleep, crappy fast food and the day from hell becoming a weekend and the week ahead and Christ knows how far into the rest of the winter.

"Clyde?" King said and Fulcher came back to himself. He took a breath, inhaling the smells of the burgers and chips they'd got from a nearby McDonalds, the aroma of the food clinging to their skin and the car.

"I told you." Fulcher folded his hands into fists, wishing for a cig. "You don't have to be here."

"Is that why you called me?" King asked.

Fulcher managed a smile. "Fuck off."

Another silence fell between them, less strained than earlier. Fulcher broke that quiet a few moments later.

"We've got nothing, Mike. Not a thing. We're sitting here like a couple of plums on the zero chance our friend comes back to check out what we've done to his scene. That print they got down by the river is useless. They know the make of trainer and reckon it's a ten, but that's it."

"That's not useless. And he might make an appearance."

"It's useless for now unless we get something to put with it. The blood on the ground was all Loui's after he broke her nose and teeth. He might have grazed himself with the hammer, but so what? No fluids. No fibres from his clothes. Fuck, he could have been naked for all we've got." He nodded towards the sheeting; the material held firmly in place to the brickwork. "Same in there. Same method. Same beating. Same shit. He dumped her there, but she'd been dead for hours." Fulcher inhaled, grateful the breath shook only a little. "And he's not coming here. It was just to get me out of the house. I had to move."

"CCTV?" King asked, ignoring the last comment. It seemed the best way. Getting Fulcher to talk was a small result, though. He wouldn't waste it.

"They're checking it from the pub. The estate agents' is useless. Doesn't cover the front. The pub isn't great; it's on the doors, not the side, but they might get something." He shrugged and his heavy coat hissed on the car seat. Neither man had removed scarves or coats despite the gentle flow of hot air.

"Hopefully by morning," Fulcher added and knew he sounded about as positive as he felt.

King caught movement far down St Michael's Road: a guy lumbering. He leaned on the window of a post office and remained there. Keeping an eye out in case the man decided he needed to piss, collapse or both, King said one word.

"Marshall?"

"No." Fulcher concentrated on his fists for a few seconds, unclenching, clenching. "He checks out. Single. Works nights. Keeps quiet. Not much going on there."

"You sure?"

Surprised for the first time in what might have been years, Fulcher eyed his subordinate and couldn't hide his amusement. "You questioning me, Mike?"

"Don't give me that." King kept his focus on the figure illuminated by the nearest street light. "I just think he's not a hundred per cent."

"Meaning?"

"Buggered if I know. Just a feeling."

"You want to talk to him, again?"

King echoed his boss's negation. "No. You're probably right. It's—"

Fulcher interrupted him, still amused. "Thanks."

"It's probably just wrong place, wrong time, but I tell you something. That beating he got is balls. No way a kid jumping him for ten seconds did that. He got the shit kicked out of him. Doesn't mean Loui Cameron or Cheryl Temple or Meg Freeman did it. Someone did, though."

"You reckon it was our boy?"

"No. Not directly." King had given the theory a lot of thought since watching Jimmy Marshall walk from the front of the station into the growing gloom of the afternoon. "I don't think Marshall knows him or did anything himself, but he knows something. We need to keep an eye on him."

"Agreed. I'll get on it in the morning."

Fulcher opened his hands for the last time, more comfortable with splaying his fingers on his legs than making fists. "I tell you one thing." He inclined his head towards the silent pub. "That place. It's got its own horror story starting right now. Nobody will give a shit about the estate agents; it'll be the pub that gets the stories. The dead girl pub. They'll do more business in the next month than they've done in the last year."

"You think?" King glanced at Fulcher for a moment before returning his attention to the man at the post office now staggering more or less towards the road's end.

"I think." Fulcher watched the sheeting flap around the lower edge. "It won't be like Fred West's house or any of that shit, but it'll be bad." He waved a hand to the pavement, picturing it full of Saturday afternoon crowds—the people who'd gathered in minutes while a teenage girl lay dead in the dirty puddles, the people who'd filmed and taken shot after shot for their fucking Facebook statuses or their fucking Instagram or their fucking Twitter or for their own fucking selves.

Realising he was close to losing control, Fulcher breathed for a moment and said nothing else. King waited, knowing the man would speak in his own time.

Passing Starbucks, the stumbling figure drew closer.

"They'll want it to be a bad place. They'll make it that way and they'll make it how that bad place affects them." Fulcher took another look at the closed off alley and imagined Meg Freeman's small, pale face beyond the sheeting, her unblinking eyes staring at him but making no move out to the pavement or road because the alley had become her home.

"Clyde," King said.

In a heartbeat, Fulcher's attention snapped from the alley and his own thoughts to their surroundings. He saw the same as King.

The man on the pavement walked with his head down, one hand holding his face and the other hanging limp. He drew closer to the estate agents building, a small patch of moonlight illuminating the stain on his free hand as it dripped from his fingers. He struck the agents door, bounced and kept moving towards the alley.

Stopped there.

Reached his fingers all smeared with red towards the white.

At the same time, King and Fulcher shoved their doors open and ran for the man, Fulcher roaring for him to stop, to get down on the ground right fucking now.

King named the figure.

It was Bill Lister.

The two police reached Lister together, Fulcher reaching for his hand. Lister twisted and it was only luck that kept him on his feet.

He faced the two officers.

"Jesus fucking Christ," King hissed and stepped back. Twenty years' experience could not stop that retreat.

Trying to look at the men through eyes that were no more than shredded holes, Lister raised a hand coated with his blood. Dozens of jagged wounds wept all over his face. Shards of broken glass jutted from the wounds. Red had soaked into his already stained clothing and run to his trousers and shoes. With dim horror, Fulcher saw the man's tracks marked the pavement behind, revealing an approach mistaken for drunkenness instead of a dead man walking.

He reached for Bill Lister again, trying to say the man's name.

Lister managed to part his lips and the sight made Fulcher recoil as King had.

Lister collapsed and splashes of red from his destroyed face and missing tongue splashed on the pavement.

Chapter Twenty-Two

Sliding the car into my space, I killed the engine and turned to Steve.

"What the fuck did you see?" I whispered while he stared straight ahead to the high wall that blocked the grounds of the block from the pavement and kept quiet. I'd barked the same question while we sped from the car park and back to the lights and late-night life, slowing only for red lights. The journey out there had taken me fifteen minutes; I got us back to my flat in about half that, convinced whatever the hell had scared Steve was somehow keeping pace with the car. Banishing the idea we were being watched was harder than I wanted to admit.

"Steve?"

He shook his head and winced. Dribbles of blood ran from beside his ear. "Nothing. Someone. . .probably just some homeless guy wondering what the fuck we were doing."

"That scared you?"

He stared at me and I said nothing more. While he was no longer trying to attack me or calling me a murderer, we were still feeling around each other's edges, trying to work out what was happening.

"You got anything to drink?" he muttered.

"You need to get to A&E."

"Fuck off. I need a drink."

He shoved the door open, stepped out and I had no choice but to follow even though the last thing I wanted was him in my home.

A few minutes later, Steve flopped in one my chairs and poured himself a large shot of Scotch while I discreetly checked the time. Gone midnight. Steve showed no signs of leaving. Oddly, this didn't bother me as much as I would have expected. He wasn't a friend or even an acquaintance; he was a dickhead I didn't want anything do with even if our situation had been normal. At the same time, having life in my flat wasn't terrible.

He took a large swig; I found some film on TV that looked crap and left it on. Steve took the tea towel I'd wrapped in ice cubes and slid it between the side of his head and the top of the chair. Long trails of water ran from the towel along the chair to drip to the floor.

"How's the head?" I asked.

"Sore as fuck." His lips curled in a mix of a smile and a grimace. "How hard did you hit me?"

"Hard."

"Yeah. No shit."

The film gave way to ads. I eyed my own glass of whisky, not wanting it, but reaching for it all the same. We drank together.

"Weird Jimmy. Fuck. I'm sitting here with Weird Jimmy." Steve managed to sound disgusted with me, himself and the situation all the same time.

"You can go any time you like."

"You owe me. I'm having my drink."

In some completely mad way, we'd gone from him attacking me and believing me capable of murder to sitting in my flat sharing a drink, and all in the space of less than an hour. More than that, we'd gone from trying to beat the shit out of each other to what would appear to others like an odd, strained friendship.

Whatever had happened in our final seconds in the car park felt like it was already a long-ago memory and that was fine with me. Imagination, lack of sleep, stress: it could have come from any or all of them and I would not question it.

Steve checked the damp towel. He'd stopped bleeding. Pink stained the material. A decent lump had already formed on the side of his head, pushing against his hair and probably more noticeable down to the guy being skin and bones. I'd offered a few pills for the pain but Steve stuck to the drink.

He caught me looking. "What?"

"Nothing."

He continued to eyeball me and I refused to look away.

"What happened at the pub? You just walk into that girl's body?"

Not wanting to talk about the fight with the drunk and discovery of the body or even think about it didn't seem to be an option. Steve wasn't going to let it go.

Aiming my words at the TV, I told Steve what had happened with the drunk (his name, Bill Lister, came back to me as I spoke) and him shoving me into the alleyway. Down on my arse, the doorman coming to sort it out and the look on his face making me turn.

I didn't elaborate or go into detail. Steve took the bare facts, picking up on the issue I'd known he would.

"That guy do it on purpose? He want you to get into the alley and find the girl?"

"I don't know." Despite what I'd said to King in the afternoon, I honestly didn't know. Too much had happened and I was too exhausted to know anything for certain.

"The police think he did? Because if they did, he's got questions to answer," Steve said.

"They told me they'd look into it."

"Yeah? Maybe I'll look into it. Maybe he'll talk to me."

Any tiny degree of humour or warmth left the flat. I looked straight at him for the first time in minutes.

"Don't give me any shit, Jimmy. I lost my niece today and if your mate knows anything about it, he's a dead man."

Steve kept his voice level when he said that which was probably something of a miracle. Stating it rather than raging also made me believe him completely.

"Yeah." I swallowed more Scotch. "I know."

We sat in silence for a while, watching the film without seeing it. Steve's head nodded occasionally as he fought either tiredness or a concussion. The last few hours for him and his family would have destroyed any strength they had; his attack on me had been powered by anger, and now that anger was fading to leave him a scrawny shape in my chair.

In the kitchen, the boiler coughed as it flared into life, and Steve stirred. He studied the living room and the little he could make out of the hallway that led to the kitchen, bedroom and bathroom.

"Nice gaff."

"Yeah. It's okay."

"Know where I am? Me, Carl and his missus . Slap bang in the middle of Sprignall. And you know why?"

"Nope."

"Because we like it. Well, Carl does. Always has. He. . ." Steve considered, blinking repeatedly. Getting a smack in the head on top of horrendous emotional turmoil and then drinking was not a great combination. "He's not the man he was. I wouldn't fuck him off. Never. He'll kill the cunt who hurt Loui. . ." He took a moment to sniff and make no attempt to wipe the few tears that worked their way down his cheeks. "A few years back, he'd have torn this town apart to find the guy. Erica stopped him from doing that stuff. He's Mr Family Man now and he could live anywhere, but he sticks to Sprignall. Sticks to the people we grew up with. Good people. You know that?"

He took a gulp of Scotch while I nodded.

"Do you fuck," he said with solid anger. "You don't know people, Jimmy. You never did. Weird Jimmy. All apart from everyone. Outside people. Mr-Keep-Yourself-To-Yourself. Why? I know what happened with—"

I cut him off. "Just the way I am. I like my own company. It's just how I'm built."

He managed to focus on my face. "Just how you're built. Yeah. I know what you mean. Know how I'm built? I'm the man who's going to kill someone. You fucking watch. That man. . .hurting Loui like that. Jesus Christ. She was. . .good. You know? She was a good kid. Funny. Funnier than me or her old man. And fucking smart. She'd have gone places, Jimmy. University. A good job. An honest job. Money. All that."

He went on for a while. I nodded, letting his words and drunken pain flow by, while the film ended and another began and the night ran away from both of us. It seemed Steve rambled about his niece for hours but the little crack in the curtains showed only total night, not dawn. I drifted, not close enough to dozing to relax fully but managing to let go of some of the day's shit.

Pretty.

The word brought me back and I jerked upright. Steve's head hung limp and stupid. His glass rested on the arm on the chair, empty apart from a tiny sliver of melting ice.

Pretty.

A single word but enough to get through and wake me up. Not the word. The tone.

He'd said something about Loui being pretty, and his tone changed. His tone, still thick with sleep and drink, had shifted into something new for that second.

I stared at Steve, not wanting to say his name, not wanting to consider the potential of terrible things that were harder to disbelieve when dawn was a thousand years away and out there, someone had watched us from the gloom.

Someone who might have been a teenage boy or a grown man.

Unsteady on my feet, I finished my Scotch, the liquid a smooth burn on its way down, and turned off the TV. Steve made no sound. Even his breathing had faded into background noise.

Sleep. That was what I needed. Sleep to shut out everything that had happened and thoughts of Ella.

Treading lightly, I headed to the bathroom door, keeping the hall light off.

Out of nowhere, a terrible stink filled my flat—the stench of burning meat. It was like being at a barbecue where the menu was decaying flesh shoved deep into the flames to emerge, blackened, turned into reeking ash.

Slapping a hand over the lower half of my face, I inhaled the sharp tang of my own sweat.

It was coming from the other end of the hallway.

Standing against the wall, I stared at the closed door to the bathroom and took a lone step towards it. The smell intensified, coating my skin and head, eager to sink underneath my hand and shove its way inside.

Another step and the choking aroma of smoke took over the odour of burned meat. Panicked by the thought of my flat on fire, I shoved on the door. It swung wide open, revealing everything.

Although I'd turned the light off, it was on, again, and almost blindingly white. There were no shadows by the toilet or sink, no space for anything to hide.

Trying to scream, I made no sound as I collapsed to the wall and slid down it.

Looming from water the colour of oil, the shape of a girl reached over the bath. Not an inch of her skin was white. Fire had turned her into charcoal and the girl's fingers were little more than ragged stumps.

What remained of her mouth fell open, letting out another wave of the sickly-sweet stink of her baked insides.

She shrieked.

The light went out.

Chapter Twenty-Three

Fulcher brought his car to a stop without turning into the driveway. Chances were Barbara would know he'd just got back; she slept lightly, after all, but that didn't mean he wanted to get the car any closer to the house than need be. The kids would be long asleep by now. They and the little patch of Lawfield's suburbia with its tidy front gardens and detached houses didn't need him waking any of it up.

Fulcher turned off the engine and made no move to leave the car even as the icy air eagerly stole the warmth all around him. He inhaled and wished he had not.

Everything still stunk of Bill Lister's blood. It was as if the man hadn't just bled on the pavement while Fulcher yelled his name and King fumbled with his phone. The stench of Lister bleeding to death from his ravaged face had soaked into Fulcher's clothes, into the thick weight of his coat as easily as it clung to the hairs in his nostrils. He could go inside and shower until the bathroom was a wall of steam and he'd still reek of the man who hadn't said a word because he couldn't say a fucking word and not only because he'd died in the ambulance.

No fucking tongue. Jesus Christ. What is this shit?

Nestled in an inside pocket of his coat, Fulcher's phone rang.

Swearing under his breath and fumbling to answer the shrill ring, Fulcher came close to dropping the mobile. Sucking in a few sharp breaths, he checked the number on the screen, accepted the call and reached for the key.

After his initial statement of his name, he listened and could not help himself: he closed his eyes as if to shut the world away. It didn't help.

"On my way. Call King. Get him there and anyone else you can wake up."

Without waiting for reply, he ended the call and glanced up at the bedroom window. No light on, no sign of life. His wife slept; his kids slept and all the horror of the outside world did not come into their home.

Fulcher took another couple of breaths, started the car and eased away from his home. Seconds later, he left Stoneleigh Way behind, turned into Cherry Road and its twisting curves and headed for New Road. On both sides, windows stared at the empty front gardens, and Fulcher's car was the lone vehicle in what might have been miles.

A mile from his destination, the phone rang again. Not taking his eyes off the road, Fulcher answered it.

Seconds later, he increased his speed to close in on the riot now engulfing the Sprignall Estate.

***

For close to three hours, he kept to the alleyways and secluded spaces filling the estate, marvelling at how easy vanishing from sight was in Sprignall. A difference in design between new housing estates and places like Sprignall built back in the sixties; he didn't know or care. The pathways that snaked along the rear fences of dozens of streets, separating the terraces from tatty sections of grass and small woodlands; the cycleways all covered in mouldering crisp packets, crushed cans of lager and dog ends; the cut-throughs that led from small squares to the estate's three shopping areas: all were his and his alone. While he made no real effort to hide, he still stepped with light feet and breathed only through his nose to generate less smoky air around his half-covered face. Occasionally, he passed an exploring cat. The animals gave him a wide berth before vanishing into areas and spaces where the moonlight did not reach. As he stood for a minute outside a newsagents to read the barrage of graffiti scrawled on its shutters, a dog in the flat above gave a few seconds' worth of barks before falling silent. No lights came on in the windows. Nobody challenged him, and he walked on undisturbed.

He thought of Bill Lister as he crept through the estate. Sending the man towards the police might have been considered a risk, but it hadn't mattered in the end. Lister couldn't have told them anything in any case. Tearing out the drunken idiot's tongue hadn't been part of the plan, and if he was honest with himself, neither was grinding the broken bottle into his face, popping his eyes like squashed grapes and opening up more rents and holes in his cheeks than could be counted.

It was done, though. Same with the murder of the girls. All done and never undone. What came next wasn't solely up to him. The police had their part to play, and so did Jimmy. Most definitely Jimmy.

He stopped beside a phone box, looking around and patting the side of his coat where the bottle of petrol rested. The high wall at the side of the large corner shop at his back; the curve of the road heading to houses, and ahead the estate's main play area for families and kids. Grass layered with frost, the slides and swings all rusting quietly, and the three benches built from wood that was slowly rotting. Beyond the grass, the path would take him into the outskirts of Sprignall. Not time for that yet, though. Work to be done here.

He checked the time. Three thirty in the morning. Pausing to take stock wasn't a good idea. It gave the voice inside chance to protest louder, to try and stop what was coming by taking over the body as it failed to do so with Meg Freeman, Cheryl Temple, Laura Flint and Loui Cameron.

And the other one, of course.

He placed a hand on his forehead, wanting to push the voice all the way down to the bottom of things where its nagging, whining pleas would be too faint to reach him, or just shut it off totally.

Burn it away.

That was what he had to do. His business with Jimmy was his business; it did not belong to the weak one, the one from before who now wanted to stop his work because it had no chance of undoing its own from all those years ago. Admittedly, he wouldn't have known about Jimmy had it not been for the other's long-ago crimes, but so what? He had work to do with Jimmy, plans to see to fruition. The architect of how Jimmy's life had turned out had his time, and that time was done. All the voice with its begging and its snivelling, false regret could do and fail to understand it had brought this on itself. It felt no real sorrow for the pain it had caused; it could not justify its actions or pretend it wished it had not done those things to the girl. All that was done and it would live in its private hell.

Let it plead. Let it cry and be a prisoner in its own form while its hands killed and its eyes drank in the squirming flesh of the young girls as they choked. Let it have no way of making up for its crimes.

Please, no more. Stop this. I really am sorry for what I did. I really am.

"You are not. Not at all. You are scared of being wiped out when I am done. You are scared of becoming nothing. Admit it. Finally admit it, you liar."

Almost nothing inside. No words. Only a faint sense of juvenile anger, a child caught in a lie.

"Admit it or I will hurt you."

Still close to nothing in reply. The life behind the voice was thinking of a way out, still refusing to admit there was none. It had refused to admit it was as much of a monster as the figure wearing its body; it could not make up for what it did long ago because creatures like it only ever served themselves. They saw no value in others so simply used them and threw them away.

"Burned them away."

Grinning, the young man with the smooth hair and nice eyes crept away into the frozen land that covered the backs of the gardens and waited.

He did not have to wait long.

Chapter Twenty-Four

A finger stabbing nine three times.

A cracked phone held to the side of a head.

Eyes taking in the scribbled messages coating the phone box's windows: girls' names, promises of sucking and fucking, offers of a good deal if anyone wanted to score, and drawings galore of genitalia.

His call answered and his voice riding over it.

"I am going to kill another."

Even in the phone box, there was little protection from the outside; his breath misted over the single pane of glass. He eyed the scratches and the scribbles of graffiti again, the threats and the promises of free sex from women who probably didn't exist.

"You know where I'm calling from. You'll know who I am if you don't already."

The voice on the other end, still calm, tried to speak over him and there was no time to let that happen. The shape at his feet was a curled-up ball. She'd been smaller than the others – Loui, Meg and Cheryl – and it had taken just three quick blows to her skull to finish the job. Her sister, too shocked to take a breath that wanted to emerge as a scream a second later, might be dead, might be alive. He didn't really care. Not for the first time, he wondered what the two girls had been thinking when they'd crossed through the estate at four in the morning and bare hours after a nutter butchered three other girls. Maybe they'd thought they were invincible. Maybe they believed the killer wouldn't strike in such a public place, and perhaps they figured they were one another's safety.

And maybe they'd still believed that when the good-looking guy headed straight towards them along the path and asked for a cigarette.

After that, he'd done what needed to be done, not caring in the least about the howls emanating from the underside of everything.

No, don't you do this. Stop it. I'm begging you to stop this and let me go, let me go, let me go, let me—

"All you need to do tonight is come and collect the body. All you need to do after that is stop me. And to stop me, you have to find me." The man smiled, appreciating his own little joke. If the other girl—the older sister—did end up telling the police anything, it wasn't going to be much they didn't already know from Jimmy.

Checking his watch, he went on. "And to do that, you have to understand that killing these girls isn't because I'm insane. It's for one person in particular. He knows who he is. You work it out and you'll find me."

With gentle care, he placed the phone down and eyed the shape wedged against the glass. Although the light was too poor to see it, he knew the red around her mouth and nose would look black given enough moonlight, and her blonde hair was stiff with cooling blood. Briefly, he wondered how long it would take them to figure out she'd been dead before he carried out his next action. Probably enough time for word to spread around the estate that she'd still been alive. Hopefully, enough time.

"I really am sorry about this," he told the corpse. "It's not what I want. It's not who I am. It's all down to the other one."

If the girl at his feet had not already been dead, she might have heard a slight change to his tone from seconds before. His voice emerged as another man's, one full of remorse and turned ugly with self-pity.

The man closed his mouth with a snap, shutting the voice off and letting it whine and beg in his head. He concentrated on the girl at his feet and brought the other to his eyes, stared directly at him and addressed his next words to the body while keeping his attention fixed firmly to the panicking image.

"Can you feel him? I give him to you. He's yours now. You can stay together. I have no need for him."

He smiled.

"He's all yours."

Without saying another word—there was nothing left to say—he backed out of the phone box, took another quick look around and saw only the night lit by the moon. Pulling the bottle from his coat pocket, he unscrewed the lid and upended it over the girl.

The stink filled the phone box, the deep freeze doing nothing to combat it. Below the splashes were terrified cries. Bottle empty, he dropped it beside the girl and pulled a box of oven matches from another pocket.

Oh Jesus, don't do this to me. Please don't, I don't want to burn, I don't want to burn, I—

There were no sirens. Not yet. Within minutes, maybe. Possibly even seconds.

He scrapped a match; the tiny flame shone like a beacon.

Far below in the undercurrents the man had come from, a high-pitched wail of someone utterly unable to stop what was coming.

Their own agonised destruction.

Backing away a couple of steps, he threw the match and spun on his heel in the same movement.

He had time to run to the thin grass that formed the perimeter of the playing field before the flames bloomed into life and the few seconds of agonised screams burst free.

The glass in the phone box detonated and the sharp frost in the air powered through the flames, giving them more strength, more life. He looked back. The shape of the girl was too indistinct to make out behind the swirls of orange and red. Fire streamed upwards and out, cooking the surrounding ground and turning the interior into an oven.

While he knew Sprignall only appeared to be asleep and that the great roar of the fire would bring people out at any moment, he still took a few seconds to watch the girl's body cook because she didn't burn alone.

The shrill, begging voice that had been with him every step of the way was gone, scorched into ash by the fire. Its self-serving lies, its refusal to face what it was or what it had done: all gone.

He was himself and he was alone.

Which meant he needed a name.

He held his hands to his face as the first of the panicked shouts sounded from nearby windows. Hands that had done so much, been responsible for so much.

Hands that belonged to a body he had taken over, and if he had done that, he could also take the name.

Running from the echo of the shrieks, the great crackle of the burning body and the rapidly increasing number of voices, the thing now called Robert Fry left the stink of a burning body and the crackle of the fire behind.

Chapter Twenty-Five

Fulcher drove into the centre of Sprignall and hit a war zone.

The noise had been clear minutes before he left the quieter areas behind and took the turning into Sprignall Road, passing the primary school and its playing field, and the sky directly overhead brightened by the streaming glare from the force's helicopter.

Seconds later, the glare of the flames consuming the shops reached Fulcher, the huge roar of the fire not quite loud enough to bury all of the ear-splitting screeching.

He parked beside two vans and ran into the bodies, officers recognising him on sight. A wall of police formed a barrier between the surge of raging figures and the firemen doing all they could to extinguish the fire spreading from what might have been the phone box Fulcher had been told about into the shops. The flats above were empty, Fulcher knew, and there'd been no reports of deaths other than what had happened in the phone box—if the call had been genuine.

Fulcher prayed it had been a hoax but his secret heart did not believe so.

Glass broke as a rock struck a window in one of the flats. The people throwing them made no attempt to hide themselves even as five officers ran to them, their anger clear in a jumble of furious voices. The beam from the helicopter swung around, painting the ugly buildings and the swarm of people—most still wearing dressing gowns and little more despite the sinking temperatures—a ghostly white. The roar of the chopper swallowed the racket from both sides for a moment before it ascended and banked right, its light raining on the field beyond the end of the shopping precinct. Voice amplified by a loudspeaker, an officer ordered everyone to move away from the fire for their own safety; jeers came back followed by a brief volley of flying bottles, all scattering their jagged shards on the pavement close to the officers' boots. While the police were keeping their blockade steady so as to not antagonise the locals, they would not do so indefinitely. As soon as they advanced, the violence would escalate and each officer knew an increase in aggression was what those chucking bottles and abuse wanted. They waited, their line resilient only to a point, and although much of the sense from the chanting was consumed by the crackling of the fire and hiss of the spray from hoses, the volume of the abuse increased.

Desperately, Fulcher scanned the nearest faces for any men he knew personally. None stood out. For the first time in his career, the urge to flee from trouble came over him, there and gone a moment later. Brief as it was, Fulcher couldn't deny the temptation of driving like a fucking loon back to his house and family.

Banishing everything but the need to get the job done, he strode to the end of the line and officers parted long enough to let him through. He saw King bellowing orders to an assembled group while a dozen firemen struggled to get the fire under control. Flames had turned the phone box into little more than a crumpled pile of waste; windows in the mini supermarket and hairdressers had blown out, sending glass in all directions. Both shops were alight. Flame turned their fronts into a dance of red and orange while the paving slabs outside both were scorched black. Holding a hand over his mouth to block as much of the stink of smoke as possible, Fulcher had to back up several paces as a leaden cloud blew close by. Luckily, the wind took the majority of the smoke away from the crowd and across to the grass where it drifted slowly upwards. Close to deafened by the storm of helicopter, cracking of fire and the overall commotion, Fulcher signalled to King to join him against the side of flats opposite the shops.

"What the fuck's going on?" Fulcher shouted.

"They're kicking off because of the latest one. Word's spread fast; most of them were out here already by the time we arrived." King jabbed a finger at the remains of the phone box. While his face had become red with exertion and exposure to the heat, Fulcher still made out the sickly cast to his colleague's features.

"It's our guy. He called from there twenty minutes ago. Jesus Christ, Clyde." King had to swallow and Fulcher held back on the urge to take the man's arm. No weakness allowed to be shown or seen. Not with so much potential for trouble seconds away.

"He burned her in there. Set her on fire."

"Fuck me," Fulcher muttered. He'd been told the same on the phone but to be around the hell of the noise and the fire made it a thousand times worse. The non-stop crackle, the steady thud of the chopper and the rotten stink of burning buildings and petrol. This wasn't a war zone; it was a bad dream.

King leaned in close to Fulcher's ear, his raised voice struggling with fresh noise as the firemen directed their hoses en masse to the flames spreading towards a third shop: the local chippy. The images of vats of fat and grease all going up and belching fresh flames out to the precinct made Fulcher wince.

"It's worse," King told him. "Another girl. Back there on the grass. Looks like it's the first girl's friend or maybe sister. He smashed her in the head. She's out of it. We'll be lucky if she wakes up by this time next year."

Standing back, King swayed on the spot and Fulcher heard himself telling the man to keep his shit together.

Inside, he turned as frigid as the great weight of winter that couldn't be touched by the fire.

When the first of the Molotov cocktails were thrown through the wrecked windows of the Chinese takeaway, the officers with their riot shields charged forward and fresh flames spread their orange fingers towards the sky.

Chapter Twenty-Six

At first, I had no clue what had woken me or much of an idea why I was on the sofa and not in bed. Then the previous night came back along with recognising the distant wail of sirens.

Police or ambulances out in the early light and tongue and teeth nasty and stale while the light I'd left on in the hallway illuminated enough of Steve's face to tell me he would hurt when he woke.

Making no particular effort to be quiet, I rose, brushed myself down and peeled the curtain back. Weak dawn light spread; the sky remained low and the moon was a fading white light. My watch read just after six. Less than four hours kip, and what I'd got had been thin. The thought of crawling into my bed was a heavy temptation; I ignored it to concentrate on the occasional flash of red and blue light down on Albion Way.

Police by the looks, and a few ambulances. They vanished from my line of sight where Albion Way met New Road, heading north by the looks. The last vehicle followed the rest of the convoy and I caught a few seconds' worth of a rhythmic thudding in the sky. Nothing showed in the gloom.

Letting the curtain go and giving Steve another once over, I crossed to the hallway and eyed the bathroom door. It remained wide open and the section of the bath visible from my position showed it to be empty.

Just like it was last night.

Yep. Just like barely a few hours before when the burned girl had reached out of the water and screamed for me.

Steve hadn't woken when I stumbled into the living room, unable to look away from the bathroom door. At some point in those few seconds, the thing brought of my imagination had disappeared in the time it took me to blink. I'd been left with my heart turned into a sprinting animal, a fine layer of ice-like sweat coating my neck and back and all my spit turned into a sour paste.

And no burned girl, of course.

"Shit," I whispered and walked to the door.

The floor squeaked as usual. A few droplets of condensation coated the seal around the window handle. No water in the bath. No scorched flesh or blackened bone jutting from open wounds.

Not a thing.

Avoiding checking my face in the mirror, I urinated, swilled a load of mouthwash and kept the door open when I left. Imagination, hallucination or what: I still didn't think I could face the door shut and keeping any secrets.

Steve had woken. He'd pulled his feet off the floor and made a ball of himself on the chair.

"You all right?" I asked.

"Rough," he croaked.

"Yeah."

"Police?"

He'd heard the sirens, too.

"I think so."

"Where they going?"

"I don't know."

He lowered his legs, rested his head on his hands and made a noise somewhere between a groan and a yawn. "I feel like dogshit."

"You look like it, too."

He eyed me. "Funny fucker."

"Better than Weird Jimmy."

"Yeah."

I sat back on the sofa and held the TV remote although I hadn't turned it on. "What now?" I asked.

"I go home and see if Carl knows anything or if the law's been round again." He shook his head. "I got nothing else."

The man had clearly sobered up since the night before and I told myself to bear that difference in mind. It seemed possible Steve wasn't a total arsehole; drink and grief had turned him into one, and while the grief obviously remained, the booze having worn off had given him a slightly more level head.

"You think he was watching us in the car park?" The question came out before I realised I'd thought it. In all honesty, it'd been at the back of my head since we ran out of the car park and pretending it'd been down to stress or tiredness had been bullshit.

Steve didn't need to ask who I meant by he.

"If that was him, then he's a cheeky cunt."

"It's more than that," I said. "If the guy who. . .hurt your niece and those other girls was watching us, then how the fuck did he know where we were?"

Steve looked like he was about to speak, but I went on. "And why was he watching us?"

"Because he's a fucking nut."

I nodded. A small answer but better than any I had.

Watching us. Knowing my name. Telling me he likes me.

I met Steve's eyes and all the stuff we should have talked about hours before came out. Without stopping, I told him exactly what had happened near the river the day before: the young guy knocking me down, his muttered words before he ran, knowing my name.

And Ella's face on Loui's body.

Even that.

I finished, Steve licked around his gums as if to dislodge the taste of stale Scotch and said the last thing I expected.

"You need to tell the police that."

"You what?"

"You heard me."

He stood and opened the curtains fully to peer down to the road. In the few minutes since I'd woken, dawn had crept closer. Night still clung stubbornly to most of the sky, but a distinct purple claimed it out to the east of Lawfield. Steve kept his back to me. Maybe a lifetime of being what just about anyone would call dodgy meant going for the socially accepted option was embarrassing for him, like telling another man he loved him.

"Maybe not that last bit," he murmured and I wanted to laugh. He made it sound like me describing the sight of a ghost was someone playing a childish joke.

"Tell them the rest, though. The geezer. The river. What he did. . .what he did to Loui."

Her name emerged as a weak sob and I wanted to offer support. A hand on his shoulder, a word of comfort. I did neither because neither would have been welcome.

"Tell the law what he said about knowing you." Steve turned around, eyes wet. "You don't know him. I believe that, Jimmy, but he knows you, right? They need to know that."

I nodded wordlessly. Steve went to the bathroom and I switched the TV on.. Seconds later, Steve raced back to the living room, his mobile in hand. He saw what I'd been watching on the screen and stood, silent.

Sprignall burning, or at least several shops and the flats above them. Fire engines, ambulances, police cars and vans; grouped officers with their shields forming a solid wall, and dozens of raging people chucking bottles, rocks and whatever they could get hold of. Above it, a thick stream of smoke burying any dawn light and turning the estate into inky gloom. The reporter with her piece to camera flinching as window smashed somewhere close by, and the text along the bottom of the screen.

BREAKING NEWS: RIOT ON OXFORDSHIRE ESTATE. DOZENS HURT. MULTIPLE ARRESTS. UNCONFIRMED REPORT OF A MURDER ON THE ESTATE PRIOR TO THE RIOT.

"Carl's left me a shitload of messages," Jimmy said quickly. "It kicked off a couple of hours ago." He jabbed the phone in front of my face and I caught a few words as Steve said the same. "Another girl. Another one. He burned her in a fucking phone box."

I had to close my eyes for a moment and I still saw the retreating form of the figure who'd knocked me down to fall beside a dead girl wearing another dead girl's face.

Moving fast, Steve grabbed his jacket from the back of the sofa and slid it on.

"Where are you going?" I asked.

"Home. I got to see Carl. I got to. . .I got to do something, Jimmy. You call the police. You tell them what you told me."

Fumbling with the zip, he watched the chaos and noise fill the TV and the same text as a moment before scroll across the lower half. In the background of the shot, a moving object sailed high, rising and falling too fast for me to name it. Flames coughed into life when it hit the ground and the nearest figures sprinted away. A second burning bottle followed it.

"Shit." Jimmy sealed his jacket and pocketed his phone. "Something big is going on. You're a part of it. Tell the law. I'll be in touch."

He ran for the door, the corridor, the lift, the outside.

I stared at the screen and I thought about Ella.

And Steve saying I was involved.

And how much of a coward I was for knowing I could not call the police, could not face whatever it meant for me or Ella to be part of the killer's world.

Chapter Twenty-Seven

Although the road that led into the estate would have been quicker, Steve stuck to the back way, not wanting to approach home too openly for reasons he couldn't specify even to himself. Forty-five minutes after leaving Jimmy's flat, he reached the end of a series of mostly silent side streets, crossed through a park and walked alongside an overgrown trail. Beyond the broken slats of the fence supported by metal railings, the disused train tracks were covered in weeds growing wild even at this time of the year. He liked this little piece of Lawfield, always had. Back when they were kids, the area was just as abandoned as now. With the nearest houses more than a hundred feet away and the pathway not big enough for a bike let alone cars, it'd been a good place to bring girls and a few tins or joints. By the looks of the crap mouldering in the bushes, people still used it for similar although Steve and his boys had never touched needles. He spied one poking from the green and spat at it.

Head down, hands in pockets, he walked while thinking of few concrete images. Loui's face came and went as did the mad panic from the night before and the sight of the figure in the car park although hours later and in fresh (if weak) daylight, it was easy to reject those couple of seconds as imagination or from getting his head scrambled by his own bat.

"Loui," he muttered.

The path ended at a grassy section, then a short path to Eastwood Avenue. Steve followed it, shoved his way through a tangle of green at the top of a slope and gazed at the back end of Sprignall.

The air was clear and as biting although he thought he could smell smoke. The heart of the riot had been a mile or so from his spot, that precinct with the decent chippy. Standing on the embankment and surveying the area, Steve watched a police car pass, neither officer seeming to notice him, and Steve sure they both had. He waited until it was out of sight down the turning that led in a long road to the precinct, and walk home with his head down and the fading noise of the lone vehicle. Seconds later, another car sped towards Steve, following the first. A tired smile touched his face. Maybe the overnight shit hadn't quite finished despite the relative quiet.

Watched from the occasional window by people who, for all he knew, had tried to destroy their own estate or simply been happy to let it burn, Steve reached Artindale Square ten minutes later. He caught sight of Carl in a bedroom window as he came to the house from the back, his brother's face blank. No sign of Erica. Steve shoved his key in the lock, guessing his sister-in-law remained asleep either through the weight of grief or more than help from a few pills.

In the living room and listening to the steady approach of Carl as he descended the stairs, Steve studied the normal things, the photos in their frames on the wall, the black of the leather sofa, the massive TV Carl had put up himself a few weeks before Christmas.

All the normal things he barely registered and now turned into strangers by the absence of his niece.

Absence wasn't right. Loui had been stolen from her home.

The out of control fire of his grief, slightly more under control since waking, threatened to explode again. Steve resolutely held it back, reached the door of the living room and heard his brother's question come from a great distance.

"Where'd you go?" Carl asked.

Steve dropped into an armchair and struggled to loosen the laces of his boots. "Out. I needed a walk."

"You need a hospital by the looks. Who did it?" Carl waved loose fingers at his brother's head.

"Don't worry about it."

"Steve—"

Steve cut Carl's warning tone off before it went further. Being treated like a kid, being forced to face all the usual things in the house and with his family—he could not take the morning like it was anything but a fucked-up nightmare.

"Leave it, Carl. Nothing happened. Just a misunderstanding."

He finally managed to kick his boots free and made no attempt to tidy them away.

"Where's Erica?" he asked.

"Asleep. Hasn't moved all night."

Carl collapsed on the sofa, legs splayed, large hands resting on his knees. For the first time, Steve realised his brother wore the same clothes as the day before, and judging by the blackish swellings under his eyes and the blank stare that clearly wasn't taking in a fucking thing, Carl wasn't doing so great.

"The police," Steve began, had to stop and start again. "The police coming back today?"

"I don't know."

"They say they'd call?"

"I don't know."

"Carl." Steve said his brother's name, tasting it as he might taste a stranger's name. It no longer fit in the house just as the big telly and photos were all mistakes. They needed to be thrown away and the rooms turned into empty shells.

Steve's first thought in almost twenty-four hours that was not buried below grief whispered to him.

I need to get the hell out of here. I can't stay here. I'll lose it if I do.

Yes. Getting out was the best plan. Everything was all over the place; he could get no hold on it or himself. Even his moods were dancing wildly between a forced sense of cynical humour and the almost overpowering urge to scream until he could no longer breathe.

He made it upright; Carl watched the movement, obviously not taking it in.

"I need some kip," Steve muttered.

His legs had become broken pieces of wood. He lurched to the hallway that led to the front of the house and the stairs, rested a hand on the cool wood of the rail and dragged himself to the second floor where he ignored the door to his bedroom and instead went to Loui's bedroom.

The door had been closed by someone yesterday evening. Erica, the police; Steve had no idea and cared less. With the weak light falling on to the little patch of carpet outside his niece's bedroom, he eased the door open, stepped into the room and made himself as small a shape on the floor as he could manage.

While he wept, he kept his eyes firmly closed.

***

Still sitting on the chair, eyes fixed on the windows overlooking their rear garden, Carl Cameron thought of nothing at all. He sank into a leaden pool where sensory input had become a bare minimum and exhaustion turned his reactions to a snail's pace.

Half an hour after his brief conversation with Steve, he shifted position to face the opposite chair.

But Steve was not there.

Steve had left.

Seconds passed while Carl Cameron attempted to process what the lack of his brother's presence might mean. And another minute ticked by in the silent living room before he was able to play back the memory of Steve saying he needed some kip.

Steve had gone to bed.

And.

Up the stairs.

But not to his bedroom.

Carl craned his neck, not aware of the strain in the muscles, and stared at the ceiling. Above the ceiling, the floor of Loui's bedroom.

The creak long minutes before.

In the secret underside of Carl's mind, a question was being born, and while the slow remains of normal thinking struggled to stop it, they had no chance.

Still watching the ceiling and picturing his brother up there, Carl whispered:

"What happened with her, Steve?"

Chapter Twenty-Eight

Crouching, the shape dressed as Robert Fry reached blindly and rested his fingertips on the freezing metal of the drawer.

So close. So secret. Not a single person knew where the girl was and all that happened right now was his choice. For now. He had not lied to her hours before: whether she lived or died was up to Jimmy Marshall even if he didn't know it. That was the time ahead; this was all on him.

Grinning, Fry ran his fingers over the drawer and paused.

Grooves in the metal.

Scratches.

He peered around, hand gripping his little torch without switching the device on. Each side of the darkness masked everything and nothing. They were alone. He was sure of it. The markings on the drawer had to be damage from any one of a dozen possibilities. Wear over time back when the building had been in use seemed the most likely.

Crouching, he pressed an ear to the drawer, straining to hear any snatch of the girl's breath. The metal, inches thick, made that impossible and the hole through which the tubing for her oxygen dangled loose was no help. Idly, he wondered if he should simply squeeze the tube, cutting her oxygen off. That was, if she remained alive.

No. This one was for Jimmy and his new friend. This one was not for him to play with unlike the girl beside the river or in the park or that one he'd dumped beside the pub. Or any of the others for that matter.

Rising, he grasped the drawer's handle, not minding the sting from the chilly metal, and finally switched the torch on as he pulled the drawer open.

She was dead.

No sign of breathing, nothing but bone white cheeks and forehead. The small mask remained covering her face and nose so she hadn't suffocated. Hypothermia most likely. Probably to be expected. After all, she'd been in the drawer for well over a day with only a little water and her sole protection from the cold her clothing and the blanket. Surprised to find himself disappointed, Fry rested a hand on the side of the girl's face. The touch was like shoving his fingers into a freezer.

Her eyes flew open.

A spark of joy burned in Fry's chest, then sputtered as the girl's eyes flickered before closing.

"Wake up." He slapped her cheek.

Eyes open again, she tried to cry out, cough and pull away all at the same time as the mask came loose. She sucked in a great volley of air and it came back, spittle flying. He didn't mind. She was alive. She was still here for Jimmy.

"You're alive. That's nice," he told her.

She saw him although he had to wonder if she genuinely believed she did or if she thought the situation was a hallucination brought on by being so close to a miserable death. The girl's mouth opened; tongue flicked at the upper lip and even with the little light of his torch, that was enough illumination to see how cracked her lips were. She'd done well to make it so far. All she had to do was last a bit longer.

He leaned in close. Still lying flat, she cringed and tried to pull away but had nowhere to go. Much as his fist clasping the hammer had filled the world for Loui Cameron, his face covered everything for Laura Flint. A few tears ran to her temples, the liquid the only warmth touching her skin.

"Think you can make it another few hours?" he asked. "Think you can hang on until Jimmy turns up? If he does?"

Not long before, Fry would have been forced to listen to the pathetic moans and pleas from the one he'd brought back to witness these events, to torture with knowing his body was carrying out these crimes. No more of that, now. The weak, self-absorbed creature originally named Fry was burned waste and he would beg no more.

Sniggering, the thing who'd taken Fry's name and body slammed the trolley back into the wall and left Laura screaming her weak cries in the terrible nothingness of the hospital morgue.

Chapter Twenty-Nine

Tom welcomed me at the gates to the site as he always did at a few minutes to nine. It took my boss one look to see that I was not all right.

"Jesus, Jimmy. You look like shit."

"Cheers." I hugged myself despite wearing a chunky coat, thick gloves and a big hat. Tom was dressed much the same; the beam of white from the light at his back made his already bulky frame look even larger.

"I mean it. Your face looks like you got hit by a bus."

"Not sleeping too well. My face is better than it looks."

That was a bullshit lie, and I could only hope the gloom shrouded me enough to mask my black eye and multi-coloured cheeks even a little bit. A once over in the bathroom mirror after my shower had shown me yellowing bruises mixing with purples, and a graze peeking its red through the stubble on my chin.

"Yeah, I bet after yesterday. Coffee. Now."

Tom led me across the site, the silent mounds of rubble and smashed brick lining the makeshift path while our boots crunched frost and pebbles. As cold as it was anyway, the site felt much colder probably because there was no protection from the steady wind and nowhere to take shelter other than the little portakabin for staff or the two others beside it: toilet and office. All the smaller buildings were gone, smashed into broken stone and glass before the dispute with the council put a stop to the work. Directly opposite where we walked, the main building grew tall and imposing. The plan had been to clear the other structures and flatten everything before they started work on the hospital itself. As that hadn't happened, we were left with a six-floor building with its long, empty corridors, silent stairs and holes for windows into which the elements entered freely. They'd sealed off the ground floor windows with massive wooden panels, so even though the hospital had been shut down for less than six months, it already looked post-apocalyptic, an image not helped by the mounds of tall weeds that had taken over the car park. They flourished despite the time of year, and spread through the long bike shelter where the metal stands were little more than flaking rust.

Tom shoved open the door to the cabin; I followed and stood in silence as he spooned coffee into two cracked mugs.

"Any more word from the police about that girl by the pub?" he asked.

"Nothing. They said they'd call if they needed anything else."

He handed me a cup and I nodded my thanks. He took the chair at the small desk, back to the three monitors. We controlled and watched the CCTV from the cabin; the most interesting thing I'd seen since we sealed the broken fence and got rid of the drunks had been a fox running towards the side of the main building, bushy tail waving jauntily before it vanished. The job was pretty tedious but it was a steady wage at least for the foreseeable. Even if the trouble between the developer and the council sorted itself out soon, they'd still need someone on site at all hours. All I needed to do was turn up, watch the cameras, check the gates, read a book and wait for time to pass and dawn to creep down from the sky. In the meantime, I had coffee, the TV and plenty of time for my imagination to picture someone out there who liked to hurt young girls. A someone who knew my name.

"Thought they would have called you after what happened with that kid in the phone box," Tom said and I forced myself back into the present and our conversation. The police. He meant the police. I slumped on the armchair where I'd dozed off more than once. Tom shook his head. "Nasty fucking way to go. Whoever who did it, he needs hanging. Sod a cushy life inside. He needs to swing."

I'd deliberately ignored all news since first thing in the morning and spent most of it walking aimlessly around the town centre, only returning to the flat to shower and change as quickly as possible. Whatever the hell I thought I'd seen, I didn't want to risk repeating it. Hallucination brought on by stress or what, I didn't know and didn't want to find out.

Tom gave me a once over, making no attempt to hide his appraisal of my smashed face. He knew better than to ask exactly what had happened.

"You have heard about the latest kid?" he asked.

"Yeah. Well, not exactly. Didn't fancy checking the TV or going online."

"He smashed her head in and burned the body. In a phone box. Another thirteen-year-old. Same as the kid by the river, the one in the park and the one you found by the pub."

I said nothing because there was nothing to say. A monster had come to our town and was killing kids, but anything I said wouldn't change that. All I wanted was to go home and close the door, lock all the windows.

"She was with her sister by all accounts." Tom pulled a face as if he'd bitten in to a bad piece of meat. "Beat the other girl with a hammer, then did the younger sister in the phone box. Sprignall went up in flames straight after. Well, some of it. The locals were fucked off. Scared. Angry. Lashing out. Took the police a good few hours to quieten the trouble down, it seems."

I sipped my too hot coffee and didn't give a shit about burning my lips. Pretending not to notice my discomfort, Tom busied himself with the cameras and monitors for a few moments. I kept quiet while he made sure everything was recording and the connections to the security office were all fine (a job I knew he would have done minutes before my shift was due to start), then downed his coffee. We kept a bottle of pretty good whisky in one of the drawers; something for me to warm against the nights, and for Dayshift Andy to see out the dead afternoons; Tom left it on the shelf next to the kettle for me and winked while I managed to laugh.

We talked for a bit longer without saying much. Tom had heard the sister of the burned girl was in an induced coma, and I could only nod at that as if it was a normal occurrence. Shortly after, he told me I was okay to finish early and go home for some decent kip if I wanted. I forced a joke of telling him I'd get some shut eye as soon as he fucked off and he laughed probably because he believed me.

We trudged back to the gates after I finished my coffee. The temperature had decreased in the short time we'd been inside and the stars gleamed in a lonely way. Although Tom had a walk of barely two minutes to his car, he'd zipped his coat and jammed on his hat and gloves. He blew fog at me.

"Sure you're okay, Jimmy?"

"Yeah. Just been. . ." I struggled for the right term and could only say: "It's been a bad day or two."

"Hasn't it just?" He surveyed the little we could make out of the site while a couple of cars passed by on Mansfield Road.

"I tell you what." He stamped a foot and shivered. "I'll be glad when we can get back to work on this place. It's like standing in a graveyard these days."

"Thanks for that thought, Tom. That'll keep me warm in the middle of the night."

He laughed. "I suppose you want this silly shit with the council to go on longer. We don't get any further with this dump, you definitely stay in a job."

"I'll be all right." The thought of my temporary role maybe coming to an end wasn't a big issue. My employment had ranged from working in pubs to building sites to courier to delivery driver for a supermarket. Shit money all round, but it wasn't like I had a family to support. If it ended at the hospital, I'd sort myself out.

"We'll find you something here if need be."

Tom fumbled with the locks, cursing the freezer burn on his fingers, and booted the gate open a few feet.

"I'll be back with Andy at five thirty, yeah?" he said.

"Yeah. See you then."

He gave me another once over, offered a slightly awkward smile and left.

Not letting myself have time to think about the silence of my surroundings or the long hours ahead, I locked up again, returned to the cabin and poured another coffee. In the warmth with only a telly for company, I gave the monitors a quick look and psyched myself up for going back out in a bit to check the fence at a couple of dodgy points I'd noticed the week before and which Tom said he'd get round to sorting. Not right away, though. Time to sit in the little cabin and drink my coffee and think about dead girls. About the screaming, burned thing reaching for me from the bath and how maybe it'd been some kind of mad psychic flash. About the gleam of sunlight on the ankles and shins of Cheryl Temple as she protruded from underneath the bin. About Meg Freeman choking on her own blood in the long grass of the park as she was strangled.

And about the last wheezing breath from Loui Cameron as she bled on the riverside path.

I found one of Pierce Brosnan's Bond films to watch; it'd been on for twenty minutes but that didn't matter. It was something to take my eyes and my ears away, and after what I realised had been best part of an hour, the only thing that brought me back to the cabin was my ringing phone.

That, and the surety the caller was the man who'd set up home in the back of my head since the previous morning. The killer of children. And Jesus Christ, I knew all about that.

My phone continued to ring.

Chapter Thirty

"I thought you weren't answering."
"I thought I wasn't, either."
Hand over my eyes, I kept them shut and listened to Steve puff on a cigarette. Neither of us spoke and that was fine with me. It gave me chance to try and slow the thunder of my heart. Convinced the killer was calling while I sat in the cabin with no help anywhere nearby, I'd forced myself to answer the phone, standing and fighting the urge to run as I held the mobile to my ear.

"You at home?" Steve said eventually. Wind blew behind his voice. Wherever he was, it was outside, and I flashed back to his phone call. He'd threaten me, tell me to meet him and I'd grab a knife before I went out to try and take some control over my life only to find control was nowhere near me and someone would watch us talk from the other side car park and we'd run and a girl burned to death waited in my bathroom before she was killed in the shit and misery of Sprignall and—

"Jimmy? Weird Jimmy? You there?"

"Don't fucking call me that," I muttered and felt Steve take a figurative step back. When he spoke again, it wasn't with respect or anything as extreme. It was more awareness of me as someone who'd left my school nickname behind years before.

"You call the police yet?"

"No."

"You going to?" He didn't sound surprised.

"I have no idea."

On the TV, Bond was busy kicking the shit out of someone. In the cabin, I had coffee and a warm sofa. That was all I needed. Filling a cup from the boiler, I stirred it and dropped the spoon into the sink. It clanged.

"You at home?" I asked Steve.

"Yeah. In the garden. It's bad here. Like really fucking bad. Law coming and going all day. Erica's like a fucking zombie. Carl's worse. Just sits in his chair, staring at the TV. I went through earlier. The TV wasn't even on but he was still looking straight at it."

I wanted to tell Steve something other than the truth: that the days of his sister-in-law escaping her life by sleeping or his brother being unaware of his surroundings would pass quickly. I didn't say that because it was a lie.

"How did you get my number, Steve?"

"You left your phone on the table last night. I figured it might come in handy."

It didn't bother me as much as it might have done under better circumstances. Besides, he had a point.

"You heard about what happened round here?" he asked. "The fire? It all kicking off?" A click sounded which I thought was either of our phones. It took me a second to realise it was Steve's dry throat. "The girl in the phone box and her sister? You get all of that, Jimmy?"

There was no obvious anger in his question, no shouting like there'd been the previous night. Whether that aggression had been down to the drink or the immediate horror of his niece being murdered, I had no clue. Right then, Steve Cameron sounded as reasonable as anyone else I knew. Maybe he was too done in to get angry right then.

"I got all that."

"Good. Because, you know, I thought you might have missed it. Maybe you ain't heard about my place burning and hey, who gives a fuck, right? Just a bunch of low lives in their shitty estate, right?"

"Steve, wait a second—"

"No, you wait." Still no anger, only the terrible exhaustion that went beyond any physical tiredness. "You hear about the people here kicking off and burning their shops and flats? You hear about how fucking angry they are because of what that bastard's done, yeah? You hear about that girl beaten and burned? You hear the precinct still stinks of her body? You get that shit, Jimmy?"

I couldn't speak.

"You hear about her sister? Got her head smashed in. Right in. She's a vegetable now. You hear about that girl, Jimmy?"

I still did not speak.

It was only because I turned on the spot, putting the TV to my back, and facing the monitors that I saw the white circle looming into view at the front of the main building.

The face.

"Jimmy?"

A slash split the lower half of the circle, its features hard to make out in the grainy image, but still clear enough for me to recognise the movement.

A smile.

"Steve." I barely had the breath to whisper it.

"What? What did you say?"

"He's here." Again, just a frightened whisper, and then a further widening of the slash as his smile grew as if he'd heard me.

"Speak up. I can't hear shit."

The night had broken into the cabin and brought the all the strength of the winter to turn me into a statue. That was the only explanation for my body temperature dropping down and down and down and my fingers welded to my phone and I would be like rock, unable to move, when the man came to the door of the cabin, came for me.

You fucking coward, you fucking piece of shit weak bastard. You get him right now. You stop that son of a bitch.

It wasn't my voice inside, or Steve's. It was nothing but pure self-disgust. When I let my next words out, they came at a normal volume instead of the shriek they wanted to be.

"He's here. In the hospital. He's here right now."

Chapter Thirty-One

The twenty minutes between Steve roaring down the phone that he was coming and his actual arrival might have been centuries of the winter stuck in that moment. Every fraction of my attention was focused squarely on the shot outside the front of the hospital. The face remained in the same place, making no move to hide from the cameras or come closer into the moonlight. I'd somehow managed to keep my eyes on the screens while backing up to the little kitchen area, digging in one of the drawers and yanking a knife free. Gripping it like the handle was part of my body, I'd also taken the heavy walking stick Tom hid beside the sofa when the trouble with the pissheads kicked off. Nobody had touched it since; having both makeshift weapons in my hands was all the comfort I was going to get, and neither felt like they'd be much good up against a killer of children.

My mobile brayed into life. I hissed and answered it without looking from the monitors.

"Jimmy? You there?"

"I'm here." I whispered it; sure the killer could somehow hear me.

"I'm at the gates. Let me in."

"Steve—"

"Fucking let me in." Steve's voice was an insistent hiss. Within seconds, he'd be making a lot more of a din and our visitor would definitely hear him. What then? He had no way out of the site.

"Listen to me, Jimmy. For the last time. You ain't hiding from this. You're part of it. You've been a part of this shit since Ella, so stop being a cunt and let me in. We're going to kill him."

Ella. Her name always in my mind. Her face on the faces of dead girls. Her dying breaths in a winter exactly as the same as the one right outside my door.

The shot of the hospital wavered; the wall at the back of the monitors did the same, both rolling in the smooth motion of a ship on calm seas. On all sides, voices whispered, their words a jumble of hissing, but all still recognisable as young, as feminine.

Ella, I am so sorry I let you down. I let you down. I let you down. I let—

Everything fell away, leaving me untouched by the weather and the whispers of the dead girls. I floated at the far end of everything and all my senses had been switched off to leave me an unfeeling, unseeing dot.

Untouchable.

The cabin and the monitors were at my back; I sprinted over the uneven ground with the stick and knife swinging, my torch bouncing in my coat pocket, and the gates rising ahead with the great sky all over me. Ella was right. Time to end this for her.

I skidded over frost and smashed into the gates, almost knocking the breath right out of my body. The pain was unimportant. Getting Steve into the site and killing the killer—those things mattered. Nothing else.

"Jimmy?" It was Steve separated from me by a few inches of metal. "Fucking let me in."

"Hold on," I panted and fumbled with the keys, convinced hands would come down on my shoulders at any second and turn me to face a figure who was not a man and not a teenage boy but both together. Holding my breath so I could hear properly, I stabbed the key into the padlock, yanked it open and tugged on the chains. They snagged on the gates, clanging together, and I spat my breath out.

"Shit."

"Hurry up, Jimmy," Steve bellowed.

Hands on the chains, I looked around, saw nothing but the piles of rubbles and silent equipment. The hospital block jutted towards the sky at the far end of the site; if anyone came at me from it, they'd make it in seconds.

"Jimmy," Steve moaned.

I got the chains free; Steve booted the gates as I tugged them open and he all but fell into me.

A second later, I saw the handgun he was pulling from his coat pocket.

"Jesus, Steve."

"Don't ask. Where is the cunt?"

"I saw him right outside the hospital. No movement in twenty minutes, but he could be anywhere now."

"Nice."

Steve moved ahead, the black of the gun turning it almost invisible against his leg.

"Wait." I grabbed his shoulder, yanked him around and the gun was suddenly aimed at my chest.

"Put that away. There's cameras all over the place," I whispered.

Grimacing, he lowered the weapon but didn't pocket it.

"Listen to me. He's in here somewhere. We can't let him out, so we need to—" I took a few quick breaths to try and calm myself. It didn't work. "We need to lock the gates. Keep him in here, yeah? Keep him trapped and call the police."

"Fuck that. We're dealing with him, not the law."

"Steve—"

"I'll go and get him by myself if I have to."

There was no argument I could give. Gates locked again, I picked up my stick, handle solid and comforting, then the knife and stood close to Steve. For the first time, I registered his panting breath and his eyes darting all over the place. If he fired the gun, I needed to be beside him, not in front or behind. No way was he level enough to aim or think before shooting.

"Come on." I kept close to him; we crossed the site towards the trail of pebbles and gleaming frost. The lights glared on the rubble and clear spaces, turning the route straight towards the main block into a white path. Illumination didn't quite touch the front of the building, meaning the entire section was effectively a hiding place even with the two cameras aimed at the sealed glass of the entrances right in the middle.

"You definitely see him?" Steve asked.

"I saw him. Smiling at me."

"Bastard."

The gun came up, held in both of Steve's bare hands.

"You need to keep that down. I can explain you being here if anyone watches the recordings, but not if you're waving a gun around."

"Who gives a shit?"

"I do."

"Pussy." He sounded like he might be smiling. I didn't want to check because that meant taking my attention from the building ahead. We passed between two diggers, both looking like dead animals in the mix of fierce light and shadows.

"Where the hell did you get it?" I asked and knew my question was pointless because I could take a good guess at the answer.

"Carl. He's not in the business, anymore, but he keeps his shit together. Well, he did before yesterday."

I let the subject go. The Cameron family being able to get hold of illegal guns wasn't anything I wanted to know about. If Steve knew how to shoot or was a good aim. . .I didn't want to know about that, either.

We crept forward, both breathing quietly. Our boots crushed frost and stones, and more of the hospital's front came into view the closer we drew to it. Grey walls, dozens of closed windows showing nothing of the building's interior; a long section of glass sealed by thick sheets of wood along the ground floor, and covering the front on the ground, bunches of tangled weeds.

About twenty steps from the front, we stopped at the same time.

Enough of the illumination from the tall lights shone on the entrances for us to see they were empty. And enough light shone to show the caved in piece of wood sinking into one of the ground-floor windows right next to the blocked doors.

"Shit."

Steve glanced at me. "He's in there. We're going in there."

"We're calling the police."

"We're fucking not. He killed my niece. We kill him."

With that, Steve broke into a lumbering, awkward run towards the entrance. Somehow, he didn't slip, boots finding level ground and the few patches without ice. Convinced the killer would appear at any second, I ran after Steve, catching up just as he left the path and reached what had been the circular road opposite the entrance. Incoming traffic on the left; outgoing on the right. Not now, of course. Just us, the quiet and nobody else anywhere in sight. Gun aimed at the ground, Steve walked on. I followed him, weapons held high. We didn't say a word until we stood right beside the wrecked window. With a light hand, Steve pressed on the broken piece of wood. A small chunk fell to our feet. Not a thing was visible inside.

"Who's first?" he whispered.

"What?"

"We're going in. Who's first?"

"The place is falling apart. You'll be lucky to get two feet, Steve. It's just rubble and wires and shit in there and—"

"I'm first, then."

He swapped the gun to his left hand, grabbed the side of the window with his right and readied himself to boost up. All I could picture was a smiling man on the other side, grinning, ready to welcome us into the belly of the building.

With no warning, Steve froze, then turned to look back at me. His face, already a ghastly white, seemed even paler.

"Jimmy," he breathed.
Then I heard what he'd heard a second ago.
Someone screaming in the building.

Chapter Thirty-Two

Even with the late hour, work in the incident room remained ongoing. Three officers stood at a whiteboard, the surface covered with names that had so far proved fruitless in generating any leads. Several men known to the Force had been questioned; all had provided solid alibis for their whereabouts while Loui, Cheryl, Meg and the latest victim—Trudy Mackenzie—had been killed. Voices kept low, the men discussed speaking to the family liaison officers who'd had the most direct contact with the dead girls' families with the working theory an extended family member knew more than they wanted to admit although very few police held much faith in the idea. While all of them had experience in uncovering a secret relationship between vulnerable children and an adult known to the kids, the series of murders did not fit that pattern. No signs of sexual violence; no attempts to make the killings appear accidental, and absolutely no effort made in hiding the body. Even Meg's body, dumped so carelessly between pub and estate agent, had been a quick job, the girl left under the bin rather than in it. They knew he'd meant for the child to be found; same with Loui and Cheryl and of course Trudy and her sister Samantha, and the bastard mocking them with such a disregard for life coupled with the arrogant surety he could get away with it made each officer in the room want him caught in hours, not days.

At several computers, officers scanned through the social media accounts of the dead girls, their tired eyes taking in photo after photo of smiling teenagers, of parents, of school mates and pets and holidays. They cross referenced shot after shot, image upon image in the attempt to find a link between the girls, and came up with nothing other than the sibling connection between Trudy and Samantha. Nobody believed that was anything other than down to the two sisters being out on the estate at the same time. As detailed by grieving, weeping parents and siblings, the girls had not known of one another. Different schools. Different sets of friends. Different lives. Still, the two women and the man at the computer screens studied the pictures and the status updates, wading through posts of lives broken in two in the hunt for a single line that would stand out: the mention of an older male friend, a secret boyfriend, a relationship no parents or teacher could know about.

Nothing.

Still, they looked and they murmured to each other when the slightest hint of unusual behaviour or a troubled life appeared in the words and the images. And when the hints revealed themselves to be simple moments of teenage difficulties and stresses, they carried on with their work.

Close to the table piled with dirty mugs and the bin full of takeaway boxes and wrappers, a third group studied transcripts of statements from the girls' parents much as the officers scanning the social media accounts did the same. Other than the family life of Loui Cameron being noticeable (every officer in the incident room knew Carl Cameron's history and not one believed all the way down the man had given up his previous life of connections and low-level crime), the words on the sheets showed normal, everyday families with normal, everyday lives of work, of occasional hard times and arguments, of raising children and wanting nothing but the best for them. Even with her parents' background, Loui Cameron's childhood and teenage years had been as uneventful as Meg's, Cheryl's and Trudy's. Okay, none of the other mothers had gone batshit during a live press conference, but nobody in the incident room put much weight or value on the woman's breakdown.

The officers studied their paperwork, their images of photos and their records of names. They drank their coffee; they answered the ringing phone, and nobody wanted to think about the man out in the bleak dark.

Nobody but Clyde Fulcher.

He twisted his head back and forth, wincing as tendons creaked. For the last twenty minutes, he'd been staring at several photos all taken at the scenes. Twenty images of four dead girls and only the surface details acting as a difference. Trudy's remains almost unrecognisable as human, a charred lump of meat, shrivelled by the fire, and none of her features remaining for Fulcher's eye to focus upon.

Below and around Loui, the damp black of the riverside path and that black contrasting with the ice-white of her skin.

Next to Cheryl, long strands of green and light brown all gleaming with dew, and the mixed colours of fresh bruising staining her small throat. Her eyes had become two red holes, blood vessels bursting as she was choked to death, and the pleasant brown Fulcher had seen in shots from the girl's Facebook page had been swallowed by that red.

Meg stuffed under the bin, shoved there like so much crap someone couldn't be bothered to throw away properly. The photos had been taken before they'd eased her body free hours later; all Fulcher had to stare at in the glare of the strip lighting above was Meg's ankles and some of the child's shins. The leg of one jean had risen further than the other, and the camera had caught a couple of tiny nicks from shaving. How long she'd been shaving her legs, Fulcher didn't want to consider just as he didn't want to think about the length of leg and the thinness proving beyond a doubt this was a child, not a young woman. Same with Loui, Cheryl and Trudy. All four doubtless thought they knew the score, knew everything that made sense and none of them had known what life was or what it could do to them whenever the fuck it felt like. And Samantha Mackenzie turned into a sleeping body that might never wake up while her parents sat beside her bed, crushed into their own silence by grief.

Each girl destroyed as if they were of no importance at all, their lives ended without any hesitation, and if any tiny comfort could be offered to their parents, it was that the killer hadn't assaulted them first.

But Fulcher didn't think for a second the relief of that knowledge would be of any help.

I'll find you. Fulcher finally looked from the photos, not wanting to admit taking his eyes from them was a relief. I'll track you down and I'll end you.

Although he couldn't verbalise the rage of his thoughts, giving them space in his head was as good as it would get right now. Present a professional face at all times; keep calm and together for the public and press while his insides shook and trembled with a sickened horror and anger and he kept his real face hidden because he had to.

But the fury.

But the horror coating his heart.

But the need to find their man and end his actions.

Fulcher knew his colleagues saw him as the man in control and that was exactly as it all needed to be. Same with the cameras and the papers. They needed a man who was concerned with the solid facts of a case, not the shit that lived below it. And if they had any clue of the mask he wore, they kept that fact to themselves.

He tried to think of Bill Lister if only to have some focus away from the images of the murdered children, wanting to take the surface of his thoughts away from the girls so the underside could get to work and find some clue he'd missed. The attempts at changing the direction of his thinking failed because he knew there was nothing to be gained with going over what had been done to Bill. The drunk was dead. Going by his loss of blood and what had been done to him, it was a fucking miracle he'd been on his feet when Fulcher and King encountered him outside The Boar.

Sitting on the messy desk, Fulcher's mobile rang.

Expecting it to be a call with some small amount of news (and if not, then a call from Barbara), Fulcher picked it up.

No name or number registered on the screen. Even so, the phone continued to ring.

For no reason, Fulcher glanced at the main section of the room as if to reassure himself his colleagues remained in sight. Hunched over paperwork and monitors, they carried on their work while his mobile continued to ring.

He answered it.

"Fulcher."

"Hello, Mr Fulcher."

The child's voice came from a void. No background noise, no interference. It was the audio equivalent of his phone screen.

"Who is this?" Fulcher asked, hand rubbing his forehead. The caller had to be one of his kids' mates pissing about. No way would his two do something like this, but it was possible one of their friends had got hold of his number somehow and thought it was a great joke to call the cop with this childish shit.

"It's Loui Cameron."

Fulcher's hand froze in its movement. "Whoever this is, I'll give you one chance to apologise and hang up. Then you take a moment to think about what an idiot you are."

Not bad especially considering he wanted to reach into the phone, grab the kid on the other line and shake them until they bled.

"It's Loui, Mr Fulcher," she said in the same mild tone. "The dead girl. The one he killed next to the river."

"You—"

"He beat me to death with a hammer. He hurt me a lot."

Fulcher swallowed. Although the other officers were less than twenty feet away, they could have been at the far side of the building, leaving him alone with nothing but the girl's voice in his ear and the growing chill emanating from his stomach.

"He's listening."

The chill fanned out to fill his entire body.

"I've got some friends here," she said. Still, nothing came behind her voice. He strained to catch a second of anything that might place her: a giggle from a mate listening in the background, wind against a window, television or music. He got nothing but a child's calm voice. "I didn't know them before. We met here."

Silently, Fulcher picked up a pen and held it over a sheet he'd already used to scrawl notes on throughout the day. "Who have you met?"

She said nothing at first and Fulcher's mind sped through options. A kid pissing about; one of his children thinking they'd have some fun with the dad who was rarely at home, or the killer doing something fucked up to his voice, turning it into a young girl's somehow. Fulcher knew enough about computers and tech to believe his last idea wasn't particularly likely. In films, yes, but life was not films. Life was where things happened for the most obvious of any reason.

It's one of Will's friends. Has to be.

"I don't know your son."

Everything stopped.

It was as if he'd been taken from the world of sense and the law and plunged into a frozen second in which any movement from taking a simple breath to blinking to standing up and getting the attention of any other cop in the room was an impossibility.

Fulcher stared at his desk, not seeing it. "Who are you?"

"I told you." She said in the tone reserved for teenagers speaking to adults who were being beyond stupid or naive. "Loui Cameron. You know my dad. You've known him for years. He's done some bad things, but not like what was done to me." She sighed.

Fulcher caught no sense of grief or hurt. Regret, maybe, but not grief.

What the fuck are you thinking? Grief? Why the fuck would she grieve? This is not Loui Cameron.

"I lived in Artindale Square with my mum and my dad and my uncle," she went on. "I'm not there now. I can't go home again."

"Where are you?" Fulcher whispered.

"By the river. It's too dark to see but I can hear it."

Fulcher's stomach became a cramped ball while the coarse hairs on his arms crinkled. He'd been into scenes of violence, seen its aftermath and he'd spent countless hours in bleak places either by himself or with dozens of other police, but picturing the night holding firm to the silent land beside the Evenham and its still surface brought the taste of childish fear into his mouth. He swallowed the sourness.

"Tell me something you didn't get from the papers or the TV," he said, and realised the chances of this kid getting any of her news from the papers or TV were beyond remote.

The girl sighed a third time. "The man walking his dog wasn't the first man to find me."

Pen tip resting on the paper, Fulcher said: "Who found you?"

"You know him. And you know the man who killed me. And—"

He interrupted her. "Who found you first?"

The girl went on in the same breath as if he had not said a word. "—I'm not by myself, not totally. We can't stay together for long because they're in the park and beside the pub and in the phone box, but I'm still not by myself because—"

No pause at all. No difference in breath, only the instant change from word to word, voice to voice, and Fulcher was listening to a different girl speak.

"—I'm here, as well. It's Cheryl. He hurt me in the park and I couldn't breathe and—"

A third change between words and no time for Fulcher to take in what was happening or say the third girl's name.

"—he dumped me in that alley. All those puddles and the ice. It's horrible. I can't smell it but I know it stinks. Dumped me under the bin. He wasn't alone. He had a friend in that van and he's not alone now even though he thinks he is. He thinks he burned the other one when he—"

"—hit me with a hammer; he broke my head and killed me and the he burned me in that phone box and he hurt my sister, I heard her screaming, I—"

The four distinct voices spoke over each other, telling Fulcher about the fire, about the puddles and about the sound of the river in the night. Mobile stuck to the side of his head, Fulcher couldn't do anything but take in the confusion as the four girls fought to be heard and each voice abruptly collapsed into silence. It was only then that Fulcher realised he'd been squeezing the pen hard enough to crack it. With fingers aching, he dropped the Biro and sucked in a breath. It trembled over his tongue and was too weak to reach his chest.

"Fulcher."

A new voice. Male. Toneless.

"Can you hear me, Fulcher?"

"I hear you," Fulcher replied. Operating on auto-pilot, he took hold of the pen again and lobbed it at the window. It struck the glass, dropped to the floor with a patter and rolled a few inches. In the main section of the incident room, several officers turned. He waved for them and they dashed to his door.

"The girl was right. You won't stop me. It's not your place to stop me. They couldn't stop me before. You won't stop me now."

Still no tone, no ranting or anything out of control. And oddly, no sense of mocking or joy. If the call was legit, Fulcher would have expected some snide humour or superiority. His caller had neither.

"Who are you?"

"You know who. Or you did. Once upon a time, Fulcher. Back in the old days."

Anger born from frustration pulsed in Fulcher's forehead. The other police had crowded at his door, none able to do anything.

"Either tell me something useful or we're done."

"I'll tell you a name, Fulcher."

"I'm listening."

"Ella Griffin."

Fulcher's mouth closed. Somewhere in the room, a phone rang, the sound shrill and awful.

"I did it before. I'm doing it now. I'll do it again."

"What the hell are you talking about?"

"Tuesday morning, Fulcher. He has until Tuesday morning to stop me or I don't stop."

"Who, for Christ's sake? Who?"

"Jimmy, of course. Jimmy Marshall. He stops me or he doesn't. It's his choice."

"What happens if he doesn't?"

Grabbing a pencil, Fulcher scribbled Jimmy Marshall's name on his sheet and held it high. Several officers ran back into main room and Fulcher caught sight of Jenny Rourke sprinting from the phone she'd answered. Even in the turmoil of his emotions, Fulcher saw trouble on Jenny's shocked face.

"I will kill," the man murmured as if musing on the subject.

"Who will you kill?" Fulcher asked, voice raised so it carried beyond the phone. On each face, he saw understanding.

"Everyone."

Dead line. No disconnection of hanging up. Just a dead line in his ear.

Fulcher rose. He held his mobile out to the nearest officer. "Find out who the fuck just called me. And call King. We're going for Jimmy Marshall right now."

Shoving her way forward, Jenny ran into Fulcher's office and barked two words before he had chance to speak.

"Hospital. Gunshots."

Chapter Thirty-Three

Gripping my weapons, I stood as close as possible to Steve. Out of the sight of the cameras, he held his gun high in one hand while my little torch shone from the other.

We'd come through the smashed in window into what had been the hospital reception. The little patch of visible floor was nowhere near the mess I'd expected. All furnishings had been removed, the shutters over the café and gift shop were sealed and the only obvious signs of the upcoming demolition were several massive holes in the walls where the electrics had been removed.

The screaming hadn't come a second time; I'd strained to hear it or place the location while we clambered inside and had no chance. Breathing through my mouth to make as little noise as possible, I shone the torch in all directions. It gleamed on the dirty white of the steps growing from the reception. Through a set of double doors, the doors to the four lifts were vague outlines. For the first time, I registered the icy air and wasn't surprised. Even without the broken window at our backs, the building's overall temperature would have made it a few degrees above freezing but not by much.

"You hear anything?" Steve whispered.

"No."

He took a breath and called out into the gloom a second before I realised that was his plan. "Okay, you fucker. We're here and we're going to kick the shit out of you. What do you think about that?"

"Jesus," I hissed. He glanced my way, dismissed me and walked forward.

Keeping close to his side, I tried to illuminate as much of our surroundings as I could. The beam spun over the floor, towards the stairs and then to the wall beside the gift shop revealing nothing more than grit below our feet and the jagged edges of the electricians' holes.

"Wait." Steve shoved my wrist. "What's that?"

I'd missed the marking on the floor, too keyed up to take in what I was seeing.

It was a clear design. An arrow spray painted on the dirty floor in bright red. Easily ten feet long with dots and splashes of paint jetting from its sides, it pointed towards the far end of the reception. Down that way, a long corridor travelled the width of the building.

"We need to get the police here right now," I muttered.

"Fuck that."

Knowing he'd go on without me, I crept forward, our shadows merging in the shaking beam from my torch. Where the reception met the corridor, another arrow pointed into the long throat of the hospital's left side. My torch was nowhere near strong enough to penetrate beyond a few feet.

"Don't pussy out on me, Jimmy. There's a girl in here somewhere. If that fucker's still here, we end him. Either way, we got to get the girl out. Got to. Got to."

I knew what he was thinking. Save the girl and make up for not saving his niece. Except he never could. I knew that very well.

Side by side, we entered the dark. It was like walking into midnight made flesh. The corridor swallowed us; the light from the torch barely touched our surroundings. I knew offices lined the corridor, but couldn't take my gaze from the path ahead to see if all doors remained shut and locked as they'd been for months.

"Carl should be here," Steve breathed. He was talking more to himself than me and I wanted to tell him to shut up, to listen for the slightest sound. A step. A breath. Anything other than the storm of my heart in my chest.

"He should find him and cut his throat. Fucking Carl."

I had to say something. "What happened with Carl?"

"He's. . ." Steve stopped and gestured for me to look at the floor. Another arrow aimed straight ahead. We walked on, speaking in little more than breaths and still the corridor was a mineshaft.

"He's off. It's like he's just turned off. Before, he would have killed anyone who fucked with his family. This. . .this has just shut him down. That's why I'm here. For Loui. I'll be her dad if Carl can't."

I had nothing to say to that and Steve's words dried up. We continued, a slight lightening in the air coming ahead. Another few steps revealed it to come from moonlight. One of the office doors had been thrown wide open and cracks and small holes in the wood over the window let in narrow beams. Not much at all but enough to turn some of the indistinct floor and walls into a weak grey, and to show the third arrow right outside the door. Like the others, it pointed ahead. I shone the torch into the room. As with the reception, the furniture had been removed, leaving an empty floor and featureless walls. The choice was clear. Straight ahead as the arrow suggested or stopping to explore the seemingly empty office.

I didn't want to enter the room. Even if it meant finding the man killing the girls, I couldn't do it. Every terrible possibility lurked in there. Trouble was, they were ahead in the corridor as well, but at least the corridor gave a small opportunity to run back the way we'd come.

We went on, neither of us speaking, and the corridor eventually turned to the left. I knew enough of the building's layout to know we were heading for the back half which meant storage, a massive canteen and the garage area for ambulances.

Another arrow pointed the way ahead, the red close to black in the wavering light from my torch.

He was playing with us, leading us like sheep and we were willingly going along with it.

"Steve," I whispered and he raised the hand holding the knife.

"You shut the fuck up about the police, okay? We are doing this."

In silence, we moved on with the weight of the empty floors above ready to come down, crush us into nothing but another section of the grubby floor. Deserted corridors and hallways above; abandoned offices and the operating theatres become like ice boxes. No life above, no flesh and blood, only the passage of ghosts to mark the long seconds and minutes and hours until work resumed and the hospital became the same rubble and broken glass covering the grounds outside.

The murdered girls walked up there for all I knew. They walked with Ella, sisters in their deaths, making no sound as they passed from room to room, listening to the two stupid men come to their place to attempt the impossible of undoing their deaths.

We were not alone. Not in the least.

It was in the air turned Arctic. It was in the horrendous possibilities inches from our faces and hands. In the slow tread of our boots and in the dryness turning my throat into stone and in our approach towards nothing, both of us like puppets.

And the final arrow.

I'd forgotten what else was situated at that end of the building. The corridor turned left which would take us to the back of the canteen and then another shorter corridor ending at the doors to the garage.

The arrow—the last painted arrow—on the ground said we didn't need to go that way. We needed to go through the massive set of doors the torch light shook over.

The doors to the morgue.

Because that's where the girl was screaming from.

Steve raced ahead, gun hand smacking on the handle and my surety the doors would be locked like a weight on my chest.

***

From the unseen space against the wall, two sets of eyes watched Jimmy and Steve run to the morgue doors.

While one watched with curiosity, the other wept silently.

Silently because of the gag around her mouth and the long blade held to her throat.

Chapter Thirty-Four

We skidded to a stop several feet beyond the doors, our boots kicking up dust and dirt while the torch light sent mad shadows dancing and skittering over the walls. No furniture again unless I counted a massive slab of table. The light found dozens of footprints in the grit; they encircled the table, crossed back towards where we'd entered and merged into a mess. Whether or not they belonged to more than one person, I had no idea and didn't want to consider.

"Hello?" Steve tried to say it with some authority, I think, but it emerged weak and croaking. The man was just as shit-scared as me.

A shriek answered him. Raw and thin, but there all the same. They came from directly ahead of us.

"Hold that fucking light steady. There."

I followed the direction of his pointing fingers and cast light on a wall. It took me a second to realise the wall was made up of dozens of handles. Each one was a drawer.

"Oh, fuck," I muttered.

The noise went on and on.

"What's that?" Steve ran ahead and the light found what looked like a dangling wire hanging from a drawer in the wall. Not a wire, I saw as I ran after Steve. Tubing. The sort of tubing usually attached to an oxygen mask.

It jutted from the drawer, poking through a small hole and joined with a small cylinder too dark to stand out without the light directly on it.

We ran together, my thoughts turned into a beam. Get the drawer out. Get the drawer open. There was nothing else in the world.

Walking stick clattering as I dropped it to my feet, I reached for the handle and Steve yelled at me to stop. The shrieking collapsed as whoever was in there ran out of breath.

"What?" I cried at him.

"Could be a trap." He held the gun towards the drawer, both hands on it like he was a cop in an action film. Except he shook from feet to head. "On three, you open it, yeah? I'll be ready."

In a single breath, I whispered: "One, two, three."

The drawer flew open with my pull and the girl inside reached a trembling hand for us, fingers too weak to pull into a fist.

***

As he drew closer towards the sparse traffic on New Road, Fulcher hit his lights but kept the siren off. Pulses of blue and red stained the ground; a taxi pulled over to let Fulcher pass while ahead, two more vehicles did the same. He caught a glimpse of the drivers: young lads, both, their faces white against their windows and both doubtless thinking he'd been about to pull them over. Shoving them from his mind, Fulcher increased his speed and fought against the urge to replay the mad few minutes on his phone back at the station.

All the voices speaking together, all the words joined in one breath and no way was that possible without an audible difference, a note of breaths changing. And the man at the end; their man, maybe. The name he'd said.

Ella Griffin.

"Christ," Fulcher muttered and slowed to take a curve of the road. On both sides, large houses, all detached, kept their owners and families safe from the night and the growing wind. Heading the way Fulcher had driven, a cab passed and the spray from Fulcher's lights turned the vehicle into a weighty shade of black for a moment.

Although he knew the mobile still rested comfortably in his inside coat pocket, Fulcher patted it. He'd grabbed the replacement from Jenny as he ran from the office and bawled for them to find out who the hell had called him. While he knew there was no reason they couldn't do that, he had a feeling they'd come up with nothing. It made no sense, but then everything felt as if it was starting to make no sense. Too much had happened too quickly; too much was off. Someone either with recordings of the murdered girls or (worse idea) with other kids who sounded the same as those girls. Bill Lister's face torn apart and the man dying minutes after making it back to the pub where he'd rumbled with Jimmy Marshall; the shit kicking off over on Sprignall after the most recent murder and the killer's blasé call before he burned that girl (the child dead before the fire for whatever that was worth) and the man getting out of the estate while it went up in flames. The mention of Ella Griffin's name had been the final kicker. Fulcher told himself they'd have some answers when Marshall was brought in. Even now, uniform was on their way to the man's flat in case he'd taken another night off. If he hadn't, that meant he was at the hospital site. And if that was the case, he was directly in the middle of gunfire.

Jimmy Marshall.

Marshall's not your name, is it? No. I really don't think it is, Jimmy.

Fulcher increased his speed again.

In a convoy further down New Road, several police vehicles did the same while in Fulcher's back seat, the dead girls watched the man glance in his rear-view as if he saw the still, watchful faces of his passengers.

Chapter Thirty-Five

Between us, we man-handled the girl from the morgue drawer. She'd more or less passed out moments after we'd got her makeshift tomb open and a few seconds appraisal made it clear she was close to death. Face turned blue, dressed only in jeans and a coat and shielded by a blanket, hands clenched into fists and arms around her narrow chest—the cold had claimed her almost fully. Unless we got her to warmth and safety in minutes, she would have no chance.

"Can you hear me?" Steve yelled at her and I wanted to tell him to shut the hell up. The man responsible for her torture was still on site somewhere, and the last thing we needed was to pinpoint our location in the building. But then the mad dance of the torch light would do that just fine.

"Hold that." I all but threw the torch at Steve who took it as I stripped off my coat and wrapped around the girl's body. Her eyes rolled, her mouth opening to reveal a tiny hole and cracked, bleeding lips. She needed water and heat fast.

"I'll carry her. You keep the light out and the gun. Be ready," I said.

He nodded, aiming the light and gun back towards the morgue entrance. Nothing moved beyond but the skittering shadows on the slope that led back to the main corridor. I crouched, arms around the girl. She stirred and made a terrible noise—terrible because she clearly wanted to scream and no longer had the power. Thin arms bashed into the sides of my head, no force in the assault, and she wheezed as her breath ran out. Harsh coughing followed and I tried to speak calmly over the noise.

"It's okay. We're helping you. You're safe now, all right? You're safe."

She relented through exhaustion, not because of any trust between us. Holding her like I might hold a baby, I rose and hoped my body heat and coat would be enough to keep her going until we got the hell out of there.

She made no new sound; I heard her scream again in my head and something about it was off, something out of my reach.

"What's the plan?" Steve whispered. I couldn't make out his face; it was like speaking to a piece of the wall.

"We get her out of here. Back to the cabin. We call the police and you fucking leg it, all right?"

"What about. . ." He left the rest unsaid and I pictured a teenage boy running at me on the riverside path, turning into a lumbering man in the time it took me to blink. We weren't alone in the hospital. And it wasn't anything to do with ghosts.

"He comes at us, you shoot the fucker." I hoped my loud voice would carry beyond the morgue and maybe act as a threat. "You shoot him and I'll say it was me." Tears of anger were much too close, and I wanted the killer in the room with us right there and then so I could watch Steve put a bullet in his head.

We left the morgue side by side, the girl close to unconscious against my neck and chest. She snorted a few scratchy breaths from her nose that brushed below my chin. There was no way of knowing how long the son of a bitch had kept her prisoner. I guessed at least a day. Any longer and she couldn't have made it. Resisting the urge to whisper to her that she would be fine, I kept my attention focused on the route in front and the surrounding space even though most of it was close to invisible. The torch stabbed at the black, marking the odd crack and hole in the walls, the arrows already appearing faded and old, and the turn of the corridor that would take us back to the reception area. Reaching that turn, Steve hissed and we stopped.

"What?" I whispered. Although she was small, the girl's dead weight seemed to be growing with each moment; the muscles of my arms and shoulders were becoming like hot rocks.

"You hear that?" Steve murmured.

Out of nowhere, I did. A footstep.

"Move." I pushed him, then wrapped both arms back around the girl. Making no effort to be quiet, we trotted along the corridor, passing office doors, the opening ahead that came to the reception and the stairs still invisible, and that's when it hit me.

Every single office door was now open.

Steve realised the same and ran ahead. For that second, his form becoming indistinct in the poor light was even worse than that sneaky footstep back near the morgue. It meant being alone with only a girl who might be dying.

"Steve, fucking wait." I came close to yelling it. The girl coughed on my neck and even though there was no possible way I could hear anything over that noise or my own panting breath or Steve's quick steps, I still heard another footstep behind. Closer. Then another.

Body turned into a wall of heat, I found strength I didn't know I had and pushed myself after Steve. At his side, we stormed down the rest of the corridor, torch light turning the darkness into spinning slants and all those doors now wide open and all the world's demons lurking in each doorway.

Skidding through the dirt on the floor, we made it to the turning at the lifts, ran on and the torch found the opening we'd come through. To get through it while carrying a half-dead child would take far too long. Steve saw that at the exact same moment I did.

"Fuck." Steve might have been crying and whether that was in anger, fear or frustration, I didn't know.

Think. Think.

That was a joke. All I knew was my aching body, the girl's life slipping out of our hands and the non-stop chill sinking through my fleece, come to undo the heat of exertion and turn us into rock hard corpses after the man who liked to kill children finished with us.

Think.

I did so but not about our escape. About the screaming we'd heard while close to this same spot and what had felt wrong with the memory of it a few moments before.

And how the hell had we heard the girl screaming from a few hundred feet away while she was locked in a morgue drawer?

"Oh, shit, Steve."

He turned at my whisper. "What?"

There was no time to think anything else, no space for new horrors. All I had was out.

The wood all over the entrance.

The gun.

"Shoot it," I said to Steve. "Shoot the wood."

Without any warning, he did so.

Three shots, seconds apart. I shouted against the shocking noise and the girl in my arms tried to bury herself into me. Half of the covered entrance blew out to the frosty ground, sending pieces of wood scattering in all directions. Moonlight fell inside, lighting on the mucky floor and giving us shadows that stretched from our backs. The last thing I wanted was to turn and see those shadows ending at another as someone emerged from the belly of the dead hospital.

While the destroyed section was not big enough to pass through, Steve wasted no time. He booted at the remaining wood, slivers and chunks exploding to the paving slabs outside. The opening widened in seconds, forming a hole surrounded by jagged edges, and a fresh wind blew into the hospital.

"Go." He stood aside. The gun was back up, aimed at the void at our backs. Holding the girl as tightly as possible, I ran for the opening.

Behind, someone else ran.

Raging, Steve fired shot after shot, the tip of his gun flashing a light that clung to my eyes even as the girl and I emerged into the open air. My ears pounded and my voice had become a croak as I yelled for Steve, then ran on further. Twisting around, I made out Steve bashing aside a chunk of the wrecked sheeting and backing away from the hospital.

"It's okay. You're okay," I told the girl.

Steve raised the gun even as he moved further from the building's entrance. My boots crunched on scummy slush and stone; the girl squirmed and I called her Ella again.

Emerging from the hole Steve had blown in the doors, a man appeared, broad-shouldered and moving with the light step of youth. His face was in shadow but I was willing to bet he was handsome with an easy smile. He came with a smaller body against his, one arm clad in a heavy coat encircling her chest.

She was another child, another young girl.

The man held a kitchen knife to her throat.

Chapter Thirty-Six

"You need to come over to me right now."

He sounded like anyone. A teacher faced with the task of disciplining a couple of troublesome primary school kids. A friend with some bad news. A family member calling to say an elderly relative didn't have long and it was time to say goodbye.

Shoot the bastard, I thought at Steve with a burning desperation. He had no chance, though. An expert marksman might have been able to hit the man without risking hurt to the child. Steve, keyed up beyond belief, half-frozen and going through a storm of emotions had zero chance.

Even so, he kept his gun raised, holding it with both hands.

In my arms, the girl had come to. Her teeth chattered; she shook even with the weight of my heavy coat.

"What—" She tried to say more but it died in her throat.

"It's okay. Just stay quiet," I breathed and sped through my options. They came down to running with the girl we'd saved from the monster ahead and letting another girl die, or facing him with his rescued victim in my arms.

"I'll count to five," he called across the site. He wore a scarf around his neck and chin. The material and a thick hat pulled low meant not much of his face was visible. That didn't matter. He was the same son of a bitch who'd decked me next to the river.

But I couldn't think about that because he was counting.

"One, two—"

"Wait."

Again, my boots crunched on the frost while shivers wanted to set in. I fought them off and whispered to the girl.

"Don't move. I'll keep you safe."

Half-dead, frozen, she understood what was happening and tried to push off my body, squealing, coughing and her spittle spraying against my face. I tried to say any words to calm her and failed. It was only when I stopped walking and she knew there was no escape that she stilled. All the fight fell out of her body and I knew she wouldn't have reacted if I'd dropped her the ground.

The girl held captive tried to speak; his grip tightened and the moonlight turned his blade into a gleaming piece of silver.

"Let her go," Steve said. "Let her go so I can blow your fucking head off."

The man's face shifted; I guessed he was smiling under his scarf, amused by Steve's bravado.

"What about you, Jimmy? Want me to let her go?"

An echo of his voice from the Saturday morning beside the lapping water of the river remained. It was the same tone as right there outside the derelict hospital. And something more, something I couldn't put my finger on.

He shifted on the spot. The girl he held stared at me, eyes huge as she wept. Unlike the child we'd rescued from the morgue, she was dressed for the weather. Clad in a heavy coat and gloves, she looked like he'd wanted to keep her safe for however long and that threw up terrible possibilities, none of which I was able to get a hold on because everything was happening too fast.

"Jimmy?" He said my name in a soft, cajoling way, and another echo ran around my head. Not from our other encounter. From years before. Inside, denial spoke up.

No way. No fucking way.

His face shifted again, the smile hiding under his scarf. Almost more than anything, I wanted to see his face uncovered. See it. Know it, perhaps.

No way.

"You got Laura out," he said. "I didn't think she'd last for two days. I had to give her a bit of water, but that was all. I knew you'd get her out. But not this one. Did you hear her screaming before you came in? She's a surprise. From Winchester. They both are. From my hometown. Brought them here as insurance."

She sobbed in his arms, clearly not daring to move against the blade on her throat. Against me, the first child—Laura—was like a frozen piece of rock.

"The police are looking for them there. The police here. . .not really. They're more interested in the man who keeps killing girls. Cheryl. Meg. Trudy." His focus shifted to Steve. "Loui," he muttered.

Steve howled and the gun in his hands rose, finger squeezing the trigger.

"Steve, no," I bellowed.

He fired.

The shot blew a hole in another piece of wood sheeting; spinning pieces of brown hit the ground and broke the frost. The man didn't make a move.

"Loui. Cheryl. Meg. Trudy." His gaze returned to me and I said the name in the same instant he did.

"Ella."

Chapter Thirty-Seven

Later, I wondered why there I had no immediate reaction. No screaming. No mad need to drop Laura and launch myself at him. I had nothing. It was as if he'd hit a switch inside me and everything had turned off.

On all sides, the wind picked up into a steady force and a few wet drops struck my face. It took another moment before I realised they were small flakes of snow, not rain. The wind took more of them and turned the gap between us into a small flurry.

"Please."

The word came from the girl the man held captive. She'd stopped crying for a few seconds; her eyes were still giant pools of staring white. Thirteen or fourteen at the oldest, thick strands of brown hair blown around her face, and still with a child's height and build. A little girl caught by a monster and stolen out of the safety of her life to end up somewhere she didn't know and stuck a second from death.

And nothing in her hands to help. Nothing in mine or Steve's even with the gun. Everything in her world belonged to the man with the long knife in his hand.

"Just stay calm, yeah?" Steve told her. "It'll be all right." He sounded near tears and I could almost feel his rage. His niece's killer so close; the man who deserved nothing but a tortuous death. I knew how Steve felt in that moment because I'd felt the same close to twenty years before.

"Take your pick. Laura or this one," Knife Man said.

"You're fucking crazy," I replied. Any feeling below my elbows belonged to pain and the winter.

"Am I?" he asked us. "Am I fucking crazy, Jimmy? Or am I just doing what I'm good at? Am I who you think I am or am I someone else? Someone. . .brought here by your old friend?"

The figure's shape remained the same; his eyes fixed on mine and I could do nothing but hope he didn't see Steve taking a sliding step to his left.

And then it all became hell.

"I'm so good at this, Jimmy. Ella knew that although she wasn't the first. Not by a long way."

I screeched at the night because the night was moving. Shadows loomed out of the hospital's front, sliding and pooling together as if they were made of oil and turning into one shape the wind battered against. The outline of a figure, a girl born from black, and her features forming just long enough for me to know her.

Then the wind blew Ella away and the man who'd killed and killed shoved the weeping girl in front of his body. In a movement too fast to take in, he slid the knife across her throat and shoved her at me.

A gunshot split the night. I went down in a pile of limbs and blood and the killer was running straight for me while I fell back still clutching Laura, screaming as Steve was, and the frost-covered ground welcomed us with sharp fingers.

***

Coughing even as I tried to inhale, I kicked at the ground, spun to my side and Laura fell from my arms. She curled into a ball, head tucked into her chest. I tried to stand, to call out and failed at both. The world was pain from hitting the ground, pain from carrying Laura, pain from all the horror of recent seconds.

Twisting, I made out the shape of the running man as he sprinted across the site and aimed for the gates.

"Fucker." Steve staggered towards me, gun waving. Blood had splattered over his face and coat, and his eyes were as wide as the other girl's had been. The other girl, who was now a crumpled pile coated with a thin layer of snow; and that snow was smeared red.

Steve fired two quick shots after the running figure who did not slow and the bullets raced into the spinning white. I tried to say Steve's name and all that emerged was an old man's croak. Steve steadied his hand, tracked the fleeing shape as he'd seen cops do in probably hundreds of films and fired. I had a millisecond of insanely furious joy, sure the bullet would hit the bastard and he'd drop just as the girl had.

He smashed into the gates with a mammoth crash. Impossible as it was, the thick chain and padlock split open as if they were no stronger than paper, and the gates flew open to Mansfield Road. An instant later, he was gone.

"Motherfucker." Steve raced over the uneven ground of the site, stumbling and coming close to falling in a way the killer had not in the slightest. I could do nothing but hiss his name and watch him sprint between the gates and into the road.

For the first time in what felt like hours, silence filled the site. Crawling to Laura, I tried to pick her up, couldn't manage it and collapsed beside her. I got an arm over her body and rolled. Rock poked its fingers into my back. I lay on it, holding a girl I knew would not survive more than another few minutes without warmth, unable to make a move from the swirling flakes falling from the sky, unable to get an image out of my head while glimmers of blue and red came from the sides of my vision.

The face in the shadows, the face of my dead sister.

Chapter Thirty-Eight

Boots pounding on the pavement, the road, the opposite pavement. The rattle of his breath a boiling pressure in his throat and turned sub-zero the second it spat from his mouth. The running shape of the man ahead, always fucking ahead.

Without giving the streets any thought or pausing for any cars out late on a Sunday night, Steve sprinted after the man who'd killed the girls, who'd butchered Loui like he'd butchered the kid right in front of them, and that man remained at least fifty feet ahead no matter how fast Steve ran.

Mansfield Road fell behind. He skidded at the next turning on the right and managed to keep going without falling. Passing a sign that did not catch his eye, he followed the killer into St George's Street where terraces grew tall on both sides. Fighting back the desperate urge to fire shot after shot, Steve veered into a sharp right and sped between two cars. The road had been gritted. Sure-footed, he doubled his efforts and abandoned all other thoughts. There were no daggers in his chest, no baking heat in his throat, no oceans of spit spraying as he ranted and bellowed threats into the dark.

For a second, sirens reached his ears. He shoved the noise away because it was not the man ahead, a black shape visible thanks to its movement and the light from the moon.

"You're a fucking dead man."

In reply to Steve's shriek, the man cackled and it seemed to Steve that the pavements and kerbs lining the fronts of all the houses echoed that cackle. Fear tried to break through. He would no more let it in than the noise of the police sirens seconds before.

The killer reached the end of St George's Street, streaked across to the far side of Queen's Walk, and Steve did the same a moment later.

Fighting for breath, he crashed against a low wall bordering a front garden and stared at either end of the Walk.

Nobody walked or ran or moved at all. He stood on a suburban street, utterly alone.

"No. Fucking no."

Negation made zero difference. While the killer could have ducked into any front garden or the side passage between the ends of terraces, Steve didn't believe for a second the son of a bitch had time to do so. Not without the noise they'd both been making giving his location away.

Steve sucked in a massive breath, spat and sucked another breath. His legs and chest were fire; the adrenaline turned muscles into rock and made his stomach cramp every few seconds. He wiped sweat from his face and realised a moment later that it was not only sweat. Blood soaked into the salt coating his lips. A dead girl's blood.

Gagging, Steve bent double and spat repeatedly. Despite the lack of illumination, lights pulsed in front of his eyes. At the same time, the chorus of police sirens reached him.

It was over. He'd lost the bastard and the police would be on him at any second.

Taking one last look to either end of the empty road, Steve staggered further along and managed to lumber towards a drain seconds before it felt as if his legs would simply drop him to the pavement.

Get rid of the gun. That was first. Then be ready to do the hands up thing as soon as the law sped around the corner. He'd be on camera, shooting at the hospital, and he had a murder victim's blood all over his face. And hey, let's not forget who his brother was. The cops wouldn't waste any time when it came to pointing fingers. Grinning even though nothing in the world was funny, Steve dropped the gun into the drain grating.

It hit the cover with a hollow clang, then slipped between the grates. Seconds later, a dim splash rose out of the hole. Trying to slow his breathing, Steve stood straight.

Metal slid out of the night to strike his throat.

He realised it was a knife a second before it cut.

Chapter Thirty-Nine

They'd given me my own cell. That was something.

While I had no way of knowing the time for sure, I guessed it was something like three in the morning. Doing nights for so long had given me a good feeling for the unique taste and touch of the middle of nowhere time between midnight and five AM. Currents grew still; the pump of blood slowed and breathing wound down. The same in my cell as it was in the cabin at work, except I had no TV to keep me company and nobody coming to take over my shift of checking the monitors and little else.

After steaming into the site, the dozens of armed officers had surrounded me and the unconscious girl, one of them bellowing about my gun, ordering me to show it to them slowly, to not fuck them about, and my yells back had felt thin and weak. They didn't believe I had no weapon and their own guns were all over me while the lead officer continued to bellow for me to drop my firearm. All through this, Laura had tried to make herself smaller on the ground, hands over her ears, the skin of her forearms turning as blue as the glimpse we'd got of her face in the morgue. I'd tried to tell them that I wasn't the killer and they needed to get the girl inside right now, but didn't have the strength or the breath. All through this, their guns were fixed squarely on my head, ready to fire if I did anything the police didn't like or saw as the slightest threat. The guy in charge came closer, still ordering me to not make a move, and only drew back when a new voice came from behind, telling him to stand down.

It was Fulcher. He jogged from the snaking path, still shouting for the armed officers to stand down, to search the main building, to get a fucking blanket on the kid right fucking now.

After that, the long minutes collapsed into a jumble of flashing lights, questions upon questions and dozens of officers scouring the site in their hunt for whoever had fired a gun and whoever had kept a teenage girl prisoner. They kept me in the back in one of the vans, at least three officers never more than a couple of steps away, and I got a quick look at the ambulance that took Laura from her hell.

Fulcher wouldn't tell me anything in those moments. Once I gave him the briefest summary of what had happened and mentioned Steve's name (there seemed no point in lying when all they had to do was check the CCTV recordings), he sent people to the surrounding streets and bellowed he wanted the helicopter out in a search of at least five square miles. I later heard they'd blocked off all of the nearby roads and got the dogs out after they brought me to the station. What had gone on after that, I had no clue because nobody was telling me a thing.

Hours in the cell with nothing to look at but my filthy hands or the walls. They hadn't let me change my clothing or wash, so blood and grime clung to me along with the repeating memory of the man who'd cut a child's throat as easily as slaughtering a pig.

Out in the long corridors, the occasional voice was audible along with the odd burst of a ringing phone. I shifted on the hard bunk and hugged myself. Holding on to the thought of a long, boiling shower and scouring my body clean from the blood, sweat and dirt caking it, I listened to the tread of approaching steps, sure they'd pass the door to my cell.

Right outside, they came to a stop. Keys clinked together and I remained on the bunk as the door opened.

It was the same guy who'd questioned me in the station after the pisshead started on me. A few seconds passed before I remembered his name. King. Another cop lurked behind him. Their faces were impassive although neither looked as if they'd got a lot of rest lately, King especially. He had a broad face and high forehead topped with thinning hair and all of his features were paler than they'd been during our first meeting. Heavy bags weighed under his eyes.

"Up," King said.

I rose and had to clear my throat before I could speak. "Is the girl okay?"

King tilted his head, indicating the left-hand side of the corridor. "Come on."

"The girl."

"You've got a lot of questions to answer, Mr Marshall. Let's go."

All at once, I hated the man despite knowing he was just doing his job properly. For all he knew, I was a serial killer who'd kidnapped a child and held in her in an abandoned morgue. For all he knew, I was getting my jollies in hoping she'd died en route to the hospital.

With them flanking me, we walked through the station, turning into another corridor before drawing level with the back of the reception, then passed a couple of toilets and vending machines and halted outside a nondescript grey door. King's mate knocked, opened it and King led me inside by the arm.

Seated at a spacious table, Fulcher looked at me.

"Mr Marshall. Have a seat. We need to talk."

King and the nameless cop left without saying a word. Fulcher and I stared at one another in silence. The only movement the man made was a tiny raise of his eyebrows, then a glance at the free chair.

"Am I under arrest?" I asked.

"No. Not at the moment."

I sat. The chair was more comfortable than the bunk in the cell but not by much.

"You are not under arrest and you are obviously free to have a solicitor present. If you would like one, we will probably have to delay this conversation for a few hours at least. Would you like to do that, Mr Marshall?"

"No."

"Are you sure?"

"Yeah."

"Okay. I would like to inform you this conversation is being recorded and you are on camera." He pointed at the wall behind me; I didn't bother turning.

"The girl. Laura," I muttered and Fulcher took a long moment to appraise me before replying.

"She's alive. They're doing everything they can to fight the hypothermia and probable pneumonia. There are no guarantees, but there's a chance she'll survive.

Physically, in any case. So's the other girl. He cut her throat, but whether by accident or on purpose, he missed arteries. She lost a lot of blood but she has a chance."

"He didn't kill her?"

"No, he did not."

I wanted to weep. Two girls, two kids brutalised by something out of my hell. He could have killed either whenever he felt like it, but they'd survived.

Fulcher went on. "By the sounds of it, we have you to thank for finding those kids. You and one another, of course."

I pictured Steve dashing to the gates after the man somehow smashed through them; I heard his desperate, raging voice and I felt the lonely touch of the weak flakes melting as soon as they landed on my head and coat while the girl I'd thought was dead lay on the ground with a wound in her throat.

"You found Steve?" I asked.

"No, not yet. We've questioned his brother and searched the house, but Steve Cameron is keeping his head down. Given his involvement with a firearm, I can't say I'm surprised but we'll find him."

Momentarily, I wondered how much concern or interest Fulcher had in the Cameron boys and their access to guns. Probably quite a bit but in the middle of what was going on, priorities had to be made. I was willing to bet Steve had ditched the weapon somewhere so they had no physical proof of it in any case.

"Can you tell us anything about the other girl?" Fulcher asked. "Name? Anything?"

"Not much. He said she was from Winchester. Said he brought her there as insurance." The word tasted like shit. "Whoever the hell he is, he's from Winchester."

My gaze skittered away from Fulcher's and he picked up on that straightaway. Knackered as he clearly was with the stubble of at least a few days' growth, the shirt undone from the neck and the strain written all over his face, the man was still police and he knew a clue when one was right in front of him.

"Mr Marshall? Anything to add?"

"No."

A lot of men would have lost their shit right then. They'd have bellowed at me someone was out there killing little girls and I was obviously involved, obviously knew more than I was saying because why the fuck else would I have been connected with at least two murder scenes, so fucking talk right now.

Fulcher did none of that. He rested the pen he'd been writing with on a small pad, leaned forward and spoke in the same measured tone.

"Mr Marshall. I said you are not under arrest and that is true. However, while I don't consider you a murder suspect, I will be happy to charge you with obstruction of justice if you don't tell me everything you can about what happened tonight at the hospital. I don't want to do that. At the moment, you're here for questioning and it is noted and appreciated that you are helping us. I would like that to continue."

Built like a tank he might have been, TV copper he might have resembled but Fulcher had a lot more going on than his appearance and physique suggested. The man knew how to talk to people instead of simply threatening them. Even so, I couldn't bring myself to spit it all out. Not with the image of Ella's face formed out of swirling shadows and spatters of snow so close. That and the slightest suggestion of a grin from the man in front of me and Steve when we'd said Ella's name. A knowing grin, I thought.

The lights flickered. Fulcher glanced up. I remained looking towards him and although his look away was for a bare second, it was still long enough for me to have time to see the outline of a girl lurking in the corner of the interview room. She faced me, small, undefined for the most part. Only her hair had detail. Long and straight. Thick and healthy.

She'd liked her hair. Spent years growing it.

Then she was gone and all of Fulcher's attention was back on me while a shouting command at the back of my head ordered me to believe I'd seen nothing because there was nothing to see.

"He's killing children. Five that we know of and another is still in a coma. She may die at any moment. I want this man stopped right now, Mr Marshall."

It was time to stop being so fucking scared. I needed to escape my own cowardice. And that would come from telling Fulcher the truth.

"Marshall is my mother's maiden name. My original surname is Griffin."

The afterimage of the girl keeping close to the wall behind Fulcher remained in my eyes and I had to be grateful her face hadn't been clear. While I knew Ella existed solely in my imagination and not as a restless spirit, I couldn't have taken seeing her in detail, not when I didn't know what would be in her eyes.

"Mr Marshall?" Fulcher said in a low voice and I answered him.

"I'm Ella Griffin's brother."

Chapter Forty

Winter.

Over Oxfordshire and Lawfield, it holds the air and the land in a tight grip. Since October, the temperature across this section of the country has not made it above two degrees for longer than a few hours. Morning only frosts are a memory; now, they cling to the roads and pavements around the clock, and icicles dangle from gutters. A thick layer of snowfall rests on the ground, mounds of it churned into messy piles against kerbs and fences. Vehicles travel much more slowly than normal, their drivers focusing all of their attention on the murky light breaking the fog, their shoulders and necks strained and aching from tension. Gritters are out in force before dawn to salt the carriageways and main roads, but they don't come to the side streets and suburbs. In Lawfield's streets and avenues, the terraces face their roads treacherous with ice and snow turned rock hard. Older people rarely venture out; a few neighbours check on them, but most keep to their own houses as much as possible, keeping their heads down and keeping warm with their central heating powering on through the days and nights.

And still the winter holds.

The supermarkets keep their shelves stocked as well as they can, fighting to fill them with fewer deliveries than usual from their suppliers. Since Christmas, there have been four major accidents between Lawfield's supermarkets and their distributors' warehouses further north. The collisions coupled with a massive run on canned goods, frozen food and alcohol mean the shops' shelves are noticeably thin. At the same time, the shoppers go through the aisles as quickly as they can, grabbing items, missing the products they can do without at a push, all keen to get through the tills and out to the multi-storey car park, then home to shut their doors against the weak sunlight and long nights.

Several of the primary schools have been forced to close. Cracks in the water pipes leading to flooded classrooms; electrical faults; teachers unable to make it out of the surrounding towns and villages due to the unsalted roads: the children rejoice at their unexpected freedom and their parents are forced to take time from their jobs or call in the help of friends and relatives.

And still the winter holds.

So far, none of the secondary schools have closed. The buildings are newer than the primaries all dating from the seventies. Their innards of pipes and wires more secure, less likely to be touched by the falling temperature or from leaks of ice-cold water. The teachers and support staff make it work each day for the most part, and the students spend much of their lessons looking through the windows to the massive sheet of grey sky overlooking the playing fields and the dead bushes forming barriers between public land and school property, all wondering when the world will grow warmer and this January will be consigned to memory.

And still the winter holds.

This thought is an unformed shape in Ella Griffin's head. Half an hour has passed since the end of the school day; she knows she is late home and is not bothered. Jimmy will be in; their mother won't be home for another couple of hours. She has time to walk through the fading light and the fog. Her house is only another five minutes ahead.

Ella, thirteen and small for her age, enters Nelson Park and aims for its centre. All around, the massive trunks of the oak trees stretch through the haze, their branches gnarled and twisted like the fingers of old men. This thought is also unformed in her head, ready to come to life when she needs it. Ella enjoys images and the development of a slight idea into a drawing on a page. For the last year, she's been sketching more frequently and occasionally attempting a full painting. These works are mostly for her and her alone. Drawings can be seen by others if she is in the right mood; the paintings are more private and maybe in the future she'll be okay with friends seeing them. Not now, though. When she's better at it.

She reaches the middle section of the park and passes the rusting fountains, all turned off since September. Murkiness slides between the pipes and struts. A street light blooming yellow for the last half an hour turns the mist into a weak soup, and the top of the light is a halo. Ella wishes she owned a decent camera and had opportunity to take a few shots of the light. It would make a great painting; one she might be okay with showing to a few friends. Doing her best to store the shade in memory and keep hold of the way the fog coats the fountains, she leaves it behind, follows the path straight on between more oak trees and draws closer to the other side of the park. Pathways snake to the left and right, heading between bushes and slopes of grass. Usually, people walk their dogs around here. Not now, though. The brittle white snapping below her school shoes has seen any dogs and their owners off for the day. She is alone and the thought is more than welcome. It's needed. Lately, she's been trying to make sense of her life and what might come ahead after exams, school and the future. While a lot of the other kids seem to care about nothing more than having a good time, Ella tries to see where she will end up and cannot envisage a life beyond Lawfield and the known streets and parks. Some days, this is a fine thing. Others—and more often—it fills her head with a throb of anger because this can't be all she will know. But what if it is? What if she never gets to the world beyond? The thought, another undefined and incomplete wondering, asks her what will happen if she lives her mum's life of work and kids and the same home as always, and she cannot take the fear and anger this creates.

Ahead, another street light turns the mist into a thin yellow and shines on the roof of a van. It is the sole vehicle parked on Nelson Road as far as Ella can see. The smart houses and the block of the old people's flats on the far pavement are covered by the mist, and no headlights from other cars illuminate the gloom. Slightly perturbed and unsure why, Ella walks on, veering to her right so can she exit the park through a set of railings. Out there, cross the road and the next left two minutes away. Their house on Windsor Avenue waits for her with its lights and warmth. Jimmy will be there and while he is sometimes a bastard to her, he can be okay. Maybe she'll tell him about wanting to paint the light around the fountains and maybe he won't laugh at her.

Focus on the railings and opening to the road, Ella lets go of her slight trepidation about the still van. At the same time, she catches the soft sound of steps behind.

She has a second to turn and catch the blur of movement before the hammer strikes her squarely in the face.

Ella's nose breaks. Every single thought is eaten by pain detonating in her head, then radiating out, up, down, everywhere. Blood floods her throat; she chokes even as she tries to call for help and sees nothing through her tears but a shimmering movement.

Something hot and quick grabs her. The world spins over and over and still, her head is on fire. Blood sprays from her ruined nose, falling to the ground in thick droplets, the gore marking their speeding journey from the park to the back of the van.

All Ella knows are images and instinct. She kicks out, hit nothing and finally manages to clear enough of the blood in her throat to suck in a fiery breath.

A second before she is able to make a sound, she is thrown into the van, strikes a hard floor and is again swallowed by pain. Body bucking, streams of blood pooling down her cheeks, she manages to roll over, hacks a burning cough and retches hot liquid over herself and the floor.

Somewhere, a door slams, an engine starts and the van is a shaking beast with her caught in its belly. Trying to cry out, Ella rolls again, hits the side of the van and reaches blindly. Her flailing hands find a narrow metal strip which she grips with all of her strength. Sobbing, still trying to cough and find a way to think through the agony of her face and bruised back, she spits as much blood as possible and screams.

The sound bounces from wall to wall, floor to low ceiling and does nothing but hurt her ears. There is no light at all to penetrate anything; this is what being buried alive must be like, and that thought makes Ella scream until her throat is on fire. Running out of breath and unable to stop weeping, she pulls herself into as small a ball as possible, lowers her head and lets the hot liquid flow.

The van takes roads she can't see. Gears change and crunch. They slow occasionally and she tries to cry for help, desperately hoping the decreased noise of the vehicle will let her voice be heard by people in other cars. Even as she cries, she knows this isn't likely. There simply aren't enough people on the roads especially after dusk comes down like a weight.

The van turns, travels straight road for over a minute, makes another turning and gradually slows.

Stops.

The engine dies and a door slams.

The storming thunder of her heart increases; the tidal pull of nausea threatens vomit at any second, and there's a bestial reek all around. She's making that stink – the sharp aroma of a cornered animal as its predator closes in. She's been scared before but never like this, never to the point of being losing anything human to the stench of her fear. She's been beaten, stolen from the public park and bundled into a van. All these facts mean only one thing and it is the worst thing in the world.

The van doors jerk open to reveal a brown wall, a glimpse of pavement and a figure dressed in a heavy coat as black as the balaclava pulled over their face.

"No," Ella croaks.

It does no good at all. The figure clambers inside, takes her howls and kicks, places a gloved hand fully over her mouth and carts her to the outside where the abruptly freshening wind and the last of the daylight don't touch the watery gloom. Ella can make out no more of their surroundings. The location could be anywhere in Lawfield.

The man presses her ruined face into the scratchy material of his coat, bringing fresh hurt and making breathing even harder. Carrying her like she's a tiny child, he slams the van doors closed and Ella hears the rough grating of metal on the ground. From the corners of her eyes, she sees a tall fence parting; they pass through it and he kicks the fence closed. They're in a wide passageway, passing more brown walls, surrounded by the awful cold turned colder by the brickwork amplifying it. Keys jangle, a lock crunches and a final door opens.

Dazzling light assaults Ella's eyes and she has to squint which sends more boiling fluid from her shattered nose. The man crouches, drops her to something soft and she can make out enough of the immediate area to place herself.

A shop. The back of one. Storage units stand tall against one of the walls. Boxes of wines and other drinks are shoved against the opposite wall, and standing on the cracked floor, four tall lights glare their white beams down. Between the lights and standing on skinny tripods, three cameras are all aimed directly at her and the lumpy mattress she's been dropped upon.

"No," Ella whispers. "No. Please."

It's as if she knows no other words. No and please are all she has. Her skittering vision jumps over the shelves as the man turns his back on her and begins to unbutton his coat. Standing straight on a high shelf, several large bottles of what she thinks is vodka are within arm's reach if she can make it upright and grab one before he turns around.

Too late.

He turns back, pulling the balaclava free to reveal a perfectly normal face, a young man older than her brother but still not what she'd call a fully-grown adult. He smiles, lips curling with nerves and awkwardness.

"Hello," he says and crosses to the three cameras.

Red lights shine on their sides when he is finished with them. The tall lights are brighter than the sun but she can't look away from him and can't stop picturing herself grabbing a bottle and smashing it into his head.

There is no time for that. He is coming to her even as she says the only two words she knows over and over and when he is finished and the cameras have broadcast it all, seconds, minutes, hours and days of darkness and pain trickle by. The unblinking eyes of the cameras show her utterly exposed, left on the floor like an insect while out in the streets and the parks and the through the frozen leaves of bushes, the police, her family, her friends and the public hunt for her.

Time becomes a piece of glass, reflecting the moonlight and the glare of the icy sunshine in equal measure and with equal disinterest in her suffering. She no longer believes the outside world exists; her place in the town, even her name, are deep inside that sliver of glass and all the centuries that come with every winking beam of night, of day, of shadows pooling, dying while she is a tiny insect on the floor.

On the fourth day of this hell, he places his hands on her throat and the blinding white of the lights begins to wind down into moving shadows where Ella will no longer be alone.

Chapter Forty-One

He knew he wasn't really Robert Fry. Never had been. He had no prurient interests in children as Fry had but calling himself by the man's name was more than a last joke at the expense of that whining, miserable animal. Taking his identity was required for the final part of the work. Jimmy Marshall needed to know his name. Needed to believe it. Anything going up in flames with Trudy in the phone box was fine. The confrontation with Jimmy at the front of the hospital building and letting the man see a glimpse of the truth had only been possible due to that burning. Turn the shrieks from the Robert Fry trapped so far below into ash, keep the man's name and none of his humanity.

It was what it was and there was no more to the world than that.

Tacky blood remained on Fry's hands from wounding Steve. While the wound hadn't been deep in the slightest, enough blood oozed from the slash to coat the knife, Fry's fingers and dribble to the frosty ground before he yanked Steve into a side alley and carted the man through empty gardens, then smashed him over the head with a metal pole before chucking him in the back of the car.

And now here: Sprignall Estate in the middle of the night. Fry peered across Artindale Square. Not a single light in any of the windows, the only illumination coming from the moon and a couple of street lights with their orange haze discolouring the mist. The police had been all over the estate after the mini riot, but when peace and normality returned, they'd been on their way only for a few to return to the Cameron house a short while ago, doubtless asking questions about the idiot Steve and his gun. Without being able to get their hands on the weapon and after finding no more firearms in the house, they'd departed. Quiet returned to the estate. The shopping precinct that had been the site of the fire and violence remained sealed off, its buildings all blackened and its windows boarded over in the same way as the ground floor of the hospital. Maybe it would all be cleared up once insurance payments kicked in, and the businesses would come back to life. Fry didn't care one way or the other. By the time the estate maybe picked itself up again, Fry's future would be decided. And that future depended on what Jimmy Marshall did after the rest of the events. And those events were all about to start as soon as Fry rang the doorbell.

Making no particular effort to be quiet, he closed the car door, righted Steve as much as possible and slapped the man's face. In his other hand, he held a long hunting knife, the handle rusting, the blade still wickedly sharp. Steve's eyes flickered. The streams of red on his neck still visible in the poor light had trickled to a stop for the most part. Fresher blood ran from the head wound Fry had inflicted. That liquid dribbled beside Steve's ear and stained his jawline. One eye managed to open, white and wild in the moonlight.

"You with me, Steve?" Fry asked. He used his own voice. No need for pretence here. "Steve?" He slapped Steve again. Hard. Steve's head rocked and the wound in his neck opened again to turn the air into a salty tang.

Steve cried out; the sound not even close to a meaningful word.

"Good," Fry replied.

He spun Steve around and marched him to the front door.

Moments after the high, clear ring of the doorbell, a lock turned and the door opened. Keeping its face behind Steve's shoulder for a moment, Fry heard Carl Cameron's voice and there was no sleep in the tone at all.

"What the hell?"

Arm jerking forward, Fry shoved its knife towards the man's chin, briefly grateful Carl wasn't in bed and came to the door so quickly. Maybe he expected the police. Maybe he hoped for some news.

Carl's eyes grow as wide as his brother's, and the sight was almost comical—a first all through Fry's long life. He saw himself through the older man's eyes: someone only a few years out of his teens, yet to really experience life and who doubtless knew nothing compared to Carl Cameron. Even so, here they were and here it all was.

"Inside." He shoved the man back, pushed Steve forward into the well-lit corridor and kicked at the door without turning. It slammed shut and a woman's voice, querulous and exhausted, floated down the stairs.

"Carl. Is it the police again?"

Carl said nothing. He stared at Fry, eyes bloodshot, bags sitting underneath them. The reek of drink and fags clung to his skin, his t-shirt and jeans. He'd clearly slept at some point and done so in his clothes. The man looked like he'd spent hours glued to an armchair with a never-ending cigarette on the go and a continuously topped up glass to hand. Cloying warmth filled the hallway; the radiator beside Fry's lower half belched out heat, and somewhere ahead, a boiler coughed into life.

"Carl?"

The ceiling creaked. In seconds, she'd be at the top of the stars. Fry knew the layout of the house. The building was the same as the majority of others throughout Sprignall, each abode built to the same specifications back in the early seventies. Entrance hall, stairs on the left beside a toilet; open-plan kitchen and dining room straight ahead, and a living room probably decorated in an ugly, tasteless way on their right.

"Call her down," Fry muttered.

"Fuck you."

As gently as possible, Fry laughed and pressed harder with the tip of its knife and the light caught the blade. Carl blinked. Heavy drops of sweat trickled down his meaty cheeks. The stink of fear merged with the heat, giving the hallway an animalistic stench.

"Carl?" The woman had reached the top of the stairs and while she wouldn't be able to make everything out from her perspective, she'd see enough to know it was not the police come at such a late hour.

Fry grabbed Carl's shoulder, turned him around and pushed Steve into his brother. Lumbering, moaning, Erica Cameron descended the stairs.

The TV conference hadn't done the woman justice. On screen, Fry had watched a fat woman momentarily go insane with rage. No neck. Rolls bulging over the waist of her thin leggings. Over that, she wore a shapeless t-shirt. Short hair pulled back from her face in a tiny ponytail, and the shape of a cross dangling under the shirt, wedged between doughy breasts.

"You scream and I'll rip his throat open."

One chunky hand rested on her mouth. Although she looked as sleep-deprived as her husband (not to mention as slow and stupid as a pig), she knew what was happening, and Fry could only be grateful for that. It would make the next few minutes easier.

"Down here. In front. You're leading the way," Fry told her.

Beginning to cry without making a sound, Erica came the rest of the way down the stairs. She reached for Carl, fingers shaking. The tips brushed the man's forearm before falling away. At the same time, Steve sagged. Fry gripped his hair, pulled his head back and shook it.

"Forward. Slowly," Fry said.

Moving in a strange shuffling motion, they passed the stairs, the cupboard below them and entered the kitchen. Fry told Erica to turn the light on. With a fumbling hand, she did so. Harsh illumination exploded above. At least eight or nine mugs were in the sink, submerged in a bowl of murky water. A couple of plates had been left on the side and a chipped cup half filled with what might have been cold coffee stood next to the kettle. Fry took a second to see all this and said in a conversational tone:

"What a shithole."

Erica made an odd noise, something that wanted to be a scream but was little more than a strained hiss. Perhaps thinking the sound would take Fry's attention from him, Carl tried to lunge forward, leaving his brother behind. Moving faster than Carl, Fry sliced t-shirt and shoulder. Carl howled, stumbled into the wall and left a bloody smear as he came close to collapse. Steve croaked Carl's name, unable to do more.

"No, don't cut him," Erica cried and reached for her husband.

Carl stood straight and gazed at Fry. In his eyes, Fry saw his own death and that was utterly fine. There was death for all of them. It was just a matter of perspective.

Erica sobbed, hands twisting together. All the anger and hate she had during the press conference yesterday was gone, puffed away on the wind. Carl, meanwhile, was not the man he'd been once upon a time. The criminal. The fists. The boots into faces. While muscle and anger remained, he was too far removed from that man to risk his family's lives by jumping into a knife.

"Everybody. Into the living room. We're going to have a chat."

Nobody moved.

"You've got until I count to three to move and then Steve is dead." Fry encircled an arm around Steve's neck, blade on skin.

Still nothing. He could have addressed the wall.

"One, two, thr—"

"Wait." Erica screamed the word, hands raised. Sound would carry through the walls. No matter. They had a bit of time.

Walking as if her feet were broken, Erica shuffled over the kitchen tiles, into the small dining room and into the living room.

Fry glanced around, amused to note the décor was as ugly as he'd imagined. The jet-black of the massive leather sofa. The tacky photos of the family with their plain white background, Carl and Erica fat and classless like people in a million other pictures, the girl forced to dress as if she was in her late teens and not still a child. The predictable and meaningless phrases about love and family and laughter in their frames. The painting of Christ above a field of lambs gazing down at the room. The massive TV screwed into the wall over the fake fireplace.

"Everyone is going to do what I say." He nodded to the sofa. "Erica. Sit down."

She crossed over the carpet to do so and Fry moved before she had chance to sit. Punching Steve in the side and landing a heavy blow on the man's kidney, he threw Steve to the floor, shoved Carl forward and dropped. As Carl twisted, Fry slid his large blade in a smooth motion across the back of the man's ankle, severing tendons with ease. He pushed as blood sprayed its thick red over the carpet. Howling, Carl pitched forward directly on to his wife who reached to catch him, calling his name at the same time. Knocked by Carl's greater weight, they both overbalanced and crashed to the sofa, Carl's leg jetting red. Grasping its knife in a fist, Fry yanked Steve to his feet and held him in a headlock. Struggling to free himself and breathe, Steve could do neither as Fry held the tip of the blood-smeared blade half an inch from his left eye.

"Shut up. Right now, unless you want me to blind him."

Erica buried herself against Carl's shoulder as he rocked back and forth, a high-pitched keen steaming from between his sealed lips. He sounded like a kettle coming to the boil.

Fry eased his hold on Steve a fraction who spluttered for breath. Sucking a deep one in, he coughed and sprayed spit. Blood continued to gush from the wound Fry cut into Carl's foot. He held his calf as he rocked and continued to make his boiling kettle noise. Erica sobbed soundlessly. Her face had become the same red as the spreading stain on the carpet. She might have a heart attack, Fry knew, which would ruin everything. She needed to stay alive for now. Afterwards, he didn't care in the least.

"This won't take long." He pulled the knife away from Steve's face an inch. "You know what I did and you'll happily see me dead. I know that. I really do."

Loui's parents stared at him with the eyes of horrified children, and Fry imagined the same expression was on the uncle's face. A few seconds ticked by. The police could already be on their way if the neighbours had called them, but he doubted that. While sound would travel through the walls, the chances were there had been a non-stop racket in the house recently. With any luck, the neighbours would believe it was more of the same.

"Erica and Carl." The names tasted ugly. "You two. You two...failures."

"What?" The first word Carl said in minutes and it was spat between his lips. The man's face had gone far beyond white while his hands, lower leg and feet were a glorious red.

"Your daughter. Out overnight. Out there for people like me to find her." Fry smiled and Steve groaned in his arms. Ignoring the uncle, Fry went on.

"Your little girl. Thirteen and still a child. Thirteen and left for me. You are failures."

Erica threw her head back, the tendons below the loose flesh of her neck jutting like cables through the fat. A heart attack no longer seemed likely; it seemed definite.

"That's fucking bullshit," Carl shouted. "You fucking. . .you cunt, I'll kill you, you motherfucker, you—" He broke apart, coughing his rage. A moment later, he sounded as if the switch controlling his righteous anger had been clicked to off. "Son, I've fucked up much worse than you in the past. Every little shit like you who thought they were the big man, the hard bastard. Fuck all, every one of them and you are no different. Just a kid whose parents didn't give a shit, right? Nobody understands you so you hurt people, right? Started off fantasising about it, about hurting others because you're just so different, right? And then thinking about it wasn't enough so you get stuck in and you fuck with me like you are worth shit."

Fry might have expected the lack of life in Fry's little speech to grow into mocking, disgust or outright fury. There was nothing, though. It was as if the cop could manage words but not emotion.

"Done?" Fry asked.

Carl said: "I am going to feed you that knife."

"You know what's funny?" Fry consulted an interior clock. If the police had been called, enough time had passed for them to arrive. He was safe for the time being.

"It's all on him." Fry flicked the blade against Steve's skin and caught a whiff of the man's terror. It flowed from his pores with the salt of his sweat and the pump of his blood. "If this idiot hadn't gone looking for someone I used to know, I wouldn't be here. I could have gone to any of the other girls' families. Cheryl or Meg or even Laura. I watched their parents and their brothers and sisters. I saw into their homes. I saw their dreams and their futures just as I saw yours. Any one of them would have done, but he made his move. He made you my target. I'm happy to leave the other families alone. They've got their grief and tears; I'm done with them for now. You lot, on the other hand, you're my business and it's all because this one—" Again, he brushed Steve's neck with the blade, eliciting a weak sigh from the man. Steve had moved far over any line of thought and could no longer find the strength to make any noise let alone plead for mercy.

"This one wouldn't stay away from my old friend. He marked all of you. He made Loui their leader."

"Wait." Carl licked his lips, face white enough to show every dot of stubble as an individual grain. "We—"

"He wanted to fuck her," Fry said and tapped Steve on the head with the tip of his blade.

Silence.

"Yes." Fry said so as if any member of the family had denied it. "Your brother. This man. He wanted to fuck your daughter. Imagine that. Imagine him going into her room while you slept."

Erica could barely breathe. Carl had reverted to making his kettle noise and Steve's entire body thrummed like a wire. From a side pocket, Fry pulled a second knife free and threw it at Carl's blood-splattered feet. While the blade was not as long or jagged as the one Fry still held, it would do the job.

"Now. Take that and kill your brother, Carl."

Letting go of his wounded leg and reaching with gore-streaked hands, the man grabbed the knife, and

Fry saw flat murder in his face. He saw his own throat split open at the hands of a grieving father, and the vision was as amusing as it was predictable.

"Don't bother. I can move much faster than you."

"You fucking—"

Flicking the knife upwards, Fry caught Steve a fraction below his eye, dragging the blade through the soft tissue of his cheek for an inch and sending dribbles of blood to merge with the man's sweat. Unperturbed, he let Steve screech while Carl reached for his brother and touched nothing. Fat, useless Erica held her face and shook back and forth.

"You've got ten seconds to stab him or I'll do to your wife what I did to your daughter."

"What? No, I..." Mad with desperation, Carl looked at his wife and back to Fry. While murder still filled his eyes, so did unthinking panic. Fry let itself see the room from Carl's point of view for a moment. Everything spun; everything shook and nothing made any sense. The terrible pain chewing on his leg had vanished, swallowed by confusion and fear and something much worse than either emotion or agony.

A suspicion that the figure with the knife, the man who'd hurt them all and invaded their home, was telling the truth. Hadn't he wondered sometimes in his most private heart why Steve was so eager to stay with them, why he made no move to find his own place? The unpleasant inkling something was wrong in his house and the refusal to admit in daylight that the speculation was anything but paranoid shit?

But at three in the morning, it was easier to wonder, to fear and to listen for the slightest noise from the hallway—a noise that might be a sliding step on the carpet or just the house winding down.

Steve choked out a word. "Carl." He sobbed, spluttered and found his voice. "It's shit. Total shit. You know that. You know I wouldn't do anything like that. Jesus Christ, what the fuck is the matter with you?"

Fry knew what the matter was. Fear was a great tool. So was the sly core of families like this one.

"You know what he's capable of. You know that and you know what I'll do to your wife, so ten seconds, Carl. One, two, three, four—"

In Fry's arms, Steve became a thrashing animal, no longer concerned with the knife near his face or the stream of blood coursing down his cheek to drip on the floor. Steve tried to speak, to say Erica's name and Fry watched him speed through all options before understanding all the way down that there were none.

"Seven, eight—"

"Carl, please, Jesus Christ, please, oh God, please, oh fucking please don't—"

"Nine, ten."

It was all over in the time it took Fry to blink once.

The knife no longer in Carl's hand, the knife jutting from Steve's stomach and Steve's fingers wrapped around the handle.

"Steve," Carl whispered.

Fry reached around, knocked aside Steve's soaking fingers and yanked on the handle. More blood splattered along with the meat of Steve's stomach. Organs tried to push their way through the wound, and Steve's fingers, probably moving on a non-thinking instinct rather than instruction attempted to push them back.

As it was a moment before, Fry's speed was horrible and wonderful.

He withdrew the knife fully free, let Steve collapse to the floor and pinned the blade deep into Carl's throat. Penetrating tissue and muscle, he twisted the handle. Carl's mouth hung open. He jerked, already dead even if the impulses juddering to a halt throughout his body were not yet aware of it.

Fry gripped Carl's chest and jerked the knife free. He advanced on Erica.

The woman had become like stone. Not a sound emerged from between her lips and all the mad rocking back and forth had ceased. Fry studied her, inhaled the conflicting aromas of spilled blood and open wounds. None were pleasant, but all were necessary when it came to his work. Same with the next part.

"Erica?"

She gave no acknowledgement he had spoken let alone offered a reply.

"You've done well, Erica. Better than you did with your daughter, in any case."

He took hold of Carl's iPhone, activated the screen and hit nine three times.

"I'm going to call the police, now. They'll come and sort this mess out."

Still nothing. She had become stone. Maybe she'd never speak again.

"They've got a challenge. They need to know something but they'll only have a few minutes to get here and find it out. Do you understand?"

The slightest twitch in her eye. There was enough left inside for her to be useful.

"Good. When they get here—if they're here on time—you tell them a name."

He crossed the soaking carpet, lifted her limp arm and gently bent the hand back. Surprisingly, the flesh of her wrist and forearm was smooth and almost dainty.

Speaker activated on the phone, he hit Call and dropped the mobile to the sofa. The device bounced once, then lay squarely beside Erica's thigh.

"You tell the police a name."

Fry leaned close to her ear as the voice over the speaker asked what service was required, the same question he been asked when calling from the phone box and the space around it like a freezer ready to receive the fire.

"Robert Fry," he whispered and drew the blade directly across Erica's wrist.

Chapter Forty-Two

Monday morning fell over the country. Throughout Oxfordshire, it came sluggishly as if the night was unwillingly to let go. As the first hint of sun touched the sky, turning it to a purple from the black, Lawfield began to ready itself for a new day and the new working week.

Street cleaners patrolled St Michael's Road, sucking litter into their machines, their engines a steady roar heard by only a few people walking on Albion Way as they headed to office buildings and shops with their heads down and their gloved hands tucked deep into pockets. The frosty morning found them, though, eager to caress any inch of bare skin, to turn lips into chapped meat and noses into non-stop drips. They hurried to their destinations, some thinking about the terrible events over the weekend, others trying to focus on their jobs and the upcoming hours while the spectres of murdered girls and burning shops in the estate a few miles away drifted at the edge of their minds.

Shortly before six, the first of the buses left the depot, their drivers all clad in heavy coats and several wearing hats and gloves even as the heaters struggled to warm the almost totally empty vehicles. Reaching the parkways surrounding the cities, they branched off in their separate directions, passengers shielding themselves from the teeth of the wind in shelters and doing their best to avoid the crumpled lager cans, dog ends and faded crisp packets.

Half an hour later, a water pipe cracked under the flooring in the classroom of a primary school. Jimmy Marshall would not have recognised the interior of the building despite having attended it in his childhood. While its layout remained the same as the days of his childhood, modernisation throughout the intervening decades had turned the school into something the child Jimmy would have believed to be science-fiction.

The passage of time, memory and a child's imagination made no difference at all as tendrils of water grew with spreading fingers from the side of the room, soaking the story time carpet and pooling towards the wall of computers. Above the monitors, children's drawings of family members and pets were the only witness to the encroaching flood. The leak and damage would not be discovered by staff for forty-five minutes, by which point another two pipes would be cracked wrecks and their engulfing water would be deep inside the school's electrics.

Outside in the school grounds and easing over the field towards the avenues of smart houses and the long parkway further ahead, a wall of falling temperatures slid in all directions. While the forecast had detailed a day much the same as several weeks' worth of temperatures close to zero and little sunshine, the Monday morning sank into an arctic freeze even as the purple sky became the grey of low cloud, all pregnant with the threat of a blizzard.

At precisely seven o'clock, the first of the heavy flakes drifted down, each one settling instead of melting on the ground, in the branches of naked trees and on the dead grass of the town's parks.

Winter held hard to Lawfield.

Chapter Forty-Three

I was within twenty feet of the main entrance to my building, the taxi already a fading roar along the road, when Tom called me. Ignoring my ringing mobile wasn't an option. Tom needed to know what the hell was going on with his site. Fishing my keys from my jeans pocket, I answered the call.

"Hey, Tom."

"Jimmy? What the hell's going on? You okay, son?"

"Tired, but in one piece."

Wet flakes pattered on to my head and shoulders. I let it fall without making any effort to brush it away. Peace and warmth waited inside. Not wanting to talk inside the building, I rested on the wall that ran the car park's perimeter and looked over it to the empty road. Too early for much traffic; still too dark to see a hell of a lot and I flashed back to fighting with Steve in my car while someone watched us from the gloom.

"What happened?" Tom asked. "I get a call from the law; they don't tell me a thing other than the site is closed off and will be for at least a week. They—"

"There was some trouble." I pictured Steve chasing after that man and wondered what Steve was doing right then. Sleeping, hopefully. Fulcher said they found no trace of him or the other guy, no sign of Steve having been injured, and the big cop believed Steve had gone to ground due to the gun he'd been waving around and shooting—a fact I'd made no comment on despite Fulcher telling me the gun was the least of his concerns. Steve and his brother would be in some deep shit when the gun did become a concern to anyone. For now, I could only hope the police were more focused on a man who killed young girls than a family they'd known were dodgy for years.

"Jimmy?" Tom all but barked it at me and I came back to the conversation.

Going through it as quickly as possible, I told Tom the basics: the guy who was killing girls had somehow got into the site and kept two girls prisoners. They were both hurt, but safe now. Christ knew what state they'd be in mentally in the weeks and months ahead.

He listened in silence and spoke only when sure I'd finished.

"That piece of shit."

"Yeah."

"And you're all right, Jimmy?"

Oddly touched, I blinked away the sting of tears. It had been too long a night and too much horror had gone on lately. I couldn't face Tom caring and I couldn't deal with anything while standing in the light of a new day.

"Yeah." I cleared my throat. "Yeah. Fine. Just shook up. Been with the police all night, answering questions. They'll be on site for a while, Tom."

As I might have guessed, Tom's priorities were on the human side of the situation. "Sod that. You get some sleep, son. I'll sort it all out at my end. We'll be back in business before long. In the meantime, I'll take care of you."

Knowing exactly what he meant, I started to protest and he brushed it off. My wages would be paid; things would be dealt with as long as I shut up and got some rest.

"Cheers, Tom." I had to mutter it. Tears threatened again.

"Don't worry about it. Speak soon."

He hung up. I pocketed my phone and watched a small van pass the side of the building. It paused at the lights, moved on with the road to itself and vanished from sight.

I headed inside, welcoming the warmth of the foyer. The relative silence of the lift and my slow tread on the carpet to my door meant I had space to think and recall every second of the mad scene with me, Steve, the two kids and a murderer.

He had a name I still would not think of and one I hadn't come close to saying to Fulcher. He could keep his interest in Steve's gun a secret; I could do the same with a name that could not be true.

The doors lining either side of the hospital hallway all open to show nothing but whatever horrors my imagination wanted to create.

The girl—Laura—and the skin turned blue from being buried alive in the morgue drawer.

The grin under the scarf, the secret shared between two people who knew each other.

Inside the flat, I stripped off my coat and fleece, thought about taking a shower and settled for forcing myself to eat some toast and swig too hot coffee. There was no urge to put the TV on or check any news sites. There'd be nothing to report about the girls we'd managed to save. Fulcher had let me know they were in intensive care and the local police were trying to track down both sets of parents. Everyone was pretty confident they'd be all right. Physically, anyway.

Finishing my toast and studying the armchair where Steve had passed out, I thought about calling him and decided against it after just a few seconds. While it didn't feel likely Fulcher would have done anything as hi-tech as put a trace or listening device on my number, phoning Steve still didn't seem like a good plan. Fulcher's people would be all over the Cameron house on the hunt for more weapons, maybe thinking there'd be some link between illegal firearms and the murders. If Steve had any sense, he'd have vanished minutes after failing to find the killer.

Someone knocked on my door.

I froze, not even breathing for a good ten seconds. Alternating between hot and cold and resisting the urge to rub my sore chest, I rose, crept over the carpet and reached the door without making a sound.

Leaning to the peephole, I expected to see Steve looking like shit after a night on the run and hiding. If it wasn't him, I'd be on the phone to Fulcher within seconds.

There was no need for that, I saw.

Fulcher stood in the hallway.

The metal of the handle and key barely registered in the heat of my hand. Everything had become too hot as if in contrast to the temperature outside below freezing. I licked sweat from my lips and stood aside without speaking. Fulcher entered, his side brushing against the wall, and his coat dotted with melting flakes. A few had landed in his hair; droplets marked his forehead.

"What is it?" I said and shut the door.

Fulcher entered the living room and faced me.

"It's Steve Cameron. And his brother. And sister-in-law."

I knew the rest without him saying so.

Chapter Forty-Four

A mile from Artindale Square and the carnage he had left in number fifteen, Robert Fry stood in the derelict shop with the rear doors wide open. Even so, the light failed to reach its way to the furthest corners or to the tops of the shelving units. Cobwebs and dust, all left to rot after the last owners gave up trying to make a go of things in Sprignall, remained in their secret places with only the breeze managing to disturb them.

Fry faced the yard and listened and saw.

Not to the immediate area; the sirens and occasional shouts didn't interest Fry. He saw further afield, a mile distant to the flat green of the square designed as a play area for kids and untouched by almost all of them for years. Around the square, the terraces with their grey bricks and their dirty windows, and parked in lines, the police cars and vans standing sentry as the officers did the same at the foot of number fifteen's drive, the only sign of movement coming from their steaming breath.

Fry saw the silent officers and heard the anger from the assembled people on the green and in the street, all hurling their anger and fear at the white tent erected around the front of the house and few seeming to care about the wind or the snow that settled at their feet. Nobody threw any makeshift missiles as they had during the riot at the shops. Fry thought it might only be a matter of time, though. The people of the estate were scared and angry. One without the other was a big enough issue for the police to handle. Put the two together and they were looking at the potential for a lot of trouble.

Fry smiled.

While officers stood guard at the front of the house, others went door to door, knocking, ignored for the most part while those who did answer refused to let the police inside. Questions were asked; cursory answers given. Nobody had seen a thing and the din coming from number fifteen so late were no more unusual than any other recent noise. A sullen woman at number twenty-two did admit to hearing a car start and drive out of the square but she couldn't say what time that had been. Late was all she gave the officers.

Fry's eye and ear took in every movement from the forensic teams working in the rear garden and combing through the overgrown shrubbery that grew over a patch of green near the backs of the houses to the waving arms from the people grouped on the square. Fry heard their raised voices, their swearing and watched the impassive men covering along the opposite pavement take the abuse. Orders had gone out not to risk antagonising any of the locals especially after the trouble at the shopping precinct although Fry knew that did not mean the law would let Spregnall's population get away with kicking off in a proper way.

The first chucked stone, the first advance from the green towards the officers and any trouble would be dealt with sharply.

Fry's attention veered towards the long road that turned into the square. A police van followed the turning, passing car after car before coming to a stop in a small parking area between two streets of terraces. While the arrival of the police dogs was notable, Fry's attention remained on the lone car following the van and he named the large guy in the passenger seat before the car stopped.

Clyde Fulcher.

Hello, Clyde. It's been a long time.

And it had. Close to twenty years. Of course, Fulcher had been a much younger man back then and further down the ladder of seniority. No Detective Superintendent for him in those days. Nope. Just a police officer faced with a horrendous crime, just another cop in the machinery investigating a child's murder, another face already becoming strained by the hours and stress of the job.

I know your name, Clyde. I always did.

Fry listened to the man speak to his colleague as they exited the car; the younger officer trotted to the wall of men guarding the front of the house and kept his eyes off the noisy locals while he asked for a report on the potential for real trouble. A woman's voice, clear and carrying, yelled fucking pigs from somewhere in the crowd and the crowd roared its approval.

Dismissing the noise, Fry followed Fulcher as the man approached the tent covering the front of the house. A mile from the rich aroma of blood and open bodies, Fry whispered Fulcher's name and felt no disappointment when the man's only reaction was to jam his hands into his coat pockets.

It did not matter. All the work was almost done and Fry's business with Fulcher would be done by the end of the day. Fulcher himself would be done by the end of the day.

Fry closed his eyes and his ears and left Artindale Square. Back to himself and back to the wide space of the shop's storage area, he strode to the rear yard, closed and locked the shop's doors and did the same to the main gates as it left.

Seconds later, a man who older people would have said was still a boy strode away from the empty buildings.

The few people out on the streets and not indoors to watch the news reports about the events in the square saw the young man's sunny smile and gave it no thought.

Chapter Forty-Five

Fulcher had inhaled a lungful of the stink inside the house when he'd still been ten paces from the front door. Even so, he refused to cover his nose and made no sign that entering the building was taking all of his willpower. One thing he and plenty of his colleagues had to learn over the last few years was that everyone was recording every second of shit like this. Even though the TV and papers hadn't arrived yet (and he had a good idea that would change within five minutes, max), the last thing he needed was a shot of him gagging shared on fucking Facebook or looped on fucking YouTube or going old-school and being sold to the fucking tabloids. That was part of the reason he'd sent King to the other men. Keep him out of the house for a few moments until Fulcher himself had seen the damage.

Through the opening of the tent and sliding protective covers over his shoes, he identified Bryce by his small stature and let the man lead the way down the short hall and into the kitchen. No trouble in there, just the team checking for fibres, prints and anything else that might be a help. Just his colleagues and the godawful stench of things never meant to see daylight and blood not designed for anything but veins and arteries.

"It's bad," Bryce said, voice muffled behind his mask.

"I figured," Fulcher replied. He'd got a glimpse over Bryce's shoulder. Red. So much red.

Through an open window, a fresh volley of abuse fell into the house.

"The peasants are revolting," Bryce muttered and Fulcher snapped his mouth shut. The comment, obviously meant as a weak joke, needled him maybe because of a slight sneer in Bryce's voice. It was easy to judge the estate as a shithole and nothing but. It'd always been rough and having Carl Cameron living there for years didn't help. Even so, judging the population in that way when anyone would react with the same levels of fear and anger to recent events was not happening on Fulcher's watch.

"Watch who you say that shit to, Bryce," Fulcher said and moved to push past the other man. At the last second, he stopped, their clothing not touching and Bryce walked further into the kitchen without comment.

Fulcher took it all in. The blood sprayed from near the sofa out over the plush carpet. The splashes of red close to the skirting board of the wall below the window. The overturned coffee table and the spilled tea from the mugs.

The two bodies of the men fallen to the floor.

Steve lay in a curl, hands on his stomach, facing the TV on the other side of the room.

Carl had dropped at the foot of an armchair. Fulcher had a clear view of the man's face from his position in the doorway. On the floor, Carl Cameron appeared to be winking at the police officer because a spray of blood had glued an eye closed.

"Christ," Fulcher said under his breath and forced himself to look at the markings on the wall. The blood had run down the white, giving it the look of a shitty horror film. The message was real nonetheless.

There was nothing else for him to see in the living room, nothing more to take in other than the reek of salty blood clinging to his nostrils. Their man had been and gone and left them a note along with a message via Loui Cameron's mother.

Turning his back on the mess, Fulcher crossed the dining room in several large strides and exited to the back garden. Moments later, King joined him, forearm covering much of his face.

"She's dead," King said without any preamble and Fulcher didn't need to ask for clarification. Erica Cameron had been their one witness to the horrors inside the house and they'd got nothing out of her but the name of a dead girl.

"Ten minutes ago." King lowered his arm and both inhaled the refreshing crispness. The house, heavy and cloying with heat and the crowd of bodies, felt like a weight at their backs. In silent consent, they edged further away, sticking to the border of patio and grass.

"This is some bad shit, Clyde," King said and Fulcher nodded.

"One of the worst I've known. And the thing is it's only going to get worse the longer it goes on." Fulcher flexed his fingers, taking in the sting of the air. Flakes brushed his hair. Although the unexpected fall hadn't been going on for longer than an hour, the garden was gradually becoming more white than green. "This guy, he's not in any denial about who he is or what he's doing. Not like some of the fuckers we've dealt with."

King listened to his superior, aware Fulcher was talking more to himself. That was fine. King had witnessed Fulcher's thought processes at work for several years. Connections made; realisations come to. It was how the man operated.

"He's got his shit together. He doesn't try and hide anything and he won't stop until whatever the hell he's doing is finished."

Fulcher's memory tried to play back the mad phone call he'd received from, apparently, three dead girls and one man, and he managed to stop it after a few seconds. Nothing had come from attempting to place the call's location and the few people he'd told about the mix of voices had theorised a cleverly done recording although that hadn't explained the precise responses he'd been given from the girls or the man.

"What about Marshall?" King asked.

"I told him face to face. He doesn't know about his sister's name being involved in this. All he knows is the family are dead. I told him to stay indoors all day and call me if anyone contacts him. He's not responsible for anything here although based on his reaction, I don't think he sees it that way. The guy. . ." Fulcher struggled to verbalise his thoughts, a rarity King did not like. "The guy is a wreck but it's all below the surface. He's been keeping everything in for so long, he doesn't know how to do anything else. I tell him his sister's name came up here and fuck knows what he'll do. He knows he's involved. Same with what happened to his sister. That's enough for now."

"You think the guys who did his sister are worth talking to?"

Fulcher shook his head. "No. I made some calls to check up. They're all accounted for inside. Two died six years ago, one's been in a wheelchair for fifteen years thanks to someone who didn't appreciate him being a nonce; one's eighty-three and can't get off his bunk to go for a piss and the main one, he hanged himself third day inside. If our boy is connected to them, he's operating outside of any of them. A relative, maybe, or an old friend."

King had heard the brief theory already; most of the investigation's enquiries were now focused on digging into the past of the four men who'd watched while a fifth raped and murdered Ella Griffin so many years before, the girl the first victim in a planned series of attacks.

Picking over the mental phone call and the jumble of voices, Fulcher shook off his thoughts even as the supposed promise of more deaths after the next morning echoed at the back of his skull. He drew close to King and pitched his voice low.

"We want this fucker stopped, don't we, Mike?"

King gave no pause. "We do."

"Will we do anything to stop him?"

That brought a pause as Fulcher had known it would. "Meaning what?"

"Meaning we need to get down in the shit with him." Fulcher's face had turned slack. For the first time, King saw an old man looking back at him. Wordless fears swam in his stomach. There were long years ahead; days and months of murders and grief, pain and anger. That was his job, what he'd put himself into for as long as he could remember and there was no getting away from it now. Not with the dead face of his boss so close, Fulcher's eyes turned as black as the bags underneath them or the dots of stubble flecked with grey.

"Clyde," King began.

"It's okay. You don't need to worry. I'm. . .I've got things to do. Just trust me, yeah?"

"Yeah," King whispered.

"Good man." Fulcher took a few breaths and life flooded his features. Not a lot. Some. King had to take that as enough.

"Get back inside. I'll be there in a second."

Fulcher gazed over the whitening grass and made no move while King appraised him. He didn't even blink, King saw.

Fulcher waited until the other man had returned to the dining room and joined the forensics team. More white fell. Fulcher listened to the interior voice he trusted in ways he trusted no other, not even his wife.

You need to get down into shit just like you told Mike. That's where this fucker lives and where he won't stop. You face him there and if you come out clean, then great. Just don't bet on it.

Fulcher would bet on nothing. Too much about the case played with everything he'd believed during his entire career and while he had no time for hard and fast rules of good guys and bad guys without any shade in between, he'd operated for years with the surety of keeping himself clean while plenty of colleagues had got dirty. For decades, Fulcher had wondered what drove his fellow officers to give up on the law while knowing the answer at the same time. Everyone had their limit; everyone might reach that limit eventually and the only way to avoid doing so was to raise your own limit as the years went on and the crimes became bloodier, the victims more innocent, the horrors greater. Never take it home. Never let his family into the darkness of his world and never let the darkness into the world of his light.

Never.

I love you, Barbara. So much.

Fulcher withdrew his phone and stabbed in a number he'd committed to memory well over a year before.

And when Kelly answered, he had to close to his eyes, unable to face the garden and the morning while he told her what he needed her to do.

As long as Jimmy Marshall agreed to it.

While Fulcher spoke, the reek of the blood spilled in the house began to permeate the trees and grass.

Chapter Forty-Six

By half ten, I'd had more than enough of sitting on the sofa, staring at the TV without taking anything in; I needed to move. The urge to get some sleep had all but collapsed after Fulcher told me the latest, his voice soft and respectful and while I was tired to the point of my body aching, getting any rest was out of the question.

I showered, head held under the spray for as long as I could take the heat, down with slitted eyes to see the memory of the burned girl reaching from where I stood. There'd been nothing like that since and while I didn't think it was just a mental vision, I'd found a way of incorporating it into everything else. Maybe so many other nightmares had come to life recently that one more was part of it all. The sight of a burning ghost, the attack beside the river, yanking a half-dead child from a morgue drawer, the rip of the skin of a girl's neck and the ghost of my sister never more than a moment's thought away: every terrible event merged into one horror.

Dry and dressed in another chunky fleece and big coat, I left the flat, crossed the bridge into Oxford Road while the Evenham streamed underneath and the traffic was sparser than usual. That didn't feel like it was purely down to the nasty weather; the morning had brought more news of murder and people would want to be where things made sense. I had a feeling plenty of sick days were being taken and kids kept home from school. Doors and windows locked. Children allowed no further than their back gardens while parents watched from windows and kept an eye on gates and fences. Wind gusting over empty parks and play areas. The pavement outside the pub and alleyway on St Michael's Road untouched by the tread of shoes and boots. The only life on the riverside path was birds hunting for worms and bugs.

Lawfield was closing down and it wasn't simply because of the sky hanging low with fresh snow or the teeth in the wind.

Fulcher had told me to keep my head down and stay in the flat; he'd call me later to check in and let me know if there was any other news, and I'd agreed without any thought. Knowing he'd probably want to beat the shit out of me for going outdoors with everything that was going on was no reason to stop. I left Oxford Road, crossed with a few others at the lights and took a right at the start of a backstreet of takeaways. A cycleway unfurled for a mile or more. I left it after just a few paces and trotted down an embankment.

Ahead, the path along the river.

In daylight, it looked much different to my last two visits. No secret places; nowhere for anyone to hide. The willows hung their long branches over the ground and into the water. The river lapped at the permanently damp weeds and greenery of its bank, and visible between the clumps of bushes, playing fields were abandoned chunks of land. Not one dog walker was in sight.

Tapping my coat against the side of my chest, I got going, eyes darting from side to side, speaking low.

"I know this could be a bad move, but I've had enough, Ella. I'm not hiding. No more."

My dead sister kept quiet. I spoke to her more often than I liked to admit. Sometimes, she answered in my head. Right then, she was nowhere near me.

"I don't know what's happening here, but you trust me, yeah? I'll get it sorted. We'll fix this. It'll be done and I'll come and see you tomorrow. I'll—" Hot tears came from nowhere. I blinked them away, carried on walking with nothing but the sky and water for company and refused to stop talking to my sister. I told her I was sorry something had got her involved in whatever the hell was going on. I said it was my fault; I said she didn't have anything to worry about and I'd make sure I tidied up her grave the next day and eventually the words in my head fell apart into an echo of an apology.

Hands in pockets and scarf bulging over my throat, I walked another ten minutes, refusing to slow as the path neared the entrance to the path of the playing fields. There was still nobody else in sight, and the only sound was the wind on the water. Thin snowflakes continued to rain, settling on the grey ground and the green of the bushes and hiding those colours. I kicked at a loose drift and caught a blur of movement passing between tree trunks.

Immediately, I stopped and readied my hands.

The shape made no effort to hide itself. It stepped between low hanging branches, knocking small icicles to the ground, and there was no surprise at someone appearing at the same point where Steve had emerged.

No surprise at all.

Chapter Forty-Seven

My body was on my side; it did not tremble or spill frightened sweat from head to toe. My insides were still. Even fear hadn't come. Yet.

I relaxed the hand in my left pocket although kept a hold on my phone. My other hand thrummed against my hip, shaking like a hummingbird. I'd practiced the movement a few times before leaving the flat and reckoned I could get the knife out within a couple of seconds.

I said nothing. Neither did the young man, and my darting eyes took in everything.

He was motionless at the treeline, taller than I'd first thought, wide through the chest and shoulders, his face unlined by age or stress. He could have been anyone's favourite son, maybe a kid who came from a good family, one with cash and a nice house with the mortgage long since paid off and savings developing nicely; holidays in hot countries away from the tourists, and then skiing holidays over Christmas when he came back from university. A dad who didn't need to work because he'd invested wisely twenty-plus years ago before the boy was born; a mother who could never believe any horror story about her precious son, and an easy life ahead because there was an easy life behind. No grief or horror or misery for this kid who was only a kid to me because I was older. The good life for him; real life for me.

Dressed in a heavy coat much like mine, healthy and shining hair free from a hat, he should have been around his equally perfect friends in one of the city's nicest areas, not out in the freeze without any indication he'd strode through the bushes and trees. No dampness on his shoulders and splashes of ice-cold mud staining his jeans. He was untouched by the day and by the winter.

Out there by the river with the dead trees at his back and nothing moving in the abruptly still surroundings, he'd stepped from a nightmare, not the greenery.

He glanced further along the path where the route meandered below thicker branches, then pointed.

"I died down there."

A child's voice, and my entire body dipped into freezing water at the sound.

"He killed me down there. He beat me with a hammer."

He looked back at me and his eyes were no longer old; they were a teenage girl's. They knew I was an idiot and that nothing in the world mattered by friends and right now.

"Are you going to stop him, Jimmy?"

He took two steps forward and I took two back, immediately hating myself. Speaking seemed out of the question. I managed it, though.

"Who are you?"

I barely heard my own question so there was no way the sound of my voice carried over the ground. He smiled all the same, exposing perfectly straight teeth.

"I'm Loui." The smile vanished and more words came, the voice changing with each name, not a single breath between them. "And I'm Laura and I'm Meg and I'm El—"

"Shut up."

I roared it, fire in my throat, fire in my heart. He fell silent. Around us, the wind picked up again, scattering the flakes and turning my back into ice as it gusted along the path and made the branches around the woman dance. His smooth hair remained still.

I told my fingers to punch my phone and dial the number I'd keyed in. They refused.

His mouth broke into a leer and he spoke in a normal voice. "You don't have long. Less than a day to stop me. I told you the rules. Stop me by tomorrow morning and I'll go away. Don't stop me and I'll kill and kill and kill and—"

A spasm down my arm hit my fingers and my fingers hit my phone. I yanked the mobile free. At the same time, I brought my knife out and Fulcher was in my ear.

"Jimmy? You okay? What's happening?"

I jabbered into the phone. "The river. The path at the playing fields. I'm with him right now. Right fucking now."

I disconnected the call even as Fulcher shouted down the line, and slid the phone back to my pocket.

"You are not who you think you are," I told him while he gazed back, curious, amused. "Robert Fry has been dead for almost twenty years. You are just some nutter who needs locking up in a nice, soft room."

He giggled, the little sound turning him into a prepubescent child instead of a man in his early twenties. I kept a mental hold of myself and the dam inside holding back the screaming outrage and terror remained in place.

"Go on," I said. "Tell me your real name. Tell me where you live. Who you are."

He inhaled as if considering but said nothing. The ice in the air crept into my skin, feeling as if it wanted to turn my bones into as much a part of the winter as snow and strong sunsets in the middle of the afternoon.

"You think you're dangerous?" My heart rate was increasing; there was electricity in my mouth and the burning need in my fists to smash them into his smug face. "You don't know a thing about danger or bad men. How old were you when my sister died? Old enough to not be shitting your nappy?" I managed a derisive snort. "I doubt that."

"You believe that?" His question was as gentle as the river brushing its banks. "Really?"

"I believe you will be in prison for the rest of your life like Robert Fry should have been except that son of a bitch was too much a coward to face it. What's the deal with him? Do you idolise him or something? A child killer who hanged himself inside?" I snorted, peripheral vision narrowing, shrinking; my focus becoming the man before me and nothing else.

"He killed himself before the other prisoners could; he killed kids and you're trying to be him." I sucked saliva, tasting its sourness on my tingling tongue, and spat at his feet. "Fuck you and fuck him. You are both nothing."

He nodded. "Fry was nothing. He was a vehicle for me and that was it. It's why I burned him." A hissing laugh. "Plus, he deserved to cook. And now it's you and me." His eyes rolled over fully white. It was as if the sub-zero air had slithered inside his head and whited out his eyes.

"You do know I can kill you at any point I choose, don't you?"

I had a second to note something about the way he spoke, something that didn't mesh with his youthful face. Whatever it was, it was chewed up by my welcome anger.

"Come and try it. I'll make you bleed like you did to Steve and his family last night."

He blinked, eyes once again a wide and clear blue. Insanely, he managed to appear hurt. Again, the child's voice. "That wasn't me. It did that. Not me. I'm Loui and—" and another change— "I'm Laura. We told you who we were. It killed us and now you have to kill it if you can, if you can, if you fucking can, Jimmy." And the children were gone, leaving only the same voice I'd heard from the figure who'd emerged out of the hospital before killing that girl.

"If you fucking can, Jimmy, you fucking remember me, Jimmy because I remember you."

Raging, spitting, he flew over the ground and come straight at me while I raised my knife, much too slowly, and he was a speeding monster screaming as he bore down on me.

Chapter Forty-Eight

The car's back right tire hit the kerb, sending a jolt through the vehicle. In the passenger seat, Fulcher braced himself and said nothing to King. They were moving too fast and at the same time, nowhere near fast enough. Jimmy's call had come through less than ten minutes before and despite running from the house to the cars with King calling for others to follow and despite the race across town through less traffic than normal at that time of day, those ten minutes felt like ten hours to Fulcher.

Veering right, they sped into the entrance of Water View, flanked on either side by all the signs of middle-class suburbia, a place where the police almost never had any reason to come. From a few windows, pale faces appeared, older people alerted to the intrusion into their lives by the roar of the four cars. Slowing a fraction to take the bend in the road, King didn't need Fulcher to direct him. There was only a single route they could follow and the rest of the way would be on foot. Inside, he got a hold on his surety that the fucker would be able to take cover in the trees and bushes or even just run down the river and out into the surrounding countryside. They knew he was here and that would be enough. The open land acting as a perfect cover for the bastard was just another problem.

They clipped the kerb again, then mounted it to skid to a halt in a wide parking area for the nearby flats, all converted from older houses. Parked tidily, four cars were parked in their bays, the majority of the locals at work. Fulcher shoved his door open a moment before the car had completely come to a stop. He and King emerged; the other vehicles sped into the area, each one spraying gravel and crushing snow. Officers jumped free, each man kicking through the white as they ran over the car park.

"The call was from straight over the field at the end of the path." The wind took a tight grip of Fulcher's words. Flakes whipped across his face. "Mike, Andy, Colin, you're with me." He jabbed a finger at the other men and all caught the welcome wail of sirens. They'd have more colleagues on site within two minutes. "Al, Dave. Go three hundred feet left. Through the trees. Rob, Ali, the same to the right. If he's hiding, we find him. If he runs, we go after the cunt. Move."

The sirens had drawn closer. Fulcher wasted no time in radioing through for the others to come over the field. They knew the score. Leading the way, he ran across a short path that ended in worn railings and opened to the playing fields. Ahead and spreading to both sides, most of the green lay below blinding white while above, the sky hung low. Banishing his nameless fear and confusion, Fulcher tucked his arms close to his sides and ran with King and the other men close by. Their movement was frustratingly slow due to the uneven land rising and falling in slight degrees and those bumps covered by white. Halfway, Fulcher stumbled and roared his anger. Panting, wishing he'd kept in better shape, he righted himself and raced on. The men he'd directed to the other ends of the path were nearing the treeline, their tread surer than his, their lungs and throats not burning quite so much. Mike, Andy and Colin ran parallel to him, none overtaking him although they clearly could. Powered by a storm of exhaustion and anger, Fulcher pushed himself to his limit, stomped through the snowfall and found the path lost from view. On more level ground, running became much easier although it did nothing to help the fire cooking his chest or to cool the sweat dripping from his head to his eyes. Fulcher spat, clearing his mouth of a sour taste and closed in on the last fifty feet of path as the whoop of sirens died behind and he knew they'd have another twenty officers on site in moments. And then the fucker would be theirs and this hell would be over.

No more killing; no more wondering what the hell was going on with a case that made no sense, and no more memories of a case from twenty years ago and the fear that case was a festering mess in his hands right now.

With his men at his back, Fulcher crashed through low-hanging branches lining a path relatively clear and emerged to the stretch running the length of the river.

Prone on the ground, Jimmy Marshall lay with red staining the snow around his head. Gasping, heart turned into thunder, Fulcher checked either end of the path and saw nobody but the other officers shoving their way through the trees and bushes.

"Ambulance, now," he shouted at King who'd had already got his radio to his face before Fulcher's order. Fog pumped from his nostrils.

Fighting the urge to rub his chest, Fulcher crouched beside Jimmy, checked for a pulse and found it straightaway, a strong beat in the man's neck. The white of the snow and the white of Jimmy's face merged into a single terrible shade marked by the bright red oozing from somewhere at the back of his head.

"Jimmy?" Fulcher barked. "You with me? It's Fulcher. Jimmy?"

Jimmy's eyelids fluttered but didn't open. Yanking his coat off and letting the sharp air smash into the heat enveloping his body, Fulcher draped it over Jimmy's upper body.

"Where's that fucking ambulance, Mike?" he barked without turning.

"On its way. Two minutes."

"Check with the others. He could be hiding anywhere. Colin, stay here."

Fulcher didn't turn as King jogged away, heading towards Rob and Ali. He leaned closer to Jimmy, pitching his voice low enough to not carry further than Jimmy's ear. "We're ending this tonight, Jimmy. You and me. It ends tonight."

Dancing over the water and blown along the path, the snow began to fall in heavier and heavier flakes.

Chapter Forty-Nine

Twilight descended fast over Lawfield.
Across the town, the population left their offices as early as possible, heading to their cars with little conversation and few smiles as they nodded goodbyes to those remaining. Parents had picked up their children from school gates, the vehicles lining streets half an hour earlier than usual and causing jams between the parents and the people who lived in those areas. Arguments had broken out in numerous places, threats exchanged and the potential for violence never more than a few moments away. On Albion Way, buses full to standing inched their way behind slow moving vehicles, the main road filling with its rush hour traffic by three in the afternoon, the drivers hunched shapes behind their wheels.

In clothes shops, staff gazed at their mostly empty premises and thought about cashing up unused tills while managers hoped for an early evening push to help sales, knowing as they did so that it wasn't at all likely. Bar staff did the same while they cleared the few glasses left on tables from the late lunch crowd, wiping splodges of ketchup clean, taking the food menus back behind the bar and all uncomfortably aware of the TVs and music too loud with fewer drinkers in.

Throughout Lawfield, older men walked their dogs and none ventured from pavements to park areas or fields. While the reason why remained locked in their hearts, all felt the same. Better to be seen. Better to stay beside roads even if those roads were quiet. The animals sniffed fences and posts, few allowed to pause by their owners all eager to get home before full dark and make sure windows and doors were securely locked against that dark. The fear and anger was locked inside their hearts, kept from their mouths and waking minds by the ways of old men.

Watching over the dog walkers, the office workers in the cars and peering into the windows of the pubs, the Starbucks and the shops and businesses, the end of the day ate the fading red of the sunset and dropped a heavy snowfall from one end of the county to the other. No more than a few miles from the block of flats Jimmy Marshall had lived in for three years, farmland had become an indistinguishable and untouched white sheet that spread further with each passing moment. Animals had been taken into shelter by farm workers, and the only light in the rural edges of the county came from the windows of isolated houses. In those homes, families checked their doors and gathered together without letting themselves think of the recent murders or the long, empty roads and tracks between them and their neighbours.

Closer to the heart of Lawfield, Sprignall had quietened since the potential for trouble early in the morning. Support from neighbouring counties had spread officers throughout the estate; a few scuffles between those officers and the locals had been dealt with swiftly. The sharp response and the deterioration in the weather dampened much of the anger although only on the surface. The crowd on Artindale Square dissipated by noon and those involved either remained in their homes to curse the police in privacy or drank in the estate's three pubs; big men lining bars and grouped around tables while harsh lighting competed with the noise of fruit machines and TVs on walls. They swore about the law; they made plans to return to the square and demand answers about what had gone on with Carl Cameron and his wife and brother. They drank and kept their backs to the windows and blizzard hammering on the glass.

By five, the last of the light had been buried alive by the new night and drifts two feet high blocked roads all over Lawfield. Gritters made their slow way on parkways and main roads, leaving backstreets untouched. Tons of salt had been brought out of reserve by the council shortly after noon when it became clear the weather would not improve, and while the parkways and miles of A-roads were kept clear, Lawfield's narrow roads and newer areas of family homes and expensive flats were left to the snow.

And the secrets it kept.

Chapter Fifty

Head down, coat zipped to his neck, Fulcher strode from the main entrance and reception to the hospital and passed the two smokers in the shelter, both puffing as quickly as possible. While he had no urge to be outside and exposed, there was no way he could make his phone call anywhere near people. Cursing the weather, he waited for dozens of slow vehicles to take the curving road to the of the car park and jogged across to the other side. A wide grass area had been placed at the side of the main building complete with new benches, their seats and struts buried by the white. It didn't matter. He wasn't out here to get any fresh air or wait for an operation to be finished. This was all about privacy.

Fulcher crossed the square and stood against a wire fence that formed a border of the hospital grounds and public land beyond. Lights cast bright beams down, and car headlights bloomed on the ground. Feeling exposed even though the nearest people were the smokers back in the shelter, Fulcher slid his phone free, pulled a glove off and dialled. In seconds, the evening stung his fingers and sank into the dry skin. Ignoring the needling pain, he held the phone to his ear and heard her answer.

"Yes?"

"You definitely still on for tonight?" he asked. There was no need—or point—for polite greetings.

"Shit." She sighed down the line, and Fulcher caught a second of background noise. Cartoons, by the sound of the loud TV. "Is your man up for it?"

"He is. He's hurt, but he's game. Went for it pretty quick. I've just finished talking to him and he's right behind it."

Fulcher fell silent, not willing to add he'd seen more than eagerness in Jimmy's strained and beaten face. Bruised the man might have been, his features discoloured and painful to look at, but there'd still been strength inside the purple and sickly yellow around his nose and on his jawline. Fulcher's earlier thought about Jimmy having kept everything under lock and key for so long that he no longer knew how to do anything else had come back like a weight during their conversation up on the fifth floor. The back of Jimmy's head wrapped in a thick bandage, the soft murmur of nurses' voices out in the corridor and the slap of flakes on the window. All that around Fulcher while he studied Jimmy for any sign of doubt once the plan was out in the open.

Doubt, no. Need, yes.

That was it exactly. Jimmy needed to get this done and he was willing to risk everything to do so. If not for himself then for what had been done to his sister. While neither of them had gone into any discussion on what the hell connection there might be between Ella's killer and the men who'd watched the broadcast from the back of a rotting shop, and the killer butchering children in Lawfield, Fulcher saw Ella's name in Jimmy's eyes. Not only in the man's eyes. In his bruised face, tainted with fading yellows and purples from the beatings he'd taken over recent days, scrapes and grazes marking his features, and the weighty bags below his eyes signifying a serious lack of sleep. He looked like shit which changed little.

Beaten or not, Jimmy needed this evil business done.

Dismissing the speeding passage of his thoughts, Fulcher said: "Five hundred quid. No questions asked."

The woman he'd called gave him a mocking laugh. "Make it a grand, and you're on."

"Fine. A grand." There was no point in haggling with her.

"You got that sort of money?"

"I've got it."

"They're paying you too much."

"Probably."

Fulcher watched the two smokers leave the shelter. Briefly, loneliness stabbed him. He shook it away.

"I must be out of my mind," she said. "You've asked me for a lot, but this is. . ."

"I know. You do this tonight and that's it. I won't call you again for as long as you want."

That brought another laugh to his ear. "You're full of it. I've heard that at least ten times."

"I mean it—" Fulcher had to stop himself. He'd been a second away from using her name and that went completely against their agreement. No names on the phone. No face to face meetings on the estate. Nobody knowing their arrangement. Just exchanged information. Just cash in hand.

"Careful, now," she said and while the words came laced with humour, Fulcher heard fear.

"You got someone for your girl?" he asked.

"Yes." Frostier now. She didn't like any mention of her personal life and Fulcher could appreciate that. In over a year, she'd asked him precisely nothing about his marriage or own children.

"A grand buys a lot of toys," he said.

"It does." Then without any chance for him to reply: "I'll be there."

She hung up.

Fulcher put his phone away and slid his glove back on. Dawn was approximately twelve hours away.

A lifetime away.

A single breath.

Fulcher headed back to the lights and life of the hospital, readying himself to tell Jimmy it would soon be time for him to risk his life.

Chapter Fifty-One

The doctors and nurses ordered me to stay in hospital at least overnight and probably would have done whatever was in their legal power to keep me there if it hadn't been for Fulcher leaving DS King behind to tell the staff I was helping the police with an ongoing investigation. I'd got some sleep, crashing out from a combination of stress, total exhaustion and the painkillers for my head. From what Fulcher told me as he came and went from the room, I'd been lucky to not be seriously hurt by the guy attacking me. I was also a fucking idiot for going outside when he'd expressly told me not to. Any weak attempt on my part to tell him the young guy talking in the voices of dead kids had been met with quick nods and no belief. King had given away little on his face, but I took a guess he felt the same as his boss. I'd had the shit kicked out of me again, and sustained several heavy blows to the head. No wonder I'd been banging on about a young, strong man responsible for all the horror of the last few days who was able to perfectly mimic the voices of teenage girls.

Once I'd got some rest and King convinced the staff I'd be under his personal care, they bagged up more painkillers and told me to go home to bed. Fulcher had gone by that point after going through his plan with me and I'd pictured myself out in the black and snow, no match for a killer or anyone who might come for me. Saying no to Fulcher wasn't an option. He hadn't needed to reiterate the nutcase's words about the next day and continuing his violence unless we stopped him by dawn. The following day and all it meant for me personally was never more than a moment's thought away.

I made it home by seven, tried to doze for an hour and failed. The TV kept me company along with every light in the flat and the knowledge King and another cop were downstairs in the car park, probably freezing their arses off while they watched every shadow, every slight movement for the approach of a stranger to the building. If the killer did come knocking, he'd be seen. The roads and pavements were practically deserted on the drive from the hospital; the thickening drifts of white clogging gutters and pavements had done a good job of emptying Lawfield's public areas. While a few taxis headed for pickups and drop offs, buses had been cancelled and most of the trains were running late. We'd come up Albion Way to Oxford Road, and I'd watched from the back seat while the two officers tried to keep conversation going.

The last of the office workers not dressed for the weather; their skirts and thin trousers whipping around their legs, and their bags bouncing on their sides as they lurched across the uneven ground.

The bar staff turned into blurry outlines through windows spattered with snow and gleaming with the yellow from street lights.

The still lump in a shop doorway that could only be someone homeless buried in a sleeping bag.

All of it Lawfield. All of it a town either hiding or finding cover from the winter.

Everyone except me. I was going back out into it.

My phone rang, a soft trill on the sofa. It was Fulcher.

"Evening," I muttered.

"How you feeling, Jimmy?"

"Like a kid who was the best impressionist in the world kicked the crap out of me."

"Still on the voices thing?" A question asked lightly but with a weight hanging underneath it.

"Like I told you. He came out of the trees. He spoke in different voices; he said he was the girls he killed and he grabbed me like he was made of rock." I came close to raising my voice for a moment and focused on my breathing before speaking again. "Just like I said."

Before Fulcher replied, I knew what he was thinking. The man supposedly speaking in the voices of murdered children was crap; he'd known their names and maybe put on a high-pitched tone. That, my stress and fear had done the rest. Otherwise. . .what? He thought he was the dead girls? Or. . .

Or they really had spoken out of his mouth and that was just ridiculous.

"I'm not arguing," Fulcher replied. He sounded as if he was holding a hand up, palm out, to calm me. "Just checking you're okay."

"And still on for tonight?" I let myself smile although the situation wasn't funny.

"And still on for tonight," he agreed.

My gaze fell on the kitchen knife I'd placed on the coffee table. The blade was dull but long. Not wanting to look at it while I spoke to Fulcher, I turned to the repeat of Brooklyn Nine Nine on the TV instead.

"I said I'd do it if you still think it's the only plan."

"Plan? It's bollocks. I'm risking people's lives for this and every single bone in my body is asking why. Thirty fucking years on the Force and I've never come close to doing this sort of stuff. We're out of time, though. If this guy is telling the truth, then we've got tonight to find him."

"Do you really believe he'll stop if we find him by morning?"

Fulcher paused just long enough to give his lie away. "Yeah. Well, I hope so. He's fixated on you and what tomorrow means for you. I think he wants you to stop him. Probably right at the last second so he can feel like he's led you to it and you've earned it."

As much as I didn't want to ask, I had to. "Is this guy something to do with the men who hurt my sister?"

There were no tears, only a pit in my chest.

"No. Not in as much as he was part of it," Fulcher replied. "He's far too young, isn't he? Maybe he knows about it and..." Uncharacteristically, he hesitated. "Could be a copycat thing for all we've got at the moment. Bastard kid gets his rocks off on old crimes, gets obsessed with something that happened when he was all of two or three years old and wants to re-enact it or do some kind of insane tribute. I did think maybe he could be related to someone who was involved in Ella, but none of those men had sons who'd be the right age now. And the investigation back then found no evidence of anyone other than the men who were sent down being involved. Plus, all those cunts are being passed around the prison showers on a daily basis or they're dead. Remember that."

"I remember," I whispered and forced the name out. It stung like an old, deep wound. "Robert Fry."

"Fuck that piece of shit," Fulcher said. "My one regret in my career is Fry hanging himself so soon after getting sent down. He deserved his time. Fry's gone. Whoever is doing this is some shitbag kid who's yet to see twenty-five and thinks he's the big I am, but that doesn't make him Fry or Bell or Hopkins or the Khan brothers. He's gone and we've got a real live son of a bitch to stop by tomorrow. . .if he really is that fixated on you and I have to believe he is."

I didn't have to believe the same. I did believe it. Whatever was happening – a man I couldn't help but think of as a kid targeting me and my past; so many murdered children, and either my head falling into pieces or the ghosts of those dead girls speaking to me – each factor proof of a connection to my dead sister and the anniversary of her murder the next day.

"Any questions about tonight?" Fulcher sounded calmer. Behind his question, a jumble of other voices came and went along with a ringing phone. He'd be wherever they were heading the investigation and I had a brief wondering thought of what the man's home life might be like and how much he'd seen of it since the Saturday morning.

"Just one," I said. The phone behind Fulcher's breathing stopped its noise; the mix of voices went on and on. "How do you know he'll follow me?"

"Because you're part of this."

He hung up.

Thirty minutes later, at exactly half nine, I necked painkillers and headed out.

But not before making sure the knives—mine plus the special one Fulcher had given me—were hidden inside my coat.

***

Shielded from the fierce wind by the warmth of their car, DS King and DS AliAli Hannan watched Jimmy Marshall emerge from the entrance foyer and stride across the car park to the narrow path that served as a route to Oxford Road. Within seconds, Jimmy's shape blurred in the flakes although both men knew he'd have to move slowly due to the weather and the beating he'd sustained earlier. They'd made it clear to him they would spend the evening in the car park; he'd showed no sign of noticing them on his way out and King privately thought that had been a conscious move. On the small chance the psycho out there was watching the flats, there was no reason to give away the police's location.

"This is a bad idea," Hannan muttered. "Letting him go. Nobody on him. No clue where he's going." He sighed. "Bad thinking, man."

"He knows the score." King kept his face turned from his colleague, knowing Hannan would see his doubt. They'd known each other for a long time. There were few secrets between them.

"He knows it, yeah," Hannan agreed. "Doesn't mean he can handle this guy. Twice, he gets jumped and twice he gets battered. You think our boy's going to let Marshall go a third time?"

"Fulcher told him exactly what to do. As long as he sticks to the plan and doesn't do anything differently, he'll be fine."

King pressed his face against the window, catching a slight movement in the abrupt easing of snowfall. It was a man walking a dog along the slope of Oxford Road. Seconds later the snow returned to its mad swirl, and man and animal vanished as Jimmy had.

The two officers waited in companionable silence for another ten minutes before pulling out to the slush-covered roads, the car's tires spreading salt through the mix of brown and white, the lights at the junction welcoming their vehicle and no others.

Chapter Fifty-Two

I spent two hours doing exactly as Fulcher had ordered: keeping to well-lit (if almost totally empty) roads, avoiding all back roads and side streets, having a lonely dinner in an Indian restaurant and unable to do more than pick at the food much to the annoyance of the staff with not much else to do, and nursed a couple of pints in different pubs while the other few drinkers made little effort to hide their appraisal of my bandaged head and the bruises still visible from my beating on the Saturday. By the time I left the last pub, the duty manager and bar staff were pointedly tidying up around me, stacking chairs on the wooden tables and laying out breakfast menus. I stood close to the doors on the street, the pub's lights at my back, hands deep in my pockets while I squinted against the wind. Lawfield, never the most crowded of towns, had become a ghost ship which was no surprise. A Monday night, temperatures dropping and pavements impassable. Anyone with any sense was safe in their home, doors and windows locked while I checked both ends of the Causeway, saw nothing but a single taxi and pictured the route I had to walk.

If I headed straight there, it would take about forty-five minutes. I checked my watch. Quarter past midnight. Way too early. Shit. On the other hand, there was nowhere else to go and nothing to do.

Pretending being outside wasn't like walking through a fire that froze instead of burned, I trod carefully. Clumps of snow had been kicked up into ice-covered slush in places but the majority of the surface layer remained untouched. It broke apart under my weight while the blown drifts filled the prints in and stung the bridge of my nose where my scarf didn't quite reach.

Leaving the Causeway behind, I followed St Michael's Road, not letting myself pay any attention to The Black Boar and alleyway beside it where Meg Freeman's body had been so carelessly dumped, and walked alongside Carling Way for a while. Occasionally, the noise of a car broke through my tiredness, and I had to hope it was either King and the other cop or Fulcher trailing me like we were in a shitty film, a thriller where every plan to stop the killer had failed and all the good guys had left was using one of their own as bait—a plan destined to fail when the killer jumped from the bushes on my left and stabbed out my eyes.

That thought wasn't enough to make me laugh or even smile, and I pretended I'd be able to do so when sunlight broke through the dark and all this shit was over.

Crossing the road, I followed the curve into New Road and began the longest part of the walk. Two miles straight ahead, then another mile along a cycleway bordered by grass and a road that would probably be just as quiet as any behind.

Odd as it felt to not be too scared to do anything but watch for every moving shadow and listen for every creak of a branch, I faded in and out of real consciousness as New Road took me along. The lack of sleep, the crippling temperature, and the fireworks in my head all combined to force my focus on little more than one foot in front of the other and hope I was walking in a straight line. Looking back after the first mile, the moonlight bloomed on several footprints that hadn't been filled in. They were the markings of a drunk unable to keep level and I refocused my efforts on heading straight.

Mumbled speech came and went. I spoke aloud to Ella, the words trapped inside and not much more than incoherent mutterings whether they were inside or out. At around the halfway point, I surprised myself by speaking clearly for the first time since ordering the second pint.

"What happens if this doesn't work?"

I stopped and turned in a slow circle, my senses dulled as if I'd drunk too much. Things were slow, dream-like. The world slept under a white carpet. I was a black dot on that white, an insect banished from all other existence, and the snowfall would bury me alive inside my own private grave where nothing would ever touch my skin or soul again.

Sort yourself out.

The thought was as sluggish as my movement, coming from all sides with no urgency or real strength. Faraway or close by—I couldn't work out which—the odd light turned windows yellow. Other than that, there were no signs of life. If the police were tracking my movement, they were hiding from sight. Long driveways sloped up to front doors and gardens and everything was closed off to me. Outside with no protection other than a couple of knives and the word a police officer risking his career to stop a killer while I risked my life.

For Ella. The mutter rose from far below, not my voice. I was sure of that. For your sister.

"She's dead," I said, giving an inarguable fact to the air.

There was no reply to that, only a sense that it didn't matter. And neither did wondering what the hell would happen if Fulcher's plan went down the toilet. If I survived it, we would have the morning to face and all that might mean. All I had right then was a little time and a little plan.

Slightly more together in my head thanks to stating such a bald, ugly fact, I walked on, treading more firmly and my attention back on the present. Time passed; my estimate of forty-five minutes to cover the distance was a fair way off, I realised, because I hadn't given much thought to the weather. By one o'clock, there was still over a mile to go. That was fine. Half two was coming up; all I had to do was be in the right place at the right time and do my job.

New Road took me on, frost and snow breaking below. A dog barked somewhere. I counted three taxis over the following hour and saw the blur of a black cat running through the white towards a side entrance of a bungalow, then heard the rattle of a cat flap. Eventually, New Road went its way and I came to the last section of my walk. The cycleway. The thin slash ahead where, unless they kept pace somehow and saw me from the road, I'd be separated from the police. The hulking shapes of storage units and portakabins much like the ones we had on the hospital site covered the other side of the cycleway. The industrial area slept. There'd be no life on that side for a few hours at least.

Swearing under my breath, I got moving.

Tatty scrubland grew at my left with the moonlight catching on the odd discarded can of lager tossed into the bushes or on a fast food container left to moulder in the undergrowth. The only good thing about the area was the size: there was no way anyone could hide in the bushes or behind the trees. Not like out beside the river.

"Shit," I muttered and tried not to think about the youth advancing on me, speaking in a mix of children's voices and his face totally blank. Then his hands on my arms, pushing them down like I had no muscle, grabbing my head and knocking me over to bounce my skull on the ground again and again. Even the memory of that hurt physically, made worse by knowing he could have kept going until my head was so much blood and broken bone.

Unable to process the insanity of the killer speaking in girls' voices and saying the things he had, I forced it from my thoughts, squeezed my hands into fists and pulled on the interior material of my coat so the knives in my inside pockets pressed on my chest. Ahead, an owl voiced a solitary hoot in the branches and something else gave a soft rustle. I froze, trying to look everywhere at once. For long moments, the surety the killer would appear out of nowhere like a ghost and come for me was like a weight on my chest. Breathing slowly, I decided the rustling had been a night-time animal. Maybe a mouse or a rat. The pickings of litter would attract either. Striding forward and listening for any further little noises or the distant noise of an advancing car, I kept my hands ready and walked in the middle of the cycleway.

Fifteen minutes later, I emerged to a path bordered on one side by a half-finished development of new houses while the back end of the industrial estate consumed the other side. The path entered Sprignall from its least populated end. Several blocks of flats loomed high, street lights offering weak illumination and a lot more in the way of shadows. Nobody appeared to be about. Somewhere, the muffled beat of monotonous music played, and further away, a car sped into the distance. When that growl faded, all I had was my breath and the faint thud of someone's house party.

"What the fuck are you doing here?" I whispered and went on before I could think of an answer.

Fulcher had told me where to go and brought up images of the spot on Google Maps. Coming off the cycleway, I walked between houses (one with all its windows sealed, and that was too much like the hospital for me to take without wanting to puke, and the fence surrounding the other's rear garden spray painted with graffiti from top to bottom), crossed a dilapidated play area and emerged on a green at the back of a small shopping precinct. Unlike the one hit by the riot and the kid it transpired had been beaten to death before being burned in the phone box, this one was untouched by any recent trouble. Metal shutters sealed the units; more graffiti stained the shutters and the backs of two benches had been removed, leaving slats for seating. My mind tried to bring up an image of Sprignall's third shopping area, one over a mile from where I stood, and I would not let it.

Movement.

A shape walking with careful steps towards one of the damaged benches.

The gleam of a cigarette shining orange against the night and the chunks of blown snow.

The woman Fulcher had set up for me.
The woman I needed to attack.
I brushed my fingers against the knives in my pocket and got moving.

***

The shifting air in the alleyway between pub and estate agent stroking the wet walls and caressing the white carpet blown in from the road.

The long grass of Tirrington Park buried under white, its surface unmarked by footprints and everything gleaming white from the glare of the moon.

The pathway next to the Evenham as white as the park but marked with the tiny prints of animals and birds' feet come to ground on the hunt while the water lapped at the tangle of weeds.

The rear section of a long since closed down shop in Sprignall, its doors closed but unlocked and the snow on the back yard stained by the passage of heavy steps.

Each location separated from the others by distance and the crippling temperature. Each its own secret place, forming its own story and legend of hauntings. Each ready to be left alone except by lurid stories growing over the months and years ahead until the names were close to forgotten, the dead girls' faces and lives remembered by their parents and families, and their lives kept out of the tales of their deaths.

From each little piece of frozen land, unblinking eyes watched, all as helpless to undo their murders as they were to stop more blood from being spilled.

Standing perfectly still, a shape calling itself Robert Fry also watched.

And saw the tiny gleam of a burning cigarette.

Chapter Fifty-Three

"Stop."

Feeling like a kid being told off by a teacher, I did as she said. She took a final drag on the cigarette and dropped it. The orange light went out before it struck ground. Thin cloud had passed over the moon a moment before, leaving the precinct even darker and making the woman's face close to indistinguishable. Fulcher had told me how old she was—twenty-six—but the instruction in the word made her sound easily ten years older.

"Who's your friend?" she asked, her accent noticeable despite her low voice. Fulcher had told me I'd know her by that accent. Pure Belfast.

Fulcher, the girl, the killer. All at once, I couldn't breathe let alone move. There'd be a knife in my back at any second and the last thing I'd hear would be the grate of metal on my spine.

Get a fucking grip. She means Fulcher.

"Fulcher," I muttered and fought the urge to look behind just to make sure she hadn't meant someone was with me, someone advancing on us and wearing any one of three faces.

"What's your name?"

"Jimmy."

"What's his dog's name?"

It wasn't much of a secret question or code, but it would do fine, Fulcher told me. There was no need for spy crap or funny handshakes; all we needed to use was private information, the sort of thing not known to just anybody.

"Tommy."

"Good enough. Have a seat."

Pulling on my coat again to test the weight of the knives, I crunched snow and sat beside her, keeping a few inches of space. Below my arse, the old wood felt like I was sitting on the ground. She'd brushed it clear before sitting, the sound a tiny hiss.

"Fulcher and some other cop are back the way I came," she said. "Looks like there's at least two cars down there, too. Anyone comes along, the police'll be all over him."

"That's reassuring," I said and sensed her understanding smile.

"You prepared?" she asked.

"Yeah. I think so."

That made her laugh. "You think so? Clyde must be desperate."

"Thanks."

"No offence."

We sat silently for a moment, flakes brushing my woolly hat and her head. I took the quiet as chance to appraise her, helped by the return of the moonlight. Thin in a way that was close to scrawny. Hair that could have been blonde pulled back from her face. Dressed in faded jeans, boots and a jacket easily a size too large. Although I could only see her face in profile, it was enough to know she was as young as Fulcher had said. She may have only been a few years younger than me, but I felt like an old man beside her.

"Kelly, right?" I asked.

"Right."

"This is all a bit fucked up, isn't it?"

"Right."

I checked either end of the precinct. Nothing.

"How long have you known Fulcher for?" I said.

"A while. I help him out with information. He helps me out with cash. It's all a big secret." She hugged herself. "And if I didn't need his cash, I wouldn't be out here. I tell you that."

"If I didn't want to stop that man who's killing kids, I wouldn't be here, either."

She glared at me and I got my first clear look at her face. There was anger there. Fear, too. With both, she did appear a few years older. Living in Sprignall probably didn't help, either.

"You think I don't?" she whispered. "I've a little girl. She's five so maybe she's too young for that fucker who's doing this, but if he came anywhere near her. . ." Her hands rose like claws and pulled into fists. "This is about more than some bastard out there. It's bad enough that we can't go trust men we know not to hurt us or some guy not taking no for an answer when we don't want to go out with him. It's bad enough nipping out to the shop after dark means taking my alarm with me and it's bad enough I have to watch my drink every time I go to a pub. This is about our daughters, our girls. He hates them. He's not going after lads, is he? Not cutting anyone's son. No. Not for him. He's hurting girls because they're girls. Same as any other bastard out there. Same as some guy thinking

I owe him anything because he's nice." She spat. "I don't want Fulcher to catch him. I want Fulcher to kill him."

She was right about all of it. The killer didn't care about men or boys. This was all about hurting girls. Kids. He hated the women they might grow to be; he would kill those women before they were in the world. Murdering Carl and Steve Cameron had been incidental. His targets were always girls and that was all that mattered to him. Kill the girls; kill the women. A man who threw his fists after a few beers; a man who'd think nothing of spiking a woman's drink in a bar; a man who murdered teenage girls to rob the world of the women they would be.

Kelly was right about every single thing.

"Same here," I said lamely.

Mollified, she relaxed. "How did you get involved in this shite?"

"It's a long story," I replied, not wanting to get into stories about my dead sister or the other murdered girls or handsome twenty-year olds who spoke in children's voices. Or about what had happened to Steve Cameron and his family barely a mile from where we sat.

"You knew Carl Cameron, didn't you?"

That made me jump but I kept my voice quiet. "What makes you say that?"

"All Fulcher said was you had a connection to Sprignall. He didn't say a word about who's killing girls, but he did say you know someone here." She brushed fresh snow from her legs. "I knew him, too. The whole family. He wasn't a bad guy but he knew bad guys. That was the sort of thing I could give to Fulcher. Who knows who. Who's dealing to who. Who's planning what."

She was an informant. It sounded ridiculous to think of something out of the London crime world in our nondescript town, but then there was nothing nondescript about what was happening here.

We sat in silence for a while, close enough to each other to feel a bit of body heat without actually touching. The night trickled by while snow dropped on us and the bench soundlessly. Everything I knew—job, flat, my quiet, empty life—dropped away with each falling flake until I felt no more grounded to the earth than a beam of moonlight.

"Someone's watching us."

She said it barely louder than a breath. My body temperature dropped even lower as I came back to myself. Mouth hanging open, hands two lumps of useless rock and the knives in my coat way out of reach because I was a frozen chunk of stone attached to the bench.

You do this right now or you lose.

It was Fulcher in my head. I hunched slightly to disguise the movement of reaching for my chest. "Where?"

"Round where you came from." She continued to speak in a whisper. "To the right of the path, there's an opening in the bushes. I saw white. I think it's a face."

While I'd been staring at nothing, she'd been on the lookout. Cheeks flushed, hands soaked with sweat inside my gloves, I twisted to look the way she'd said.

Nothing but black beyond the falling snow. Even so, something watched me as I watched for it.

Something? Someone, Jimmy. This is a person.

Fulcher sounded way too desperate in my head for me to believe him. Abruptly, the night and the high windows in the flats above the shops felt like they were bearing down on us. Same with the massive sheet of sky flecked with the pinpricks of starlight, the small squares of unused grass and twisting alleys and roads throughout Sprignall. Same with the miles of family homes and avenues and lives between me and the locked door of my flat. Same with Ella's face, small and pale and forever thirteen, and her eyes glancing at me, her big brother, through the heavy fringe she always kept hanging over her forehead.

Same with the never-ending months and years since Robert Fry kept her prisoner for days and raped and murdered her on camera for the entertainment of men like him, men I wished were there right in front of me so I could use my knife on them and turn the white as bone ground into steaming puddles of their blood.

"You going to do it?" Kelly murmured.

I saw it. The same white of a face in the black that had lurked in the shot from the camera peering down at the front of the hospital before Steve and I had somehow ventured outside to find a girl buried alive, before Steve had gone after the murderer and been gutted by his own brother as a reward.

I saw Robert Fry peering at us from the bushes.

I went for my knife. Then I went for Kelly.

Chapter Fifty-Four

Lean fingers grabbed the sleeve of my coat. She pulled and I crashed against her narrow chest, the knife wedged between us while she thrashed. Grunting, I managed to turn the blade and our eyes met.

The knife smacked into the ground right beside her waist.

She made a horrible shrill sound, and bucked against me.

My fist struck snow, saved from the pain of the impact by the thick material of my gloves.

Kelly wailed even as her hand, covered by my greater weight, fumbled in the side pocket of her baggy coat.

Red splattered over the white. Kelly twisted to face towards the greenery. I hit sludge again and again; she grasped my shoulders and hissed a word between her fake cries.

"Roll."

I did so, spinning over, Kelly on top of me, and rolling further so we kicked up snowfall stained red and the knife fell from my hands. Panting, I tried to throw another punch, but it made a weak splat as all I could do was thump a melted puddle.

Gasping, Kelly shifted under my weight and swore. "Nobody's coming," she said.

I peered back towards the left of the little bench. She was right. Nothing ran from the shrubbery. No white face floated in the gloom. If anyone had been there, they'd probably just been someone on their way home who'd seen a couple on a bench and wondered what we were doing. Nobody challenged me or came to rescue a woman from being attacked. Not a single light shone in any of the windows of the flats. Our brief struggle had either been ignored by the locals or they'd heard and not given a shit. Convinced it was the latter, I remembered what Steve had said about the people of Sprignall being better than any image given to the rest of the town. All bollocks, it turned out. They were just as selfish and careless as anyone else.

"Fuck." I spat it, suddenly furious, exhausted and frozen all at the same time.

"Get off me," Kelly panted.

I rose and extended a hand. Our pretence of violence no longer had any point. She brushed her coat, took my hand and staggered upright. The stage blood she'd squeezed from a bottle made her sleeves sticky and turned the faded blue of her jeans into a load of black stains. Around us, splashes of red were as dark as they'd been on the pathway beside the river and I couldn't look at them for longer than a couple of seconds.

Steps approached from the same direction Kelly had approached, and a clear voice called to us. "It's okay. I'm with Fulcher. It's King."

The man came into view. For a second, I didn't recognise him. Breathing too hard and alternating between roasting and freezing, I had to spit.

"Where's Fulcher?" I asked.

"On his way." King eyed both of us. "Worth a go, eh?" It didn't sound at all genuine.

"No." I shook with reaction and the last of any heat faded to be replaced by bone-deep chill. The pretence of the attack and struggle had taken it out of me. The comfort and peace of my flat seemed like they were much further away than a few miles. Twenty past three in the morning and everything I wanted might as well have been on the moon.

"You okay?" I asked Kelly.

She nodded and spat. "Worth the money," she said and that sounded no more like she meant it than King attempting to convince us the staged attack was worth the attempt of drawing the killer out. She made a move towards King who was already turning away, presumably to lead us to a car or van on the quiet road.

Where's Fulcher?

In my head, I asked the question I just asked King and while no answer came, sudden fear did. Fulcher should have been with us, not King. Not King who'd come alone like he'd been waiting for his moment.

I got between Kelly and King. He heard my lurching steps and the crunch below and turned back, eyebrows raised.

"Do me a favour," I said. "You get Fulcher here right now. You tell him I want to speak to him."

At my back, Kelly tried to move past. I shifted to block her; she came to the other side, little boots kicking through the crumbling white. I reached for her. She shook my hand away, either dismissing me as any kind of safety or dismissing the need for it.

"It's all right, mate." King raised a hand. "Just stay calm, okay? He's on his way. Give him a second."

As if in support of his words, King's radio crackled. It had probably been doing so for minutes when all I'd been listening for was the approach of a man who liked to kill girls and who could be working alone or working with anyone.

Anyone.

I swallowed piercing breaths that burned my throat. Something in my chest ached and it wasn't the temperature or the struggle with Kelly. Everything that had happened since the Saturday morning was out of my control. Every single thing in my world had been taken over by nothing I understood or wanted to think about.

"Where were you watching us from, King?"

"What?" King stared at me. I didn't need to see Kelly's face to know she got it.

"Where did you watch us from?" I kept my hand at my side like I was about to draw a gun from a holster. Although King was close, I estimated it would take him three seconds to cross to me. Three seconds to get to my real knife.

Silence punctuated a moment later by the whisper of the cop's breath while all around, the winter sank its claws into us.

"Back the way I came," King said eventually. "All right? Just down there. . ." He glanced at Kelly, then back to me. "Relax."

In the second of King lowering his hand, I promised myself I would not become involved in the world again after this.

Let the world go. Let it burn.

"Yeah. Okay." I inhaled another frost-filled breath. "Just. . .not having a good night."

"I understand. It's all right. This way."

He set out towards the precinct, big boots stomping. Kelly gave me her first genuine smile and a brief nod I took to mean respect, and followed the cop. I moved to do the same.

King's head exploded.

Chapter Fifty-Five

Ignoring the loud questions from the first of what he knew would be many reporters with their cameras eager to catch every second of the latest crime, Fulcher crossed to the edge of the scene and signalled for several milling officers to join him. Faces pinched by their rage and the cold, they did so.

"This is as bad as it gets." Despite the great waves of noise from the vehicles arriving, their sirens singing to the estate, and the abusive chants from the angry locals kept back by close to thirty officers with riot shields and their dogs, Fulcher pitched his voice low. Anything carrying to the people beyond his colleagues would just make a shit situation even worse.

"I won't bullshit any of you. One of our own is down and I want our guy dead. Not nicked. Not charged. I want that motherfucker dead. You hear me?"

They heard. He saw his own rage reflected on every face, in every pair of eyes slitted against the massive flakes blown back and forth by the gusting wind. He glanced at Hannan, one of the first on the scene after the call went out. Like the others, the man had been off duty since midnight and probably asleep in the safety and comfort of his home. It hadn't stopped the boy racing to this mess, though. Ditto the half a dozen others. Grief and hurt made Hannan's face a strained sheet and Fulcher knew he was probably feeling King's shooting the most. They'd been tight.

"He won't have got more than a couple of miles through this shit. We've got the roads sealed; the dogs are out and—" Fulcher jabbed a finger directly above as the chopper swooped low as if on cue. "They'll see the fucker if he's out there. Keep your shit together. Keep calm and in order, yeah? We'll make this right."

"Where the fuck did he get a gun?" Rourke asked, her voice high and cracking on the last word. "Who the fuck is this piece of shit, Clyde?"

"Enough," Fulcher said, not quite yelling it. Where the snow-covered grass met the uneven paving slabs of the precinct, the TV vultures bellowed their questions and panned their cameras back and forth, hopefully not picking up much more than the shapes of police indistinct in the swirl of flying flakes. Along the jumble of shrubs surrounding the play area, officers with their dogs tramped over the land, the animals sniffing pieces of spiky bushes, dismissing the green as unimportant and moving on a few inches. While he scanned other police on their radios and phones, and the arrival of several more vans with their lights blazing through the milling flakes, Fulcher tried to picture the snaking alleyways that fed off the estate's main road, connecting squares and car parks with flats and miles of ugly terraces. A genius of sixties planning totally unsuited to the twenty-first century and keeping the scum off the streets. And the scum who'd murder an officer before abducting a girl who had nothing to do with the case, a girl Fulcher had got involved in this fuck up which meant he was responsible for every single second of what had gone wrong tonight.

He gave nothing away on his face as Rourke got herself under control and someone shouted Fulcher's name from off to the side.

"Your priority right now is keeping it calm here," Fulcher told them. "It's getting ugly." He jerked his head at the crowd, easily fifty of them and more coming by the minute. "They're fucked off with all the shit that's happened here and they see this as payback on us. Just remember they want you to kick off. Don't let them push your buttons. Get with the line. Keep it." He took a breath and repeated his words from a moment before. "We will make this right."

They jogged to the uniform line, bulking it out, and the volley of roars from the locals grew louder now they had fresh targets.

Fulcher heard his name again, yelled from his right. He caught sight of a waving hand and marched between the rusting swings to DS Alan Lamb who came off a call on his mobile as Fulcher reached him. Lamb's narrow features, made thinner by the freeze, gave him the look of a panto villain.

"What is it?" Fulcher asked.

Behind Lamb, three of the dog handlers and their animals pulled to the sides, exposing a piece of grass. The dogs yipped in excitement; their chunky paws kicked up puffs of white.

"Just found this," Lamb said. "Didn't want to make a big deal. The cameras are all over the fucking place."

Fulcher appreciated the man's thinking. While there was little chance a shot could be taken that would reveal anything, they couldn't risk it. Keeping his movements calm and slow, he paced forward and peered down to the land between the dogs.

"Fucker," he hissed, then glanced at Lamb. "You got forensics coming?"

"Any second." Lamb waved his radio. "Most of them are on the path that goes out of the park." He looked over Fulcher's shoulder. "En route."

There was no need for Fulcher to turn. The white suits would come; they'd seal off this few square feet and the TV fucks would see the investigation focusing on the area beside the bushes and the bullshit speculation would be online within seconds.

"Soon as you know a thing, call me," Fulcher said and turned away.

Head down, he crossed back to the ground of the shopping area. From the assembled officers, a voice boomed, ordering the public to back up, the command met at once with mocking jeers. Ignoring any attempts at eye contact from colleagues who wanted to know what the hell King had been doing in this dump so late, Fulcher made it to his car, yanked on the driver's side door and slid inside. Seated in the passenger seat, Jimmy Marshall made no move.

"You warm enough?" Fulcher asked and pulled a glove off to test the hot air. It made the hairs on his knuckles feel like they were crackling and that was fine with him. Anything was better than walking through the freezer of outside.

"Fine," Jimmy replied. He did not stop hugging himself, Fulcher noted. He kept his gaze ahead on the milling bodies, unwilling to look Jimmy in the eye as he spoke.

"There's no sign of him. Or Kelly. Only a few prints that end in the bushes. After that, they just vanish."

Jimmy said nothing.

Fulcher discreetly checked his watch. Twenty to five. He couldn't get a decent grip on any sense of time. Just as it felt like long hours had passed while the police descended on Sprignall yet again, bare seconds could have elapsed since he ran from his car at the shot. King dead on the ground for over an hour and while that would normally have been long enough for their boy to have made it miles away, they had to bet on the weather slowing him down. Either way, Fulcher had to move, to do something other than give orders to his people while the dead hours of the night ticked closer and closer to the new morning.

"We've got the dogs out, the roads are closed in and out of the estate and the bird up there, it can cover miles so if they're on foot, we'll see him."

Still, Jimmy said nothing.

"There's one thing, though." Fulcher watched two idiots from the crowd of locals lumber forward, closing in on the wall of police. One swung a punch and three officers brought him down. Even with the doors and windows of his car shut, the roar of abuse that followed reached Fulcher. He steeled himself for a surge of bodies meeting his officers and their shields and reached for his radio to order more bodies to the line. Within seconds, the wannabe troublemaker had been carted to a waiting van and the snarls and barks of several dogs sent the crowd back a good few feet. Not for the first time, Fulcher had to wonder what motivated the sort of thinking that said go outside in this godforsaken hour, most dressed in coats too thin for the temperature, to record every second of the noise and movement and to curse the very people trying to keep the peace.

Speaking without taking his eyes off the scene ahead, he said: "On the snow back near the side of the playground. Blood sprayed on the ground to mark it. He wanted us to see it. And the message. Written in sticks, twigs, dog ends and blood."

Finally, Jimmy shifted. He looked at Fulcher.

"Same as in the house?" he muttered and Fulcher fought off the memory of standing in the Cameron's living room with the bloody writing smeared on the wall.

"Same as in the house," he agreed and forced the words out. "'I killed Ella Griffin.'"

Chapter Fifty-Six

Hearing it spoken so baldly threatened to undo me. For the first time since the long months after Ella's murder, I felt my mind wanting to come loose. It was a uniquely horrible sensation; everything clear and good inside that made thinking logically possible snapping from one end to the other with only a few bolts holding it in place and keeping me from going insane.

"Robert Fry," I said, barely aware I'd been going to speak.

"He thinks he is," Fulcher replied. He remained facing straight ahead where the street lights and the moon illuminated dozens of angry bodies, barking dogs and a wall of police doubtless all ready to smash some heads if anyone tried any shit. They'd lost a colleague and friend tonight and barely any of them would know what the hell King had been doing in Sprignall. Fulcher's little plan involving Kelly and me would only have been known to a very select few and now a police officer was just as dead as the four girls. Five if I counted my sister's murder.

I didn't know the man, but I knew what Fulcher was thinking as clearly as if the thoughts had been in my head. An operation out of the official investigation that had involved two civilians, putting both at risk, had resulted in the murder of a police officer and the kidnap of a young girl. Fulcher's career and probably his freedom were over.

"It's over. We find the fucker and we kill him. End of story," he said.

"You'll go to prison," I croaked and he stared at me.

"I will anyway. And if I don't, I might as well. That bastard is a dead man either way."

Something inside Fulcher had changed; some switch had been flicked. The police officer was gone and this new man had come in his place. Law was forgotten or at least shoved rudely to one side. Whether Fulcher had always possessed that potential or what was being done in our town had flicked that switch, I didn't know. Either way, we'd both gone over the edge.

Light bloomed above the car and surrounding area for a moment before coating the slush kicked up by dozens of running feet. The helicopter. It dropped until it was maybe only fifty feet over the nearest houses, then ascended before moving into a large circle. Fulcher took the noise as a moment to collect himself while I peered out of the windows.

So many police. So many cars. The estate's locals were in the process of being pushed back to a makeshift barrier. iPhones were raised above heads, a few flashing but most silently recording. Women in dressing gowns under coats; men holding their kids up to get a decent look, and teenage boys on bikes circling the crowd. All around the people, the dirty drifts looked like muck in the little illumination, and all of the windows in the flats over the shops blazed their light. We'd finally woken the estate. And all we needed to do was get a man's head blown off and a young woman kidnapped by a killer.

"I'm done, Jimmy. You get that. Thirty-five fucking years and I'm over."

Fulcher grabbed my shoulders and pulled me close like we were about to kiss.

"I get that," I whispered and he searched my face.

"Sunrise at about seven thirty. We've got two and a half hours."

We've.

I knew what he meant but still had to hear it. If nothing else, it would make the thunder of the helicopter and the fury from the officers grieving the murder of one of their own go away a tiny amount.

Fulcher saw all of that on my face. He let go of my arms to open his coat. He didn't need to do it fully for me to see the shining metal of the gun. It was a small weapon but chunky. Any make or model of it were a mystery; its purpose showed clearly in the gleaming line of the short barrel.

"We find him. We get Kelly back if we can and we shoot the cunt. Understood?"

I'd never held a gun in my life let alone fired one. It didn't matter. I wanted Fulcher's gun in my hand. I wanted that weight.

I wanted to put a bullet in that thing's head. For the dead girls. For Ella. For myself.

"Understood," I said.

He nodded. "Right. The river or the hospital. The two places he's found you. We found nothing by the river. Not a trace of anything out of the ordinary and we went over every fucking inch of that pathway and riverbank."

"You think he's at the hospital? You think he's hiding there?"

In my mind's eye, I saw the long corridors, all turned into a murky ash by the sealed windows and the total lack of power. I heard footsteps echoing and I heard him laughing at me, at all of us.

Come and have a look, Jimmy. Come and find me. Come and stop me before I do it all again. All those dead girls. Every single one begging me to stop hurting them. Each one just a waste of skin and bones and something for me to play with. All of them the same, Jimmy. Fucking wastes. So, you come and find me here. I'm waiting.

I had to close my eyes at the mad ranting. Doing so didn't help.

"Jimmy? You there?"

Eyes open again, I met Fulcher's gaze and tried to ignore all the angry life a matter of feet away. They'd already sealed King's body from view. That didn't stop the locals from raising their phones even higher, all desperate to get a shot of the dead man or a glimpse of his spilled blood.

"I know where he's going."

"Where?"

"The same place he killed my sister."

Fulcher's face twisted as he tried to come up with a reply to that which didn't involve acknowledging what I'd said was impossible. "The shop?" he muttered.

"Three shopping areas in Sprignall. One gets torched the other night; this one is a murder scene. He's in the third. It's on Middleton Place. The one. . ."

I had to stop for a few seconds. "The one Ella died in, it used to be a corner shop back in the day. He's there."

"How can you be sure?"

"Because it's part of his game." The surety wasn't a simple emotion. It was like a light going on behind my eyes. "He started it there, didn't he? He'll end it there. If he's telling the truth about finishing it by dawn."

"If," Fulcher echoed. While the interior of the car was thick with gloom, I still made out enough of the big copper to see his exhaustion. I was with a man just about done in.

"Yeah. If. But I think he is. He's said it's a game. I think he's playing with certain rules. They're fucked up. They're as mental as he is, but they're still his rules. He started this with my sister. He's got Kelly. He'll try to end it in the same place." I had to wonder if so little time really had passed since Saturday. Not even four days of this hell. Of course, the fourth started at dawn.

Ella's anniversary.

"He started it with my sister. He'll want to end it with me."

Chapter Fifty-Seven

They were nowhere.

The snow crumbling and breaking below Kelly's dragging boots and the constant prick of the sharp air stabbing at her exposed skin where her t-shirt, fleece and coat and ridden up to expose the skin of her lower back were all gone. Same with the scratch of spiky bushes he'd shoved her through raking their claws on the hands. And same with the incline of the land that ran alongside the sleeping industrial estate. Everything gone and all she had to hold on to was the raw pain of the cut he'd dug into the side of her thigh a second after knocking Jimmy to the ground with a fist wrapped around the gun and all she'd been able to hear was the crashing echo of the shot that took off the cop's head and all she'd known was her terror burned to ash by the bolt of fire racing up from her leg when he wounded her and her blood spurted on to the snow.

And now nothing and now nowhere.

It had come a moment after reaching what she thought was the level ground of the pavement and road.

What little light illuminated their surroundings and the shape of his body so close to hers winked out and what Kelly could only think of as a hole took the place of everything. They fell without dropping, collapsed without breaking their stumbling lurch, and the snapping of ice slipped away as easily as a tired breath leaving Kelly and the man who was not a man alone at the bottom of a thousand-mile-deep hole.

But not alone.

Kelly could make out nothing and didn't want to. Having the stabbing pain filling her leg along with the horrible grip of his hand clasping her forearm was enough to take nearly all of her focus. Even so, she knew they were not alone. Not here in the hole the killer called home. Wind, much colder than the northerly gale that had streamed across the county for hours, slid fingers through her hair, caressing each strand with a curious touch and a thing that was not a bird yet still flew and swooped and streaked in the space above. In that space, the world she knew was far away enough to be forever out of reach. She was dead and alive in the hole and all she could hang on to, as much as it terrified her and angered her to do so, was the staggering, panting creature who'd hurt her, who'd killed children and a cop right in front of her and Jimmy.

The detonation of bone, skull and blood. All raining in great sprays.

The millisecond of sight when she'd been unable to blink and so, in that fraction of time, she'd had an imprint flashed on to her eyes: gleaming white flash of the gunshot turning the white of broken pieces of bone into shining stars and a suggestion of meat that belonged buried under the man's head now exposed to the elements.

All of it gone in less time than it took to realise what had happened. Then the shriek rising from her leg when her abductor swiped a knife over her thigh and blood splatted over her shin, shoe and the ground.

And now nothing.

Kelly closed her eyes and tried to ignore the possibilities of what might be above and around, the sense of life much worse than the man who'd abducted her, the intelligences darkly curious about her and her place in their home, something terrible unseen but felt along with their insanity. They stabbed and hammered at the thin surface of the world, madly eager to break through to winter and flesh and blood where that blood could so easily be spilled.

Wandering in her mind without words, not willing to think of her daughter in this place, Kelly held on to the burning that cooked her leg, and the squelch of hot blood soaking through her jeans into her boot and sock.

Down below her ankle where she kept a small knife strapped underneath her jeans.

The man dragged her on through the nothing place, moving further into its absence, moving closer to the crumbling surface between one world she knew and another where a great unknown walked.

Chapter Fifty-Eight

Ten minutes after speeding away from the scene of King's murder, we skidded over black ice, bounced off the kerb and finally came to a stop at the rear of Sprignall's final row of shops. As much of a depressing hole the first had been even before the girl's killing and the fire, it was a palace compared to where we'd come as my watch read close to half four. Goffsmill Way pushed through Sprignall for about a mile at its edge. If we continued north, we'd cross the parkway that joined the A98 and end up in miles of fields, woods and not much else. I had the idea the police didn't like to come to this part of the estate. Too secluded, too many alleyways, too few working street lights. And I knew I wasn't imagining the atmosphere. It slid out of the cracks in the paving slabs, from the bricks marked by damp and mostly from the rear of the eight shops. There were fingers in that rank awareness and I knew it wasn't only imagination that felt crawling things burrowing out of the stone walls, spreading their filth to the ground and eager to welcome me to their home.

To the dark.

Wordlessly, Fulcher got out of the car. I took a few breaths and did the same. We'd parked in a narrow car park, not bothering with any of the bays. There were no other vehicles in sight which wasn't a surprise given the hour and all the shit going down on the other side of Sprignall. Plenty for the locals to see out that way; not so much here with the high gates sealing every yard at the back of each shop, the paint peeling from the slats in the gates; the broken windows in the flats above, and the only sound for Fulcher and me to hear the hiss of wind skittering over the white ground.

Still without speaking, Fulcher crunched to the boot of his car, opened it and pulled out a thin object. It took me a second to realise he was offering me a police baton. I took it, glad to feel the sturdy weight that meant business. Keeping his eyes locked on mine, Fulcher slid his coat zip down a few inches, pulled it open and let the moonlight catch on the barrel of the gun secured to his chest.

"We do this properly," he murmured and pulled the gun free. In his large hand, it should have been swallowed by his grip. As it was, he gripped the handle and kept the weapon aimed at the ground as he slid a small torch from another pocket.

"Whatever happens, he dies today." Fulcher put no emphasis or anger on his words because there was no need for either. "You smash the fucker's head in. I blow his face off. Either way, he dies and I take full responsibility. Happily."

"You'll go to prison."

"I'm fucked either way, Jimmy. What happened tonight with Mike and Kelly, it's on me. Completely on me. At best, I lose my job and my pension and my thirty-five years on the Force. At worse, I get sent down. As long as that piece of shit is dead, I don't really care. If he's in there and we get chance before he makes his move, he dies."

Under one of his heavy boots, snow crumbled.

"Clyde."

Fulcher stopped. I wondered briefly if it was the first time I'd addressed him as Clyde.

"We have to admit something here. It's our last chance to do it."

"What?"

"He's not human. Call him a ghost or whatever the fuck you like, he's not human."

It was out in the open and free from my chest and throat. The secret thought trapped inside for long hours and days while children were murdered and Steve Cameron grieved for his niece and a poor drunk sod had his face shredded after serving his purpose and I was haunted by my dead sister just as I was haunted by a monster that dead girls spoke through because he had killed them. . . all that kept from my voice and all of it made flesh by a few words.

"Jimmy, I know this guy has fucked with your head—"

"How does he disappear? How does he just vanish? How does he speak in different voices? Christ, he even speaks like he's much older than he is. Like he's. . ." I couldn't verbalise the rest of the thought I'd had during our insane conversation before he came for me earlier that day. It remained stuck to the inside of my head.

Like he's old. Like he's nowhere near being young. Like he's been around for years.

"How the fuck did he get in and out of the hospital?" I lunged across to Fulcher, my heart like thunder and my hands eager to swing a hammer into a monster's face again and again. "He's Robert Fry. He killed my sister seventeen years ago. He's back and he's killing more girls."

Fulcher licked a flake from his upper lip. "Say he is, Jimmy. Say he is. What do you want to do about it? He's killing girls. Little girls. What do you want do about it?"

While curtains of white fell and any number of eyes watched us from the unilluminated windows and the slight suggestion of the police helicopter's flight rumbled a mile away, I spoke the only words that needed saying.

"Kill him."

***

By the looks of the old gate, there should been at least two bolts and padlocks, one at the top and one at the bottom. Neither remained and the sliding bolts were broken chunks of rusting metal.

Fulcher signalled for me to move and I wanted to tell him to do it. With the gun and the torch, that wasn't happening. Gripping the handle of his baton, I flexed fingers close to freezing even with wearing gloves, and pushed on the gate.

A build-up of snow at its foot made the old wood drag almost silently. Clumps broke apart, revealing the edge of a drain cover. Grunting, I gave the gate a final shove and it swung open all the way.

Fulcher's torch panned across the yard and the back doors to the shop. The yard was narrow. A small storage shed filled the left side. An industrial bin blocked its door. I flashed back to the alley next to the pub on the Saturday lunchtime and the sad sight of a dead girl's bare ankles gleaming white from below the bin.

"You okay?" Fulcher whispered and I realised I'd made an odd noise that wasn't anywhere near a word. In response, I made a move to go ahead and Fulcher raised an arm to stop me.

"No heroics, Jimmy. Our friend won't hesitate to kill either or both of us. You're not Iron Man. Don't storm into this."

"Together, then."

Fulcher grinned and I briefly wished I'd known him outside all the shit. He was a good guy.

We took a couple of steps forward and it hit me, really hit me, where I was. My sister's death right here and it didn't matter that so many years had passed. This was it. She could have been killed the day before, not in a different decade, and I was entering her last place, come to taste, smell, hear and see that day brought back to life.

"Jimmy?" Fulcher breathed and his torch light landed on markings straight ahead.

Despite the size of it, we hadn't been at the right angle to see it from the gate. A few feet into the yard and there it was, spread below the snowfall. A jumble of debris, a pattern of rubbish taken from bushes and gutters and pavements to spell out two words that had waited for Fulcher and me but mostly just me.

Written in the carpet of the blizzard: WELCOME HOME.

"I can't go in," I said.

Out of nowhere, wind blew straight across the yard and sent a dancing drift of white over the message. It vanished a second later and it didn't matter. We'd seen it. It was gone.

"Jimmy, listen. We're running out time." Fulcher showed me his watch. "If this guy really is playing by some rules, we've got a couple of hours left. So, you with me or not?"

I didn't answer him. Inside, I asked the same question to Ella.

You with me or not?

Blinding light cast by the tall lamps.

The thin mattress under her back.

The fire in her centre, in her stomach.

The ruptured body she no longer knows is hers.

The stink of the mouldy walls and the shelving units.

The camera with its black eye.

Hands on her neck. Air fading, fading while growing, growing, an absence.

A giant hole she is falling into.

"Jimmy?"

I glanced at Fulcher and raised my baton. It—and I—were eager to bash a skull into bloody pieces. Over and over and over.

Together, we advanced on the shop's back door and Fulcher swept his torchlight over the handle. What remained of the handle. It hung by a twisted piece of metal; the door shut but clearly unlocked. Fulcher scanned the rest of the door, then signalled for me to crouch against the wall by its side. When it opened, I'd have some cover from the inside of the building. Fulcher tapped himself with the light then, nodded at the wall to the right of the door. I understood. We'd frame the entrance and if anyone came running, they'd have their backs to us.

Taking my place, I breathed as quietly as possible and watched Fulcher reach for the handle with his gun hand. Still holding his torch, he extended three fingers.

I nodded.

Three fingers became two. Then one.

He pulled on the door.

It flapped open, caught in the wind.

A second later, I was on my feet, sprinting into the back of the shop, baton swinging while the building's insides swallowed me.

Chapter Fifty-Nine

"Down."

Fulcher's order was a war cry at my back. I dropped, hit rock hard ground and dust. In front, the light from Fulcher's torch found a bare wall stained with flaking plaster and a few squat cupboards. The white beam spun all over, offering glimpses of decay devouring the wall and floor. No furniture, no signs of life. If the place had been used as a shop, it hadn't been for a long time. Looking back, I saw Fulcher crouched, making himself a small target, gun outstretched, his mouth set in a firm line.

"You silly fucker," he said, not unkindly, and rose to offer me a hand up.

Standing, we saw it at the same time. A huge stain marking the floor a few inches from where I'd dropped. Oil-like, it spread in all directions, the liquid splashing a foot across in a messy blemish.

"That's blood," Fulcher muttered and scanned the wall at our side with his torch. "And I'm willing to bet it's from Bill."

"Bill?" I croaked, feeling slow and stupid.

"Your mate from the pub Saturday afternoon. I'm guessing he was attacked here and left to walk back to The Boar. Our friend has been here, Jimmy, but he's gone now. This place is—" He broke off, clearly about to finish his sentence with the word dead before remembering my connection.

"He's gone," Fulcher said.

I crouched again, reaching for the stain and not daring to touch it for a jumble of mad reasons. Maybe it'd still be hot. Maybe the red would burn my fingertips. Maybe I'd get some fucked up vision of Bill having his face shredded by a broken bottle. And maybe it wasn't Bill's blood at all, but rather my sister's. A ghost of a memory come back to mark the building and welcome me here for the first time in years as the message out in the yard had before the weather erased it.

A sob rose; I swallowed over and over until I was able to keep it right at the back of my throat where it stung like vomit.

Fulcher shone his torch on a second door, this one separating the storage area from the main part of the shop. "I'll try it and we get the fuck out, okay?"

"Okay." I managed the word and that was all.

Fulcher crossed towards the door and a mad, desperate scream punched my ears.

Screaming back, I lunged upright, baton swinging, hitting nothing but the dirty air, and Fulcher was a lumbering shape racing back towards me. The noise went on, lungs seemingly filled with infinite breath and hurt, a non-stop note of terrible pain, and the torchlight cast a shaking white on the brown walls and floor.

"Out, get out," Fulcher hollered over the noise, and managed to punch my arm without the baton decking him.

His torch caught a shape on the opposite wall, a small piece of white caught in the illumination and I tried to yell at him. There was no need; Fulcher saw the same and somehow managed to steady his hand.

On the far wall and held in place by thick strands of tape, a mobile screeched at us.

We met each other's eye and Fulcher's face was the same shocked realisation as mine.

The ringtone was a looping shriek of agony.

***

It was time.

Fry glanced down at the prone girl and smelled the tang of her sweat, blood and fear. She hadn't spoken since their speedy exit from the playground and the dead police officer. While he'd known her thoughts and denial as they travelled and he'd taken her to the underside, they'd been of no concern. They were even less so now they'd reached their destination. Standing at the window and facing the town while she lay at his feet, a shaking mess with one hand on her shin, her fingers splayed towards the knife under her bloody jeans, Fry imagined the first lick of purple touching the sky. The ever-present snowflakes, falling and blown, made it much harder to picture than at any point over the last few days, but it was there all the same. Coming out of the black, Jimmy's last chance to stop Fry's work.

Coming out of the black, either its work would go on forever or it would have to settle for bringing Jimmy back to the world.

Further into the eastern sky hanging low over Lawfield's fields and secret spaces, the night would soon begin its slow, steady departure.

Morning was closing in.

Resting a hand on the seldom used landline, Fry picked up the receiver and dialled a number.

Chapter Sixty

We went for the phone at the same time, our boots tracking melting snow and kicking through the dust. Fulcher hit the wall ahead of me, tore the mobile free and ripped a dangling piece of tape loose. Answering the call and silencing the screaming, he shouted down the line.

"Where are you, you motherfucker?"

My ears still full of the shriek, I tried to look everywhere even though the torchlight shone on me and a section of the wall.

In a flat tone devoid of any anger, Fulcher said: "Wait."

He pulled the mobile from his head, studied the display for a second before stabbing it with a finger.

"You're on speaker," he said in the same flat tone and mouthed to me: it's him.

"Hello, Jimmy."

Robert Fry. On the phone. Alive. Completely, totally alive and speaking to me.

"You there?" Fry asked.

Answer him, Ella said.

"I'm here." Shaking, I said his name. "Robert."

"Robert?" Fry managed to genuinely sound confused, an emotion I didn't believe for a second.

"Robert Fry. Don't fucking bullshit me."

"Robert Fry." He could have been tasting a strange food. "I was Robert Fry. Or I'm not and he was just with me. I thought I burned him away with the girl in the phone box. Always in the back of my head with his noise. Always wanting me to stop, to go away and let him stay dead just like the others used to say. So many of them. I've lost track of their names and what they did, but I can tell you that not one really regretted what they did in life. Not one. All a bunch of selfish, lying shits trapped in the dark until I found them and we. . ." He trailed off; his silence amused. "Until we took our little trips. Anyway, Fry might be dead again now. I don't really know. All I can tell you is I haven't heard him since I burned him. If he's not dead again, then he's burning. Is that what you like to hear?"

Fulcher answered for me, moving his mouth closer to the phone. "Who the fuck are you? Some little shit who thinks he's a bad man? Get your jollies off on old murders, do you? Go on; tell me. You're Fry's long-lost son." He scoffed. "Are you bollocks? At best, you turn out to be some bastard kid of one of the others Fry knew."

"Don't be stupid. They're all either dead or in prison." He rattled off the name of Fry's group, the men who'd been teachers, doctors, an estate agent; men with lives and relatives and houses and blood on their hands. "I'm not related to any of them."

"Then why do you kill the girls?" Fulcher demanded. "Tough guy hurting children. I mean, seriously. It must take a rock-hard bloke to torture and kill teenage girls. Fucking hell, you're a coward. No proper rucks for you. No chance of going up against someone who might be able to beat you in a fight. Nope. You're too scared of that just like you're scared of those girls. Kids. You're frightened of kids. Girls. Same as any other shit who bullies people. You just take it up a notch because you're scared of them." He was on a furious roll. "Let me guess. Didn't like your mummy. Or maybe liked her too much, yeah? Or a sister? Christ. What a fucking waste you are. All those kids you hurt, each one with more potential than you would ever have. Same every time with fuckers like you. You've got nothing to offer the world, so you think the world shouldn't have those who can do some good. Hurt kids and you hurt the world, isn't that it? Let me tell you, son. If you're so dangerous, then why go after girls who can't fight back? I know why. Because you don't have the nuts to do anything else. Hurt girls and feel like you matter, right? Well, sad news. You don't matter in the least."

"It's nothing to do with you," Fry replied, and in the same breath, he changed to a child's voice, a girl racing through her words without a single pause, and it was like hearing a recording come to life or a memory made flesh. "This is between me and my brother. This is about us, not you, Clyde. Me and Jimmy and his world where he's safe and I'm not, where he keeps it all out, even me. Even me after what Fry did to me on the ground where you're standing with his hands on my neck, choking me, choking me and the camera watching and—"

"Shut up." I howled the words, my throat on fire and still unable to warm any part of my body from the early morning air and the bricks turned into chunks of ice. Bending double, I closed my eyes as tightly as I could, saw all the way down through a giant hole of a void to where Ella lived now, forever thirteen, and I was forever the brother unable to save her from the world.

The world.

The world where I was safe.

Jerking upright, I came close to dropping my weapon as I reached for Fulcher, staring at the man. Fry—in my sister's voice—had fallen silent at my insane scream, and there was nothing for a second before I tasted the words I know where he is, and took a breath to hiss them to Fulcher.

Then Fry spoke again and it was all his own voice, the one I'd hated within seconds of hearing him speak at his trial sixteen years before.

"You're all so easy to manipulate. I wish it was more of a challenge, but it's really not. Not after all these years. These long, long years."

"What the hell are you talking about?" Fulcher hissed.

The reply came back immediately. "This isn't anything to do with you. So, kill yourself."

Fulcher rolled his eyes, a man who'd doubtless heard mad shit like that for years. "Yeah. Of course."

"Kill yourself or I start cutting bits out of Kelly."

Fulcher stared at me and I saw something terrible.

He didn't know what to do.

Chapter Sixty-One

"Your choice, Clyde. Your life or Kelly bleeds some more. I've already knifed her leg. Want me to start hacking at her properly?" There was a pause, then a faint sobbing. "She's crying right at my feet. I know she's a bit older than my usual lot, but I'm not fussy at this stage. And that's the other thing. You're running out of time. Dawn in what? Two hours, maybe. You know the deal. I'm sticking to my rules. Catch me by dawn and it's all over. Don't catch me and I'll never stop killing. Ella's anniversary will be the start of more deaths than you can believe. I'll make Ella famous. She'll be the first girl out of all the girls so what are you going to do?"

Fulcher wiped sweat from his forehead with the back of his arm, coat soaking up the liquid. He closed his eyes for a few seconds, then opened them to stare at Jimmy.

"I need to think," he whispered to the phone and Fry said nothing for a moment.

Then:

"There's a knife on the floor by the wall you should be standing beside. See it?"

With a shaking hand, Fulcher shone his torch straight down and there it was. A steak knife, the blade lined with sharp teeth. Fulcher held the phone close to his chest, shoved his face to Jimmy's ear and whispered: "In the car, there's a McDonald's bag on the back seat with a bottle of Coke in it. Get the bottle. Quick. Go."

He brought the mobile up again and spoke with a trembling, frightened note. "Listen, you have to listen to me. I can't just kill myself."

At the same time, he slid the gun into a coat pocket with a smooth motion and pulled his keys free. Holding them so they didn't jingle, he pushed his hand towards Jimmy who took the keys with a dumb, animal movement.

Car. Go, Fulcher mouthed, praying Jimmy would move fast and without any noise. He held to the side of his head and raised his voice to cover Jimmy's lumbering steps back towards the doors and the yard. "You can't expect me to just kill myself, for Christ's sake."

Fry kept quiet.

"I mean, it's insane. We're talking, aren't we? I won't give you any shit about I know you're good inside. You've done terrible things, but we can talk about them, about why you've done them, can't we? For God's sake, you can't just expect me to commit suicide like it's nothing."

He was babbling and it wasn't purely down to acting or any pretence. They had one shot at this and what happened after that pretence was carried out, Fulcher had no clue. He faced the gates and the snowstorm. How long would it take Jimmy to get to the car, get the bottle and leg it back? A full minute? Half that had to have passed already.

"Are you listening to me?" Fulcher cried.

"I'm listening. I also don't care. Your life or the girl bleeds. Carl Cameron would have done the same if I'd told him to. He'd have done it to save his wife."

Fulcher caught something secret and amused in the voice. Intuition borne from his long years on the Force spoke up.

"You made him kill his brother to. . .what? Save his own life?"

"I made him kill his brother because I could. Like I said, you're all so easy to manipulate. His brother was a weak idiot for trusting his flesh and blood and Carl was a suspicious animal. There was nothing to be suspicious about, not really, but since when did that stop people from believing the worst?"

"For fuck's sake. . ." Fulcher had to wipe more dribbling sweat from his head. Where the fuck was Jimmy?

"Look, we both know my career is over after tonight, right? I brought two civilians into a murder investigation—" Eyes on the door, his heart a rattling piece of rock in his chest and the clock ticking through the last minutes of the night. "I did that and I got an officer killed. My career is done. I'll be lucky not to get sent down. We both know that so what the fuck is the point of me pretending? I haven't got a fucking chance of catching you but I can help you. I can get you away. Out of the country. They'll keep looking for you unless you're overseas and then you disappear." Movement at the doors, a shadow pushing through the white. "I can get you a few quid, too. Not loads. I'm not rich, but I've got a few grand. Enough to get to Europe and further, right? You—" A piece of gloom entering the rear of the shop, a small chunk of the pre-dawn darkness come to life.

Jimmy skidded on the wet floor as he lunged inside. In both hands, he held the bottle of Coke.

"I want," Fry said as if he hadn't just listened to Fulcher's promises. "I want you to cut your wrist right now."

"Fuck." Fulcher signalled for Jimmy to shake the bottle and come closer. Understanding the small plan, Jimmy did so, and the fizzy liquid foamed near the underside of the cap.

"You going to do it, Clyde?"

"Yeah." Fulcher turned his voice into a resigned mutter. "What the fuck have I got, right? Everything is over. If you promise to let Kelly go unharmed, I'll do it."

"My word. Same with all the rules. I want you out of this. The rest of it is between Jimmy and me. Right, Jimmy?"

"Fuck you," Jimmy croaked. He held the bottle by the lid.

Fulcher raised the knife and again extended three fingers from the hand clasping the torch.

"I don't want to die," he screamed. "I don't."

"You die or she does," Fry told them.

"Oh, Christ. Oh, God. Oh, dear Jesus," Fulcher wailed and couldn't stop his smile.

Jimmy returned it.

Fulcher's fingers. Three. Two.

The faintest movement at the door again and Fulcher understood it was over in the second before Fry spoke.

From the phone: "If you stab that bottle and pretend you're slicing your wrist, I'll cut her throat."

Chapter Sixty-Two

Even now, I can see the precise second Fulcher gave up. It wasn't while he looked at me or the phone and Fry's voice making it clear he knew our stupid plan.

It was when Fulcher peered past me towards the open doors and the trail of wet prints I'd dragged in along with snow dying on the floor.

He gave up. He switched off, went down, lost his fight, stopped believing, was drowned out, threw in the towel, waved his white fucking flag, turned away.

He gave up.

Letting out a scream that held no words, Fulcher shoved the knife in his right hand down to his left wrist. The torchlight bounced off the ceiling and my hands flapped like birds as I reached for him and heard a terrible wet sound, a tearing, then a great hissing and the air and my face were full of boiling blood.

Still screaming, Fulcher went down, feet kicking while the torchlight still coated our surroundings with insane, dancing beams. And the hissing and reek of his blood was all over me.

I yelled his name, managed to grab his shoulders and shoved him backwards. It was only later that I realised I wouldn't have been able to shift his body without the wet ground acting as a lubricant.

We smashed together against the wall, sending more dust flying. I hacked out a great cough of dirty air and blood, spraying both into Fulcher's face. He'd dropped the phone and the fucking thing hadn't smashed or broken in the least. Still on speaker, Fry bellowed my name over and over. Ignoring the bastard, I fumbled with the waist of Fulcher's trousers. He'd stopped kicking and that was only down to the blood loss, I realised. Caught in the light for a second, his face was a white far beyond pale and his tongue hung limp over his red-splattered chin. He tried to say my name and I told him to shut up.

My soaking fingers were close to useless but I kept attacking his belt, screaming at the fucking thing to come on, come on, come on while Fry did the same with my name and the hiss of spurting blood would not lessen.

By some miracle, I managed to unbuckle Fulcher's belt.

"Tourniquet, Clyde. It's a fucking tourniquet. You with me?"

His head lolled back as if his neck had broken and in the spinning light, his face shone, every inch as white a bone.

"Fucker."

Gritting my teeth in a vain attempt to stop any more stink of blood getting inside my mouth, I yanked as hard as I could on the belt and half came loose. The rest remained behind Fulcher's meaty back and coat.

Leave him. He's dead.

Ignoring the thought that spoke in Robert Fry's voice, I buried my face in Fulcher's chest and shoved my hands around his back to the end of the belt. It squirted out of my grip; I went for it again and pulled. For a second, there was nothing but knowing Fulcher would be dead within minutes unless I stopped the blood loss and called an ambulance. Then the belt flew free, the buckle smashing into my cheek as it came loose.

I barely felt the pain.

Grabbing his soaking forearm, I looped the belt over it, tightened it and jammed the other end into his free hand.

"Fulcher, you hold it, okay? You hold that fucking belt."

It seemed like he'd simply collapse. Then his hand closed around the belt and he managed a weak smile. The squirting blood had decreased although the building still stank of it. I stank of it.

"Hold that belt. I'll get help." I fumbled with the phone, trying to not feel every precious second flying by. How long did Fulcher have? Five minutes? Ten? How long did I have? An hour forty-five?

On the other end of the line, Fry stopped repeating my name.

"You motherfucker. You're dead, you—"

"Shut up. If you want to help him, you've got another few minutes to do that and less than two hours to find me," Fry said.

"I know where you are," I whispered.

"Then come and get me, Jimmy."

The phone clattered on the wet ground by my feet. I slapped a hand over my chest, finding the shape of my own mobile, and ducked to Fulcher's side.

"Listen, Clyde. Stay awake. I'll get someone here in a couple of minutes, all right? You stay awake for that long, yeah? That's all you have to do."

I sobbed the last sentence and beyond my shaking vision, Fulcher managed to nod.

"Kill him," he breathed and looked to the floor.

His gun.

I scooped it up, touched Fulcher's shoulder for a tiny moment, then ran for the door and the teeth of the winter and the dying night.

Chapter Sixty-Three

Draining.
That was the word.
Draining.
Fulcher knew it was all over and that knowledge wasn't only down to the draining of blood and life from his ruined wrist. It was an understanding that had been with him for longer than he'd dared to admit. Even before the fucked-up phone call with the differing voices all claiming to be dead girls. . .and there'd been no claim. He could finally admit that now it was all over. No claim. Only truth. Dead girls had called him the other night.

Before that, though. On the path and grass next to the murky surface of the river. In the lonely land. In the late morning. Loui Cameron's hurt body sealed from view. And the area holding its breath while he and his people went through the broken blades of grass and the churned up muddy surface that met the riverbank's weeds. The area lifeless in the middle of winter. The area a graveyard.

That was when he knew this was all wrong. That was when he buried that understanding under decades of experience and thought and knowing bad people did bad things.

Then the calls about the other girls. Cheryl Temple. Meg Freeman. Poor Laura Flint left to scream and slowly freeze in a morgue drawer before Jimmy and Steve got her out. Trudy Mackenzie with her head smashed into pieces, her body consumed by fire. Samantha Mackenzie still trapped in a coma, perhaps never to waken to a world without her sister where she'd be lucky to know how to spell her own name. The child from Winchester with her wounded throat. All children. All stolen out of their lives and their families by an inhuman filth dressed like a man.

Now here he was.

In this dirty, stinking shop with its rotting walls and the snow blowing in through the doors where Jimmy had disappeared a minute before. Here with the moving shadow entering just before Jimmy had raced back in with the bottle of Coke and their plan to trick a monster.

Fulcher's gaze, shaking and full of hot tears, landed on the mobile. It had fallen silent; Fry was gone, the fucker making everything ready for the last moments now Fulcher's part was done.

He tried to think Jimmy's name, to shout in his head that Jimmy should not stop until he knew for sure Fry was dead again, and had no interior voice. Or exterior.

The moving shadow crept closer. The chill biting his exposed skin had faded as had the fire of his arm and hand. Same with the draining. While blood continued to jet from the wound, it did so with less angry force and that wasn't due to his hold on the other end of his belt. There was simply less blood to spray now.

Blinking a few times, Fulcher managed to clear his eyes as much as possible and kept them on the shadow drawing closer inch by inch.

The closer it came to him, the further away the derelict shop went. As did the night, the cold, the winter, the estate.

Fulcher's hold on his belt eased a fraction.

He thought of his children's names.

Somewhere, sirens sang their song.

Chapter Sixty-Four

The woman who'd taken my 999 call was trying to speak over me. I screamed into the phone, an animal noise of rage and frustration. It did the trick; she went silent. I clipped the kerb, fought to bring the car back under control and struck one of the few parked vehicles on Middleton Road. The shop, the blood and Fulcher were only a minute behind and that minute felt like it'd been an hour.

"Listen to me," I yelled. "Clyde Fulcher is bleeding to death. He's in the shops on Middleton Place. The one that used to be a corner shop. He's in the back, dying. Get a fucking ambulance to him right now. The guy who'd been killing kids, he did it and—"

He's mine.

The lie bloomed without the slightest pause. "He's at the river. He told us on the phone. He's at the bit where he killed the first girl. Loui Cameron. He's there and I'm going to kill the son of a bitch so you better send everyone there right fucking now."

I ended the call, turned the phone off and threw it at the passenger side window where it bounced and landed at my feet. The reek of Fulcher's blood was glued to my nose and mouth. The spray had soaked my coat and hair, and a quick look in the rear-view mirror showed a staring, mad figure looking back at me. Ahead, the road turned into a snaking curve and I was forced to slow for a few moments. Middleton Road fell behind. Cleatham Avenue took its place, a narrow section of the estate, cars and vans parked haphazardly on double yellows. I didn't slow and could only hope nobody pulled out as I neared the very edge of the estate. Out there, almost no street lights worked and every inch of the pavements and scrubby grass areas felt deserted. I could have driven into an expanse of Sprignall untouched for decades and my mind tried to throw up images of unseen, inhuman things lumbering through the alleys where not even the moon shone down.

Although my garbled rant to the emergency operator had finished less than ten seconds ago, the wonderful noise of sirens broke through the early morning. With the road levelling out, I increased the car's speed, wheels churning up slush while I prayed I didn't hit any icy patches. The awful noise of Fulcher slicing into his wrist repeated in my head along with the hiss of his spurting blood. Unless the ambulance made it to him within a couple of minutes at the most, he'd have no chance.

Hold on, Clyde. You just hold on.

And then Fulcher was out of my head and Ella took his place and I didn't want to look at the backseat to see the unblinking eyes of dead girls looking back at me, the children turned into sisters by their murders.

You can't think about that. It's out of your hands. Fry is your business now. Get to him and blow his fucking head off.

Ella had never sounded so full of raw anger in all the times she'd spoken to me. Nor so close.

I followed the road to the next turning, knowing I couldn't leave Sprignall by any of the normal routes, not without running into dozens of frightened, angry cops or rioting locals.

Racing into a cul-de-sac and speeding past the most rundown houses Sprignall had to offer, I shot towards the end of the road and held the wheel as if it was part of my body.

Steeling myself, I mounted a kerb, crushed grass and struck an old fence.

Rotten wood scattering, Fulcher's car broke through to a tangle of bushes, snapped their spiky leaves, hit a sloping embankment and churned up masses of snow. Veering madly, I brushed an emaciated tree, tore the wing mirror off and careered down towards the parkway.

Ice or uneven land, I don't know. Either way, the car skidded way off course, spun while I yelled madly and fought for control. An instant later, I hit a group of small trees, lunged forward in the seat and saved myself from hitting the windscreen by the belt. Even so, I cried out at the ugly jarring sensation and tried to blank out the pain.

The engine died.

"No."

I tried everything I could and got nothing but the gradually slowing sound of the ticking engine and my own desperate pleas. Fulcher's car was useless.

"No. Fucking no."

Staggering out to the embankment and the mess of ruined fence, mashed snow and my careering tracks from the crash, I tried not to breathe too deeply. Every inch of my body from waist to head felt like a torn muscle and the freezing air stung as it went down my throat.

The time. Six. I had an hour and half at most to get to him. Running back into the estate was out of the question. The streets and paths of Sprignall were no help; even now, the police would be on their way to investigate the storm of noise I'd caused. Below, the parkway remained free from vehicles while the sea of snow carpeted it.

Staggering, trying to keep quiet even as I wanted to sob, I lumbered down to the hard shoulder while the stink of Fulcher's blood all over my face and hair surrounded me.

***

Keeping his back to the entrance, Fry watched the night drop out of the sky fraction by fraction as the minutes passed and dawn approached. The stars were invisible again for the most part, and spread out like a sheet below, Oxford Road, the bridge and the flowing river were all easing their way back to life. The faintest white blur on the water as swans emerged from under the bridge and the riverbank; a gradual increase in the number of cars and vans heading into the town with their early workers and deliveries; one or two men walking their dogs and keeping an uneasy eye on any bushes or secluded areas they passed. And all of it through the mostly unmarked snow, all of it under the falling flakes and speeding wind. Any forecast given or checked had been proved wrong, and gritters were already being sent out for a second day while parents checked their phones and email for messages about school closures before their children woke.

Fry stood over the town, his town, and let himself feel the possibilities flowing through this day and the days beyond. There were countless lives out there, countless faces to wear and countless victims. All for him. One at a time until there were none left. It would take decades, centuries and that did not matter. He had time. If Jimmy didn't play his part properly, he had all the time in the world.

At his feet, Kelly tried to shift without making a sound and he let her pretend that was happening. Whether she lived or died over the next few minutes was all on Jimmy and the choices he made. If she finally went for the knife strapped to her ankle and tried to use it, Fry didn't much care so he let her have the comfort and torment of knowing the weapon was close and out of her reach unless she dared go for it.

He breathed in the taste of her terror and her blood dribbling from the wound in her leg, relishing both, and consulted his interior clock.

Bare minutes before dawn and Tuesday. Ella's anniversary.

Ella. Do you remember me? Do you know my name?

She was close although not yet beside him or coming at his back. She'd come with Jimmy and then. . .well, they'd see what was what.

Fry waited.

But he did not have to wait long before the door exploded.

Chapter Sixty-Five

The detonation in my hands was beyond heaven.

The handle and wood around it shattered, all scattering down and to the sides. I smashed a shoulder to the door and it swung open wide, letting the light from the corridor plunge into my living room.

Staggering, a sea of aches drowning my body from the crash in Fulcher's car and my lurching race through three miles of the winter, I fell against the wall, righted myself and furiously blinked away streams of sweat running over my eyes.

I fired Fulcher's gun again, the shot flying into the wall beside the TV. Another shot turned the TV itself into so much flying glass and plastic and sparks. My hearing boomed and somewhere beyond the booms, Kelly was yanked to her feet before squirming forward, bending and going for what I realised was a tiny knife attached to her leg. She twisted as if made of fog and swung her fist. The knife hit him in the stomach, turning her fist red while mad shouts broke out behind my neighbours' closed doors.

Kelly shrieked again, this one full of agony, and collapsed. At once, she tried to get up, fell flat and crawled. He'd stabbed her in the back of her thigh, opening a wide wound that poured blood even as the blade in his gut wept red.

Rising, rising, the shape at the window somehow turned without making a move, facing me without any face, only an outline built like a man. And although I saw no features, I knew it was smiling.

I fired straight at it.

Every single light in my flat exploded into life, illumination burying the shadows and revealing all. Kelly was crawling from the man who'd turned her pretty face into so many bruises. Jagged lines streamed blood down her neck and her shredded clothes revealed more wounds above her breasts. He'd poked her with the knife, bored as he waited for me but not yet ready to wound her in any way he considered serious.

Hair hanging in her face, she managed to lift her head. "Please."

"Get up," I shouted, ears throbbing with the echo of my shots and my voice sounding muffled to me. "Move it."

She kept crawling, hands and knees pushing her past my sofa and the coffee table. One blood-smeared hand struck the floor with a heavy thump and left the print of her palm on the wood.

"Move," I bellowed and staggered further into my flat.

The man at the window remained on the same spot. For the first time, I saw his face. And everything inside crashed into pieces.

Robert Fry stood in my living room. Still only twenty. Still the same smile. Still with the boyband haircut. Still alive. Still the same kid who'd raped and murdered my sister and filmed it while other men watched and enjoyed her pain day after day.

I blinked and Fry was gone. In his place, the youth I'd first encountered beside the river while he beat Loui Cameron to death; a man only a year or two into adulthood with the rest of an easy, pleasant life ahead because he'd been born into right family at the right time and had the right luck to succeed.

A man who thought he was a monster from my past; he believed all way down that he was Robert Fry.

Kill her.

The man didn't speak and neither did I. The voice came out of the walls, a low, guttural sound. It was like the winter that would not leave the town had learned to speak.

You want to know the truth. You want to know who I really am. Kill her.

Other voices, all snarling and full of angry mocking, picked up the words while Kelly sobbed and crawled. Pulling herself along on her elbows, she slithered while her body trailed its blood and the raging voices boomed from the furniture and lights and walls.

Kill her. Kill her. Kill her. Kill her.

I fired the gun.

A hole opened in his chest. Blood and bone flew. He fell backwards, twisting and shimmering for a second. In his place, Fry returned. I cried out – no words, only sickened denial. He hit a bookcase and went down. I grabbed Kelly's shoulders.

"Go." I screamed it in her face. "To the hallway. Go."

Sobbing, she made it past me while I advanced on the body already trying to stand. The howling storm of voices had died with my shot. Somewhere beyond, more voices full of panic and fear broke through along with what might have been sirens. All I really knew was the feeling inside that dwarfed anger or animalistic rage. It had no name. It swallowed everything and turned me into a machine.

Fry turned over. He was smiling.

Hello, again. Nice to see you.

I levelled the gun at his face. My hand shook as if we stood in a storm and even holding the weapon with both hands did little to steady it.

Fry's smile did not falter.

I'll tell you everything. How I am here. What I am. What I want. You do one thing for me and I tell you everything.

"Fuck you," I croaked.

Kill the girl.

Fuck you. I couldn't speak it, could barely breathe and not simply because of my exhaustion or wrecked body. Whatever the new thing that went miles above rage was, it had swallowed the beat of my heart and the air in my lungs.

You're nothing. You don't exist. And you lose. Your rules, remember? I stop you before dawn and you're done.

In my head, he giggled: a child amused by a dirty joke. I might go but what's stopping me from coming back? Again. Again. Again. There are gaps, Jimmy. You wouldn't believe how many ways there are of breaking through and I know them all so I can come back whenever I like. I've been and gone a thousand times and I'll do it again.

If it was possible, Fry's smiled widened. Again without moving, he changed position, going from a prone body on the gore-splattered floor to standing directly in front of me and spreading his arms wide, turning his whole body into a target. The wound in his chest flexed and pulsed in time with his rapid breathing. He blinked and I saw through his eyes for a tiny moment.

Kelly is a crawling insect, inches from the doorway while the fluid of her life streams from her shredded leg and from the wounds it inflicted while waiting for the end.

Another blink.

We're in the derelict shop, Fulcher and me, staring at each other and desperate to know how the hell Fry knows about our plan with the Coke bottle. There are no cameras, nothing to show us to the outside world and there is no need for anything like that. There is my sight that this thing uses. It is behind my eyes. It is in my head and it lives there in the pieces of whatever I have left.

Let the world go, Fry whispered. Let it all go, right? That's what you said to yourself after Ella died. You shut them all out. You shut them all away and you kept doing that until you didn't know how to do anything else. And now here we are. You and me. Together. Always together. And I owe this to you because I'm good at this thanks to people like you. And I want to stay. I want to keep doing what I do until there's nobody left.

"You are nothing," I whispered.

And that was when he finally spoke aloud, once again in the voice of my dead sister.

"He hurt me. So much. You can't stop him. You can't keep him away from the world. You can't stop him from killing girls like me. You—"

"I can stop him." I whispered it and saw the fading darkness in the sky and in the corners of Lawfield's secret spaces as Tuesday landed. It was all there right in front along with the snowflakes and the surface of the world stretched thin like old glue.

Gaps, Fry had said. Gaps where anything might slip through, slip inside and inch its way closer and closer to the sky right outside my flat.

The howling wails returned: countless insane voices singing in a chorus of their savage glee, creatures like the thing who'd taken Fry's name and face, all lurking out of sight as they pressed their thousands of fingers on those weak patches, pushed with all of their strength to break them wide open so instead of having all the narrow openings and silvery cracks through which the thing dressed as Fry came and went, they could burst their own world apart and fill the same sky I stared at.

A second, a minute, an hour: I believed what the murderer before me believed. He was something inhuman that wore Robert Fry like rags; he'd come from outside everything and the mad screeches of things I could not see were not imagination or the shriek of police sirens.

I believed it all while knowing the killer was flesh and blood and would die when I blew his head off.

Wind blew out of the walls and the floor, a hurricane without form to crash into the furniture, knocking over table and chairs, sending the sofa into a spinning, crashing weapon that hit the far wall and smashed a corner unit into pieces.

Wind blowing through the thin places.

A hundred voices screaming.

Far out over the town, the sky now a blazing red as if the sun had exploded and turned the snowfall into raining clots of gore, a tidal wave taller than my building spread from one end of the horizon to the other, a silent torrent of blood smashing trees, roads, buildings aside, drowning the land and the air as it sped down on me and turned Lawfield, the county and the country into a red ocean.

And still, the screaming creatures stabbing their fingers into the cracked walls of their prison.

I fired the gun into the window and let the return of the shrieking voices into my flat, the world breaking in, the world finally welcome.

It's only for a second but long enough: dozens of clamouring voices approaching and the unmistakable sound of the police storming along the corridor. The gusting wind blows all over my body, scattering broken glass and wood in every direction, and the broken hole in what is left of my window has become a hungry mouth.

Running steps behind. Kelly crying out for help. Both noises fading away as if they're dropping into the opening ahead.

Then only the two of us, facing each other.

You're nothing. Not a demon. Not a ghost. You are nothing.

You made me. I am your father, your son, your brother, your past, your future. You made me.

You're the same as every other monster out there. You're not a demon or a god. You are nothing good and you never were—

I was, Jimmy. Long ago and faraway and over the hills and come to play. I was everything in this world and I learned how to leave without dying. I never died, Jimmy. You understand that? Never died. Never my ashes to ashes and my dust to dust. I went out and I saw this world from the outside. I saw what you can't and now I come and I go and I come back again. Because of you. Because of everyone like you.

And Fry still smiled his infuriating, horrible smile.

I am your father, your son, your brother, your past, your future.

He said or thought the same words, mocking me with whatever mystery and truth they held, but for the first time, what might have been a genuine emotion crossed his face, brief but definitely there.

Fear. Not of me. Not in the least. Fear because of whatever he thought waited outside in the night. And I didn't believe he was scared of the things he'd created in his head; he was scared of them breaking out because that would mean. . .

He wants this all for himself. He doesn't want to share it.

I didn't fire the gun again.

As the thunder of running steps crashed down through my flat and came at my back, I lunged forward, colliding with Fry and both of us wrapped around each other.

It was like holding smoke.

Freezing smoke.

Freezing because the wind was no longer storming its way into my flat through the wrecked window.

Freezing because I was in the wind. I was in the air ten floors over the white carpet coating the town.

I held something suddenly hot and squirming, not cold at all, a boiling piece of living meat with nothing human inside it. We were suspended over the deepest ocean, one formed from the bloody tidal wave Fry had brought to bathe everything in his touch. We swam in the blackest hole and all of Lawfield had been swallowed by an absence of space and light and noise while we rolled and rolled and the snowflakes exploded silently, offering a tiny glimpse of a space between us and the way to the place he called home. Stars winked out into nothing; suns blew away as if they were tiny flames, and at the other end of everything, a raging storm tearing away the wall that kept them trapped from the great nothing between two worlds.

In the last second, there was only falling and a writhing figure dropping away from me to be turned as white as the snowfall heading on its now quiet, soft way to the streets below.

Epilogue

It's been a long time, Ella. I'm sorry.

Chilly here, isn't it? At least the sun's shining, finally. I like the trees, and the quiet. Nice to be at the back of the cemetery. Furthest from the road. I saw the forecast earlier; they said it should get better early next month and we might be in for a decent spring. Sorry. Who cares about that? Jesus. Like it matters.

I'm glad the sun hasn't set yet. Telling you this story has taken longer than I thought it would, but then I've got to be honest. I'm telling myself as well as you. I'm trying to get it clear in my head and that takes some doing. Maybe by spring, I'll have a better idea. Maybe by then, I'll understand what I saw in my flat before we went through the window.

They're working on his body, trying to find out who he was, but it's a hard slog, they tell me. They're having a job with dental records thanks to how he landed when he dropped from my window, and fingerprints haven't come up with much. When they have a name, it won't mean anything to me or the police because I know Fry was telling the truth. He can come back and he will, but he's gone for now. He's out there where he lives, and all that other stuff he said about me making him, about never having died. . . I don't know, Ella. I really don't know a thing. I don't know if I can call that place Fry came from Hell or what. Maybe it doesn't matter too much now he's gone.

I should go soon. I need to take my pills with food, they said. I suppose a broken shoulder and broken fingers is nothing, is it? Lucky for that cop who dragged me back through the window that he was bigger than me. Lucky for me he was fast, too. I can feel his hands on mine right now. I can feel myself swinging against the wall below the window and the pain in my arm is like an explosion but I'm not thinking about it because I'm watching that smoke turning so white, Ella. So white.

Until it hit the ground and turned red.

Fry's gone. Again. Whatever he was, he's gone. They won't put a name to what was left of his head or face and I don't care about that. The copper who got me inside, his name's AliAli, we've started seeing each other and he tells me a bit even though the rest of the police don't want anything to do with me. AliAli says the case is open but going nowhere and I'm not a suspect but I shouldn't move away even though that's all I want to do. I was awarded a few quid for my injuries and AliAli reckons a lot of the police aren't happy about that. I don't like to think about any of that stuff so I don't. Same with what was out there in the snow. I can't handle the thought of things worse than Fry and the only reason they're not here is because they can't work out how to escape from their side of things. But there was something else.

In that last second before AliAli grabbed me, I don't know. I got a sense of something big happening right next to me and thousands of miles away at the same time.

A fight.

A war that would make any war we've had look like two kids going at it in the playground. Fry and the others, they weren't just having a ruck; they were destroying their space.

I hope for something, though. Fry was on a time limit, wasn't he? Back here on the anniversary of the day you were taken and back to his home on the day you. . . the day you died. All that crap he said about stopping if I found him by the Tuesday morning, it wasn't the whole truth. He had a time limit, a window, and I don't know if he went away because I did find him before it was up or because he wanted to stop those things from coming through and ruining his plans. If I did stop him, then maybe he won't be back. If he really is out there, fighting them so he gets this world to himself, then I don't know who to hope wins that fight.

I did try asking Kelly about her time with Fry when he took her from Sprignall to my flat; I thought she might have seen something because no way did Fry just walk away after killing King. He went somewhere else and he had to take Kelly with him so she must have seen it, that other place, but she wouldn't say what happened or if she saw anything. Just told me to get out of her room and then cried. They let her out of hospital after a few weeks when she was as healed as she could be. I didn't see her after that. Last I heard she moved back to Belfast, which isn't a surprise. She had no connection to the police, anymore, and the investigation was dead. What was keeping her here?

Sprignall is even worse now. It's a total no-go area. They knocked down the shops that got burned in the riot and planned on building a new area, but that hasn't happened. The other bit. . . your bit, that's still there, but it's nothing now. I think kids go there on a dare or to drink or mess about, but nobody lives there or uses the area as shops.

I went to The Black Boar last week and tried to have a drink but I couldn't stay. It all looks normal and people drink there but not many. People tend to stay home after dark although I think it's getting better. Kids are allowed to play in Tirrington Park again. There's a plaque there. I saw it the same day I went to the pub. The locals paid for it. It's a memorial for the girls. I'm sorry your name's not on it, but nobody knows you were part of this. Maybe a few people Fulcher told, but it's not official. I'm sorry, sis.

Whatever happened, I can tell you I'm not looking forward to next winter even though if it snows then, it'll just be snow and nothing else. I honestly believe that but I still don't like to think about it. My doctor said that blocking it out is a bad idea, but it's the only weapon I've got. I talk to my neighbour; I feed her cat when she's goes to visit family. I go to work and I see people. That's enough for now.

I should make a move, sis. It'll be dark soon and the lady in the flat above mine is away all weekend. She's nice. Must be eighty and treats me like I'm a kid. She tells me I need fattening up and I tell her I'm fine.

I'm working tonight, as well. Got the night shift at the new hospital. Being a porter is all right. It pays the bills and I get to feel like I'm doing something that helps.

I should go.

I hope you're resting. I hope it's warm enough for you. I hope you like these flowers. I wasn't sure what to get so I bought different ones. I'll come back soon to tidy them up and all that. Keep them watered.

Can you do one thing for me before I go? If you see Fulcher, tell him I'm sorry, too. He was all right. I hope you look after each other.

Stay safe, Ella. I love you.

About Your Author

Luke Walker has been writing dark fiction for most of his life after getting hold of paperbacks belonging to his dad and brother and reading Poe, King, Herbert and Lovecraft when he was far too young. His books include the horrors The Unredeemed, Hometown and The Mirror Of The Nameless as well as the dark fantasy Dead Sun. Several of his short stories have been published online and in magazines and books.

When not writing, he can found watching bad films or reading good books. He has novels and short stories to be published soon and is currently working on new fiction.

Luke welcomes comments at his blog, which can be read at www.lukewalkerwriter.com and his Twitter page is @lukewalkerbooks. Sign up to his newsletter at www.tinyletter.com/LukeWalkerWriter.

He is forty-one and lives in England with his wife.

Other HellBound Books Titles
Available at: www.hellboundbookspublishing.com

Kidnapped in broad daylight from a busy Edinburgh street, Hannah Wilson has no idea what her abductors want with her, as they chain her in the back of their van and speed out of the city. They tell her she's perfectly safe when she's terrified for her life.

Transported to the far north of Scotland with dozens of others, all yanked from their lives across Britain, Hannah is taken to an isolated compound they call Pandemonium, which is an ultra-secure prison ruled by creatures that should exist only in nightmares - a place no one has survived for more than a few months.

Hundreds of miles away from help, her family's lives at risk if she disobeys any order, Hannah knows the key to surviving her captivity is to bond with strangers and teach them all to refuse to be victims. But, she's running out of time to convince the other captives to take their fight to the black heart of the prison and its inhuman warden; Hannah is yet to discover she is not the only one about to start a war.

In Pandemonium, all Hell is going to break out.

The Dead Room

A week before Christmas, terrorists detonate dozens of dirty bombs throughout Britain and release a man-made contagion, leading Nicola Allen to begin a frantic hunt for her husband and daughter while a nation burns. Fleeing from a horrendous event she refuses to speak of and desperate to find shelter in a dying country, Nicola's sister-in-law, Cate, takes cover in a partly destroyed hospital. Terrorised by visions of mutilated bodies and the screams of phantom children, Cate joins a group of survivors, all of whom are under attack by ruthless scavengers and looters. If Nicola is to have any chance of finding her family and if Cate is to escape from the siege, they must reunite and then descend into the belly of the ruined hospital where the horrific truth of what truly connects the two women is waiting for them. Waiting for them down in the dead room.

The Unredeemed

Four hundred years ago, Benjamin Harwood butchered whoever he saw fit to kill, knowing that sacrificing his murder victims to a demon would keep him safe from eternal punishment. But now, their agreement has been torn in half and the demon is coming for Harwood's soul, coming to set him to burn.
Preparing for war, Harwood gathers the worst of the worst, the monsters and murderers he calls friends. With this group of damned killers, Harwood must return to the crimes of his past and seek help from his most recent prey: a teenage girl whose family he destroyed, a girl with more reason to loathe him than anyone in his life or death.
Only then he can try for a redemption that may be impossible or face a universe of suffering.
But Harwood doesn't know there is a hole in the floor of the world. And something much worse than the dead is down there…

Ascent

When terrorists target an American air force base with a nuclear bomb, Kelly Wells races to find her sister in a nearby office block, desperate for them to be together in their final moments.

At the same time, a handful of others fight their way through a panicked city to reach the building-frantic to make it to loved ones before the device ignites less than fifty miles away. In the frozen instant of the detonation, Kelly, her sister and three strangers are locked in that moment and trapped in the offices.

But they are not alone. An ancient god from the deepest pits in the earth has woken and knows their most private secrets and guilt.

Now, horror takes the form of their darkest dreams to draw sustenance from their terror, and the beast stalking them will dine well.

Because everybody is afraid of something.

Copyright © 2021 by HellBound Books Publishing LLC
All Rights Reserved

www.hellboundbookspublishing.com

www.ingramcontent.com/pod-product-compliance
Lightning Source LLC
LaVergne TN
LVHW040132080526
838202LV00042B/2881